REDEMPTION

For all Content Inquiries, please visit my website:

Dedication

True family loves unconditionally and rarely judges.
Blood or not.
I hope you find yours if you haven't already.

Prologue

"Yes!" His voice rings loud and clear from the other side of his closed office door. "Jack Craven, holding for Antonio Torres."

I can hear his fingertips begin to *tap, tap, tap* on top of his desk, a nervous habit he could never quit. I know who Antonio Torres is. He's a mobster from New York.

"Antonio!" he bellows good-naturedly into the phone, the sudden pitch change in his voice startling me. Unfortunately, it's not on speaker and I can't hear what's being said on the other side of the line. "All is good here, my friend. How about you?"

The dealings with this mob family have been shaky at best from the very beginning. The *friendship* is new, even though Jack is still digging around to see what dirt he can find on the Torreses in particular. The more you know, the better the blackmail.

"The family is doing well. How about your sons?" He lets loose a jolly laugh and I can hear him pat his stomach. "Boys will be boys," Jack responds.

"I actually need a favor, Antonio. For my family." There's a pause. "I need protection for me and my daughter." Another pause. "My older daughter. The younger one can stay with her mother. I need her and I to disappear. Not now... at a time I specify."

Why is he planning this with Rebecca? Why is he leaving Debra behind? So many questions, yet I have no answers. This is how it is when you're a female in this house. You aren't privy to any information.

"I would need new identities for us and to effectively erase the current ones. I know it's a lot to ask. I have the money and I have the connections to get you situated here in Canada. Imagine if you went international?"

The pause is long this time, and the pit at the base of my stomach only grows. There's no one I can tell here. Everyone is in Jack Craven's pocket. I have to find out more and protect both Rebecca and Debra.

"I can do that." He exhales, and I can hear his relief. "How about I pay you a visit? Great! I will see you in two weeks."

He replaces the receiver on the phone, and then the distinct sound of his decanter being opened filters through the wooden slab. I can hear his bourbon being poured and then his greedy gulps.

Backing away from the office door, I turn and walk to the back door where I see the two sisters playing in the yard, so young and so innocent.

What does he have planned for them?

9

CHAPTER ONE

I once referred to Whitsborough as a Disney Princess, but I was fucking wrong. This place is the complete opposite. More like Ursula, Maleficent, and Jafar combined... times one thousand. Every villain in the entire Disney Universe comes here to fucking party. The worst part? It looks like my family may have had a hand in a few pots of evil stew.

Sitting in Shelby across the street from Travis' childhood home, I watch as the bulldozers and wrecking balls prepare for demolition. Piled in the backseat are the totes Emmett and I hauled from the storage unit. They contain diaries belonging to our mother and business documents belonging to our grandfather, most of which someone has redacted. The amount of shit I have to investigate and figure out is growing by the day. Not to mention how many people I have to kill. That list also grows by the day.

Vin turns away from our little family circle, his eyes catching mine, and his plush lips curve into a small smile until the dimple appears on his left cheek. He begins at

Metropolitan University in the fall for dramatic arts. He deserves it, and I can't wait to see what he decides to do for his career. Adrianna will start at a community college so that she can stay here close to us. Emmett, Travis, and me? We put off further learning for the time being. Travis now owns a company he'll have to begin training at, and as for Emmett and me, we have family business to sort out. After that? I don't know. I don't even know if there will be an after that for me, but I'll make sure there's one for everyone else in my family.

I get out of the car as soon as I see one of the construction workers get behind the controls for the wrecking ball, wanting to see this up close and watch the euphoria I know I'll see on Travis' face. This house is a true den of evil and the demons that reside here need to be permanently abolished. His father was the Whitsborough Rapist for many years, raping over fifty teenage and young adult women. His mother loved to help lure those females to him, and the evil piece of shit continuously raped and impregnated his birth mother. I still, to this day, regret letting him die by simply cutting his wrists. I wish I could go back and do horrible things to him.

Standing between Travis and Vin, I grab each of their hands, forming a solid line of support. Travis squeezes mine and takes a deep breath as the large metal ball swings. We all stare with bated breath as it slams into the second story, the loud noise drawing the neighbors out onto the street to watch the scene.

"Damn, that just gave me a chub," Emmett groans, grabbing his crotch lewdly.

"Seriously?" I glare over at him, bending my head forward to see beyond Travis.

"Don't encourage him," Adri says before shoving Emmett's shoulder.

The wrecking ball swings again, stealing my attention once more, and this time the roof crumbles in as glass sprays outward. Thankfully, we're at the beginning of the driveway, so nothing has reached us this far out.

"I'm expecting to hear voices like the witch from *The Wizard of OZ*. '*I'm melting*,'" Emmett says in his very best witch voice.

I snort at that one. "'*I'll get you, my pretty!*'" I mimic the witch as well.

Adri snorts next, then quickly covers her mouth with her hand, her eyes rolling dramatically.

"Hold on!" Emmett exclaims, bouncing on the balls of his feet. "I can keep this going. '*And your mangy little dog too!*'"

Vin is the first to detonate and erupt into full laughter, Travis not far behind, and Adri has her hand still covering her mouth. Emmett and I share a similar snort, then roll our eyes at each other. That's been happening a lot lately. We catch each other doing the same thing at the same time, finishing the other's sentences, and sometimes even waking up and meeting each other in the hallway in the morning at the same time. I can only imagine how much more eerie that would've been if we were raised together. I would take us being creepier if it meant we had been in each other's lives from birth.

Travis is the first to stop, turning his head to look at something to our right. I follow his line of sight to a hideous sphinx statue. There are two of them flanking the driveway beside the gates. He drops my hand and walks across the street to his car, pulling out two baseball bats. No way... Is he going to get destructive too? He comes back and immediately passes me a bat, like he knows this is something I would find pleasure in with him, and he's fucking right.

I wait and watch him with the others as he walks up to the first sphinx and swings his bat into its face with enough force to shatter the head into crumbled pieces of concrete.

"He had them commissioned to his likeness," he growls, the anger in his tone sending a chill down my spine.

Turning to look at the one remaining sphinx face, I nearly choke on my saliva. He really fucking did. Robert Greene was a narcissistic cunt who thought way too highly of himself without paying much attention to what everyone else thought of him. Like I said, cunt.

As much as I want to bash in the concrete version of that piece of shit's face, I know someone else who is more deserving of it. I hand the bat off to Vin and motion for him to beat the shit out of his father's smug mug. He takes the bat with a look of pure disgust and stalks toward the fucking statue. Then I watch his bulky arm muscles bunch and flex as he swings the bat back, slamming it with all his strength into its face. The whole top half of the statue literally explodes into a cloud of dust and pebbles. My man is a force.

As they bash in the statues, the rest of us turn and watch the wrecking ball hit one last time on the second floor before the whole structure crashes down, then the bulldozers flatten walls and move debris. It feels like a colon cleanse but for the soul. I'm purging all the evil in Whitsborough, one piece of shit at a time.

Emmett is with me in Shelby as we follow behind Travis' Civic and Vin's Hummer. "Call Carm on speaker," I instruct him. He doesn't ask questions and does as I ask.

"Little bro, what can I do for you?" Carm's velvet-smooth voice flows from Emmett's phone.

"I need an update, *bro*," I say loudly, my tone brokering no argument.

"Ah, my sadistic little sister." He chuckles. "I have one. Wade bribed the guard, who was watching your opponent, to give him a knife. I killed the guard slowly and I expect you will want to do something about Wade?"

"You bet." My fingers grip the steering wheel a little tighter. "Call a Head's meeting for this weekend."

"On it," he agrees. "What will you do?"

"Not sure." My eyes briefly meet Emmett's. "Let's just play it by ear."

"Okay, I'll see you Saturday, and bring my little brother with you too."

"I'll see if I can clear my schedule." Emmett grins as he looks down at the phone, his voice revealing just how much he misses Carm.

"*Ciao.*" Carm snickers and hangs up.

"So Wade is a dirty little bitch. Are you really going to play it by ear?" Emmett asks me as I quickly look at him and then back to the road.

"Of course not. I have every single detail already planned, but I will only ever let my immediate family know that. Understand?" He gives me a confused look as his eyes flick back to the phone in his hands.

"But Carm—"

"Is in New York with enough going on," I cut him off. I know he's fiercely loyal to Carm, being that the man is his older brother, *our* older brother, but I need to look after the family I have here in my house first.

"Yeah," he relents with a long exhale.

"I'm never going to do anything to put him in danger, and if by chance I do, I will always get him out of it. No matter what," I promise as I roll to a stop at a stop sign.

"I know." He nods and flashes me a smile. "I just worry about him there on his own. At least he has Trent now."

"Yeah, it's good that Trent decided to live in the compound and take over as head of security." Much to

Carm's disdain. We all know he had Emmett trained for that very position, but him finding me put a wrench in that plan.

I pull into our driveway just behind Travis and Vin. All of us being here eases some of my stress as I can properly watch each of them when they're all under the same roof. It's time to roll out my plans, and it starts this weekend with Wade. I made a vow to rid Whitsborough of evil, but I can start this weekend in New York. I refuse to back down and let this place mow me over. To do that means I need to sink back into the numb abyss. I need to go dark and turn my sole concentration on Jennifer Talia. She seems to be the beginning and the end of many of our problems.

"Let's get these totes inside," I say to Emmett as I step out of the car.

Once we have the totes piled in the foyer, Vin, Travis, and Adri join us. "These are our mother's old diaries and notebooks. I also have a tote of my grandfather's things. I was hoping we could go through everything with a fine-tooth comb because I think we'll find more answers than we expect here."

"Let's get to it." Travis claps his hands before grabbing a tote.

"What exactly are we looking for?" Adri asks as she follows us into the family room.

"My mother was a victim of Robert Greene. We suspect he raped her in high school. We went by the storage unit today and found a bunch of her diaries. In one of them, I found her venting that they sent her father a VHS tape of the incident, and instead of believing her, he called her a slut. He believed it was consensual," I explain.

"I also found some disturbing shit in a few of her younger diaries. Things her father was doing to her," Emmett adds.

"Looks like our grandfather hired our father to help fake his death. A lot of the information on this sheet has been blacked out, but this was about a month before Raphael came to Whitsborough and met our mother," I fill them all in as we take seats and begin opening the totes. "Raphael admitted to me about killing my grandparents when they refused to have anything to do with our mother and disowned her, but what if he didn't actually kill them?"

"Could they still be alive?" Adri asks, sounding astonished as her eyes widen.

"I don't know. Maybe they died that day, or maybe they lived out the rest of their days and died naturally. On this paper,"—I wave a sheet over my head—"it states that my grandfather wanted to move to New York and offered to work for The Rampage or an affiliate."

There are a few photos of my grandparents in the family albums, so I pull those out too. Flipping through the album, I find a wedding photo of them and pull it out of the sleeve. They're young and it's black and white. I search through until I find a colored photo of them with a younger Debra and my mother. This one shows a much larger man, his belly rounded and his hairline receding while the woman has platinum blonde hair and olive skin.

"Here." I hand them both to Emmett. "Recognize them at all?"

"No." He shakes his head and pulls the older version closer to his eyes. "Something about the lady looks familiar though. Or maybe it's because you kind of look like her."

I take the photo back and inspect her face. I've always been told I had my mother's smile and her eye color. I can see the eye color in my grandfather, but Emmett is right, our smile is similar to our grandmother's.

"Maybe," I mutter, still not fully convinced.

"I've seen no one at the compound who looks like that." Emmett sounds adamant and I believe him. "We should bring them to Carm though."

"Speaking of." I look at each of them as they lift their

heads to give me their attention. "I have a Head Meeting this weekend. Carm found out that Wade gave that guy the knife. I will call in favor of a fight to the death between us."

The room is quiet, then Vin is the first to speak. "So, you will bring in your knife too, right? Fair is fair."

"Nah." I throw both hands in the air and shrug. "I like the feeling of killing with my bare hands." I wiggle my fingers for emphasis.

Adri looks worried and I know it's because she never really got over what happened at the first fight she attended when I was slashed in the stomach. She has yet to come and see another fight and would rather just hear the highlights afterward. I don't push it, understanding that what I do isn't for everyone.

"I want to be at that fight," Adri states, surprising us all as her concerned look melts into determination. "I want to see that guy die."

"Okay." I nod, my voice filled with pride.

"Will the other Heads agree to that?" Vin asks.

"They won't have a choice," I retort as I go back to searching through the tote in front of me.

"Our mom was really pretty." Emmett sighs as he looks through the albums. "I'm glad I at least have the chance to see her face. Carm has never known what his mother looks like."

"He told me Raphael raped her and then after Carm was born, he killed her," I repeat a condensed version of what I was told.

"Close," Emmett replies, his head tipping to the side in thought. "She was a regular."

"What's a regular?" Vin inquires as he looks through a diary.

"She would sleep with the guards or whoever was

around. I don't know about her being raped, but I can see our father not being kind. After she became pregnant, our father waited and had a DNA test performed and obviously Carm was his. He looks a lot like him. Not too long after that, his mother disappeared." His brows fall over his eyes with contemplation as I grunt.

"If she disappeared, then why did Carm say for certain that our father killed her?" I press, knowing the answers I was given previously were far from the truth.

"Because Raphael admitted to it when he got out of prison. He must've been looking for some sort of redemption because he confessed to many things. Like the fact that I had a twin sister and he was bringing her to meet me." His eyes meet mine as a small smile grows along his mouth.

"Kidnapping," I murmur the correction, my voice sounding bitter as I refuse to reciprocate the smile.

"Yeah." Emmett rolls his eyes. "Even while looking for redemption, he was still deceitful."

"This diary is creepy," Vin mutters, and we all look at him. "Your grandfather, Jack, was a weird man. Many people still talk about him. My mother said he and Rebecca were close, and Debra was always jealous of it. Reading this, I know why."

"Yeah, that's the one I read too," Emmett says sadly. "Looks like our grandfather was sexually abusing our mother."

I get up and force my way onto Vin's lap so I can see what he's reading. He kisses my temple and points to a section of the page. *'Today, Daddy made me brush my hair over and over again without a top on.'* My heart aches for the little girl who endured this treatment. She was raped, then trapped, and ultimately murdered, all by brutal, disgusting men. She just couldn't catch a break.

"Hey, it says here that they sent your grandfather a VHS tape of the rape. Do you have that? I would consider it evidence," Travis interjects while reading a paper from our grandfather's box. "Looks like my father wrote this. It's his writing."

He's reading the anonymous letter that was sent to my grandfather, telling him to watch the tape of his daughter as the town whore and that he should consider sending her away.

"Why was my father so set on getting your mother out of here?" Travis mulls it over as his eyes rove over the sheet of paper in his hands.

"Maybe because she remembered who raped her, and she was building something against him?" I theorize. It's hard not to be affected by everything in these totes, but being in Vin's arms helps soothe my temper.

"You're probably right. Then she meets Raphael and falls in love, deciding to leave this place behind her." Anger rumbles through Vin's voice as I lay my head against his shoulder.

"Only to be subjected to another type of hell at his hands," I grind out.

"Why wouldn't she go into witness protection though? Especially with you as a small child. She must've known Raphael would come looking for her when he got out." Travis scratches his chin in thought.

"I think she was always trying to find a way back to Emmett. If she went into witness protection, she would have to let him go forever. Or maybe she knew Raphael had too many people he paid under the table and he would find her regardless." My voice trembles with rage as Vin rubs circles into my back, the open diary sitting in my lap.

"This is a good start." Emmett nods at the open totes.

"Let's get Wade and that problem out of the way first. Then I can completely focus on this little disease of a town. I plan on raising my kids here. It needs to be purged." Their heads all snap toward me as the room falls silent. We're all too young to be thinking about families, but I can't help thinking of the future.

"Once the first one's in here,"—Vin pats my flat stomach—"the others will follow soon after."

"Oh, yeah?" Emmett gets a mischievous gleam in his eyes. "When will that be?"

"After we get married." Vin shrugs and my heart soars.

"And when is that?" Emmett continues to badger him, giving me some satisfaction.

"Two years, tops," Vin states, and I gasp.

"Two years?" Our eyes meet and I get lost in their stormy green color.

"Tops," he reiterates before kissing my mouth. "I better head over and check on my mom." He places me on the couch and gets up, then saunters out of the room, his swagger full of quiet confidence. The way those particular jeans hug his ass has me watching as his glutes flex with each step.

"From the very first day, that's how she's looked at him. Nothing's changed." Adri smirks as I pull my eyes away from Vin to look at her.

"Except when I made out with Travis." I drop a bomb, liking the aftermath of the shock.

Travis chokes on his Gatorade and Emmett has a shit-eating grin on his face. "Adri, how did you take that?"

"She was honest with me about it." Adri recovers quickly and smiles at me. "Plus, she said she didn't really feel it."

"Nope, neither of us did." Travis leans over and places a sweet kiss on her mouth.

Few people would understand their relationship.

Fuck, I barely did in the beginning, and I was almost sure this shit was doomed to fail, but now I see how the three of them work. Adri and Travis are like fire and gasoline, and Emmett is like cool water, always buffing out the tension that's between them. If it weren't for him, they would end up killing each other.

"What do you guys think of the Black Slaughter?" I ask as I twirl a piece of my hair around my finger.

"What is that?" Adri's eyes are wide. "Someone else you have to hunt down?"

"No, baby." I drop my hand from my hair and lean forward. "She *is* the huntress… The Black Slaughter." I spread my hands over my head.

"Sounds a little corny." Emmett purses his lips as I narrow my eyes on him, then he rolls his eyes at my reaction and adds, "But scary too."

"How'd you come up with this name?" Travis turns to look at me from his place on the floor.

"Andrew Cox told me the perv committee in Whitsborough started calling me that when I began hunting them down. Silly little rabbits!" I fall over laughing.

"My sister is mental." Emmett chuckles as he does his best Elmer Fudd impersonation. "*Be vewy vewy quiet, I'm hunting wabbits.*"

"I'm hunting my bed." Adri stands and yawns. "Love you, Ember. Good night."

"Love you," I say as Emmett flashes me a wink, then chases behind her.

Travis gets up from his place on the floor and sits on the couch beside me. He looks slightly troubled, and I know it's because he's been through so much. He and I have a connection that I don't have with any of the others, and my love for Travis is different. He sees me and my very soul— as black and depraved as it is—and he loves me as if I'm pure light. It's hard to explain. Vin loves my dark soul and everything it encompasses. No matter what I do in life, his love will never change, but Travis sees it for what it is and still deems me worthy of something higher. He makes me feel like I'm pure and that my dark soul is untarnished.

"Hey, I have a question." Turning to face him, I place my hand on his shoulder.

"Shoot." He throws me a grin.

"Is marriage something the three of you envision in your futures?" He grabs my hand from his shoulder and holds it in his lap as he nods.

"One of us will make it legal with Adri, and then we will have a private ceremony for the three of us." He's thought of this and I love that for them.

"Can I be Best Black Slaughter?" I flutter my eyelashes at him.

"This name is going to stick, huh?" He chuckles. "And yes, you are my best everything."

See what I mean? He just sees me differently, and I love him the most for it. I don't care what anyone thinks. He's my favorite, but I wouldn't tell any of them that. Travis was on the verge of death, in a coma for ten days, and when he finally came back to us, I watched his eyes change as they landed on me. He was searching for my light.

"So, Black Slaughter? Is this what we'll name the skull-faced alter ego?"

"I think so." I nod and smile at him. "It sounds so ominous. Just like me."

"You're not dark." He leans over and kisses my cheek. "Don't stay up late."

Then he stands and leaves the room as I settle back down on the sofa to read the rest of my mother's childhood diaries.

Chapter Two

Vin

She's sleeping when I get back to the house, her body wrapped around the pillow I use on the bed. She's wearing one of my T-shirts and nothing underneath, her plush lips opening softly as she breathes deeply. She's asking for my dick, that's what that means. She's so fucking gorgeous it hurts.

The first day I laid eyes on Ember, I knew my life would change forever. I was finally hand-delivered my soul's mate, and it was like God himself said, *don't fuck this up*. If I knew then what I know now, I wouldn't change a single thing. Everything we've been through, our close brushes with death, only solidified what I already knew: Ember and I were meant to love each other with every fiber of our being.

I rip my shirt over my head and drop my sweatpants to the floor. I was hard as soon as I stepped into the room. I brought a surprise with me tonight and I don't plan to let it go to waste. Crawling up the bed, I move her onto her back, and she lets out an adorable little snore. I chuckle softly as

I slowly lift the shirt she's wearing, because her tempting pussy sits there on display for me, and I lean in to run my nose along her slit.

"Mmm." She squirms a bit as she begins to wake up. "Vin?"

Her voice sounds so fucking sexy when it's raspy with sleep. This is why I love waking her up just before I fuck her back to sleep. I spread her legs and lick a straight line from her asshole all the way to her clit and listen to her moan in appreciation. Her pussy becomes wet, the pretty little thing glistening with her arousal. Wanting more of it, I press my finger against her opening and push it inside, feeling her clench around me. Then I add two more fingers and her greedy pussy sucks me in. Her wetness coats my hand, running along my palm, the sight turning me on further, so I pull out and rub the moisture along her puckered hole. Ember loves anal play, especially when my dick spreads her to the point of pain.

She sits up—now fully awake—and shucks her shirt off and onto the floor. Her tits bounce with the movement, and my mouth latches onto a nipple while my hand grabs at the other. She is my one weakness. Everything I do, think, see, smell, and taste is all Ember. Am I obsessed? Yes, I fucking am, but so should any guy who's completely in love with someone.

She lays back, running her fingers through my hair as I hover over her stomach. There's a fresh scar here now, and the sight of it makes me want to murder the man who tried to kill her. Ember arches her back, bringing her stomach near my mouth. I lick along the scar and listen as she gasps, then moans. She's never shied away from me to hide her scars. They're her battle wounds and she is beyond proud of each of them. Yes, Ember is physically beautiful— like I said before—painfully so, but it's a miniscule portion of what I love about her. I don't care what her skin looks like or how her face looks, because it's the Ember inside who really makes my heart pound.

My face is back in front of her pussy as I dive in, her essence like honey, sweet with a hint of tang, and I want that nectar coating my tongue. She doesn't disappoint me as her juices run into my mouth, and I slurp it up like an addict needing my next fix. My hands slide under her ass and my fingers clench into her crack, pressing into her rear hole. When she finally comes on my mouth with my name on her lips, I lift her up higher and push my tongue into her ass slightly, causing her breath to hitch as she tenses up.

"Gotta work it out, baby." I look up and grin at her. "We're having fun with this tonight."

"Oh?" She raises her eyebrow.

I kiss my way back up her body, leaving a trail of her juices as I go. Finally, I'm hovering over her face as I smile wider. Her lips twitch with a grin in response and her legs fall to either side of my waist, then she thrusts her pelvis up as she rubs her soaking wet pussy along my shaft. It jerks, hitting her sweet spot, and I watch as her eyes roll back before closing on a moan.

"Keep your eyes shut," I demand, watching as her breath quickens, but she complies with a slight nod. As tough and commanding as Ember is, she knows when to obey me in the bedroom. She fucking loves it.

I reach inside my pants pocket and pull out the vibrating butt plug and a small tube of lube. I still remember Ember watching that porn in the Columbia library, an explicit scene of a woman taking double penetration. She was curious and said she wanted to try, but not by adding another man. If she wanted another man, I would kill him in front of her and make her watch, then I would fuck her over his dead body. No other dick will ever come near her again, not without me ripping it off and feeding it to whomever it belonged to.

I flip her onto her belly and she squeals in surprise. "Lift your ass up and show Daddy what's his." She exhales loudly and does as I say, spreading her legs. "Pretty pink pussy." I lean in and suck a lip into my mouth before biting down and releasing it with a *pop*. Ember wriggles and moans. "Stay still." She stiffens and doesn't allow herself to move an inch as I rub the lube against her puckered hole, slowly sliding two fingers in. "Good girl," I praise her and continue fucking her ass with my fingers. Once she's loosened, I lube the plug and gently insert it into her. She exhales once more, but her ass is no virgin. It takes my dick's pounding like a fucking champ. Once it's fully seated in her ass, I give it a tug to test it before turning on the vibrations, making Ember almost leap off the bed, but I clamp my arm over her ass to keep her in place as she continues to squirm.

"Holy shit!" She gasps, then groans into the pillow. "That feels... so good."

"That's good, baby," I coo as I rub my hand over her ass cheek. "Now open those legs. My dick is ready to destroy that pussy."

She does as I ask, and I spread her cheeks open and push myself inside. Her head hangs as she pants, and tingles assault my cock as I groan, feeling the vibrations through the thin membrane. I can't go slow tonight. She'll just have to forgive me later. I slam the rest of the way into her until my pelvis hits the plug in her ass.

"Oh, fuck!" she screams out as her pussy contracts around my cock. She's coming hard if her quaking body means anything. Her pussy is literally trying to suck the cum out of me, so I pound into her, reveling in the screams as she comes one more time before I spill myself so fucking deep inside her.

Pulling out, I grin at the amount of wetness coating my cock and thighs. I love making her come this hard, even if it leaves our sheets a fucking mess. Right now, she doesn't give a fuck what she's lying in as she continues to twitch through the aftermath of her release.

"Thank you," she mumbles into the sheets when I reach over and switch off the vibrations, and I chuckle as I gently remove the plug. Her stretched asshole slowly tightens and it's so fucking hot. I want to slam my dick in there so badly, but I know she's done and would have none of it. Not for a few more hours anyway.

Then I pick her up and carry her into her bathroom to run a bath in her girly, claw-foot tub.

"Add those smelly salts." She still has her eyes closed as she speaks, and I laugh as I kiss her nose.

"Okay, baby." I place her down in the tub and pour the salts under the running water, then I kneel on the floor beside the tub and watch as the most important thing in my life soaks in a hot bath.

She's all mine.

I tend to be the first to wake up in the morning, then Travis appears once the scent of brewing coffee wafts through the house. After that, Emmett and Ember's twin senses have them creepily making their way down together, and Adri is usually the last to get up. I start making the coffee and can't control the smile that keeps ghosting my mouth. I'm the happiest I have ever been at this moment and it's because of everyone in this house, but mostly because of the first girl who stole my heart and claimed it forever.

"Are you humming?" Travis leans against the counter beside me. He's shirtless, wearing only a pair of plaid pajama bottoms.

"No," I scoff and clear my throat. Was I humming?

"Yeah, you were." He chuckles sleepily and rubs his tousled hair out of his eyes. "You guys were louder than usual last night."

"Sorry, man." *Not fucking sorry at all.*

"Emmett says his dick and balls have crawled

back up inside him." I nearly choke on air with the visual, shuddering at the imagery.

"He's fucking weird. Are you sure you like him?" I question as I lean against the counter, knowing Emmett and Ember will be up soon.

"Right?" Travis laughs and pours a cup of coffee. "I must be the weirdest person alive. I fucking love the guy."

I knew there was something between those two before we even left for Spain. I had an idea we would come back to something going on, but I never imagined they'd be in a throuple—Ember's word—and it actually working out. It really does fucking work, they're one big happy throuple.

"Vin!" Ember screams from the top of the stairs, her shrill tone making me smile.

"Yes?" I call out, my voice nonchalant as Travis' eyebrows come together with confusion.

"Get your ass up here!" Her pitch is only increasing as panic runs through her words.

"Can you come down here? I just poured my coffee." I'm not concerned with her panicked state, she'll have to accept it regardless.

Travis looks at my still-empty coffee cup and then up to my face with a raised brow. I shrug and grin as I finally pour myself some.

"Vincent Greene!" she screeches, and both Travis and I wince at the sound.

"Wooo!" Travis chuckles while rubbing his hand along his cheek, his eyes flicking from me to the kitchen entryway. "She called you Vincent."

"Haven't been this excited in a while." I wink at him as he shakes his head.

She stomps down the stairs and straight into the kitchen. Emmett is close behind her with a confused look on his face, and Adri drags along behind them, looking like she's downright half asleep.

"Is there something you want to say to me?" Ember looks at me wide-eyed, her face a little pale.

"No?" I raise a brow. "I'm just making coffee." I hold up my cup, the liquid sloshing inside.

"Vincent!" She forces my name out through her teeth.

"Twice," Travis mutters before coughing to cover it up.

Emmett, though, is not so smooth as amusement flits over his features. "Damn, Vin! She's calling your ass *Vincent*. What the fuck did you do?"

"I haven't done anything wrong." I feign confusion as I take a sip of my coffee, my eyes meeting Ember's over the rim.

"This, Vincent!" She lifts her left hand and flashes the ring I slipped on there while she was sleeping. "What the hell is this?"

"A ring?" I smirk and look at her like she's crazy.

Everyone has gone completely quiet and is staring at the diamond ring on Em's ring finger. It looks stunning on her hand, as if the band and stone were crafted with her in mind.

"Whose ring?! Why is it on me?!" Her voice becomes panicked again as she continues to wave her hand in the air.

"That's Nana Germaine's ring. Ma has been keeping it for when I decided to marry someone. I asked her yesterday if I could have it and she agreed," I reply.

Adri hops on the spot with her hands over her mouth to cover the squeal that's leaking out while Emmett and Travis still stare wide-eyed at Em's finger.

"Are you proposing?" Ember asks quietly, her body trembling.

This girl can take down men twice her size, kill anybody for the right price, and basically stare into the devil's face without breaking a sweat, but a piece of jewelry makes her quake in fear.

"Nah, baby, I ain't proposing shit." I put my cup down on the counter and move to stand in front of her. "I'm telling you. We're getting married. I put that on your finger because you will be my wife. Fuck proposing it."

A sob breaks free from her mouth as she jumps up into my arms, her legs winding around my waist.

"That's how it's done!" Emmett claps and whoops. "Vin just laid claim, no matter what her answer was."

"What if I say no?" Ember whispers quietly into my ear while everyone is screaming and clapping around us.

"You never had a choice. Don't fool yourself." I snicker and lick a path from her throat to her mouth, then I devour her. Just like I plan on doing for the rest of my life.

Chapter Three

The Eastside Rampage operates out of a mostly underground compound in Hunts Point, New York. The area is an abandoned industrial part of the city, and my father, Raphael, bought out most of the area decades ago. His father came to New York in the fifties to establish a legacy for his sons, and Raphael ultimately killed him and his two brothers to take over the Rampage and make it into the bustling illegal empire it is today.

Carm sees no need of reforming it, despite the fact that the Rampage distributes drugs, whores, and assassinations. He likes the income and doesn't deem it worthwhile to change. I strongly disagree, but unfortunately, if I wanted that change, I would need to be like Raphael and kill my brother.

"I've upped the training in combat for the guards and doubled them in the ring for this weekend. It's going to get messy," Trent tells Emmett as the rest of us follow behind them.

"Nice." Emmett claps him on the back. "How are you getting him in the arena?"

"He thinks he'll be watching another Blur fight to the death." He chuckles and shakes his head.

The first time I met Trent, I thought he was a grade A asshole. He basically gave me a once-over and found me wanting. When I needed to spar before the fight I got slashed, he tried to convince Carm to let him go up against me, but Carm vehemently disagreed. I don't like letting people get away with assuming I'm weak because I own a pair of tits and a vagina. I love proving them wrong with at least a broken nose or sore testicles. I still want to break his fucking nose even though he's apologized multiple times. It's just who I am. I'd rather punish than forgive. Emmett loves him though, and for that reason alone, I have to bury the hatchet and—to everyone's preference—not in his back.

"I want to go in as the Black Slaughter," I reveal.

"What?" Emmett turns quickly, almost causing me to collide with his chest.

I pop my fist out and jab him in the stomach. "Watch it."

He bends over and coughs, then looks up at me with a grin. "You want to go into the ring with your makeup on?"

"Yes." I nod adamantly. I'm not asking. If that's how I want it done, then that's how it'll be.

He sees the look on my face and knows it brokers no room for negotiation, so with a shrug, he turns back around to resume his talk with Trent.

"The Black Slaughter," Adri hums behind me. "I like it."

"Wait until you see her in her makeup. You're gonna like it even more." Vin chuckles.

My Black Slaughter face is reserved for the people

I kill on jobs, or for myself and my family. Wade is one of those jobs. He tried to have me killed, now it's time I repay the favor. The Heads are already here, and our meeting begins in about an hour. I need to get to my room and apply my makeup because I'm going in there for the sole purpose of setting someone up to die by my hands.

"How did you get the guard to confess?" I question Trent. According to Carm, one of his guards was paid to slip my opponent the knife by Wade.

"I didn't." Trent looks back at me, his expression turning perplexed. "Carm got all the pleasure. From what I heard, he didn't take it too easy on the guy."

"Carm got his hands dirty?" Emmett asks, sounding surprised.

"Yeah, he refused to let anyone else in that room with him." Trent turns back to Emmett, his attention on him.

"I'm so lucky to have such a brother, huh?" I slap Trent on the arm and walk by.

"Yeah, you are," he agrees behind me, his voice holding a hint of humor.

I get to the room they once held me prisoner in, and Vin follows closely behind me. For most, sleeping in a room that once doubled as a cell would be unheard of, but for me, it's therapy. I refuse to blame these four walls for the trauma I endured. That respect was given to my father, who I repaid with a bullet to his head. I also stay in this room because they held my mother here, and in some ways, it feels like she's here with me.

"Are you pissed you didn't get to question that guard?" Vin closes the door, shutting out any listening ears.

"Not pissed." I stop and think over exactly how I'm feeling, knowing Vin would want the complete truth. "It would've been nice to do it myself, but I know Carm can do the job."

"I see," he answers and flops down on the bed.

Sitting on the counter in the small bathroom, I apply my Black Slaughter makeup. I'm going into that meeting to call Wade out for trying to kill me, and I'm going to be as intimidating as I can be, the makeup provides a layer of anonymity.

The white makeup coats my skin like paint, blocking out all colors in its path. When Adri found out I was using Halloween makeup, she nearly threw a fit. The next day she had ordered a bunch of special effects makeup and top makeup brand products. I don't know too much about makeup, but I can give her the respect she deserves. This shit is pretty amazing.

I begin by drawing the spider webs on each jaw and the corner of my forehead in black. Next, I work on the skull's eyes, cheeks, and nose. The pattern flows from my mind through my hand, my face the perfect canvas. I paint a blood red rose on the top left corner of my forehead, right above my eyebrow, then apply the same color to my lips. When I'm done, I sit back and admire my work. It's frighteningly beautiful.

I get dressed in black leather pants and a matching corset top, and around my neck, I wear a satin choker with a knife pendant hanging in the hollow of my throat. Every detail matters because, after today, every motherfucking Head in that room will remember The Black Slaughter.

"You look so fucking hot," Vin groans from the bed as he reaches inside his pants and strokes his cock. "I feel so morbid."

I laugh at him and blow him a kiss. "When I get back, I'll mess up this makeup all over your dick."

There's a quick knock on the door, and then I hear Trent's voice as Vin removes his hand from his pants with a huff. "Ember, I have to escort you to the meeting."

I open the door and revel in the quick flash of fear in

his eyes before he covers it and smirks. "That's a bit creepy."

"Trent!" Vin calls from his place on the bed. "Make sure my fiancée makes it back here untouched." The threat in his voice is clear.

"Fiancée? Congrats." He looks from my face to my stomach, his brows crinkling in the center. I don't resent his thoughts of teenage pregnancy, since outside of that reason, it's utterly absurd for eighteen-year-olds to be engaged. Not that I correct him because it's none of his business. "I'll have her back here without so much as a hair out of place on her pretty, evil head."

I follow him out the door and down the hallway to the large double doors that house the Head meetings. Two guards stand on either side, their faces void of any expression. "Are they all here?"

"Yeah. I made sure you were the last to arrive. Carm informed me of your preference." He turns before opening the door and looks at me, his hand resting on the handle. "You remind me of your father. I know you hate hearing that, but you do. I can also see how you're different, but it's slight. It's not a bad thing to be like him. He was tough, respected, and feared. He ran an empire that one man shouldn't have been able to command all on his own and he killed like it was his favorite hobby. All I'm trying to do is warn you. Don't let it fuck with your mind. That's where he was weak, and also in here." He taps his chest over his heart. "Continue to love the people around you and never let the pleasure of killing embrace you like an old friend. The more you revel in the high, the longer you stay there."

I'm not offended to be compared to my father. I've already accepted it a long time ago. Maybe even before I met the asshole. I understand what Trent is telling me, and I appreciate his words. Not many people around me knew my father, save for Emmett and Carm, but I don't want to dredge up Emmett's dark past and Carm refuses to speak of him. So it's good to hear how not to turn into our sperm donor completely.

"Thank you, Trent," I tell him genuinely, and he pats my back before opening the door.

The hushed conversation stops abruptly and everyone's eyes slowly widen as they take in my face and attire when I walk inside.

"I've been quieter and more subdued for the last few meetings. I'm new and wanted to get a feel for the position and the people I am now associated with." I stand at my usual spot at the table, directly to Carm's right, and lay my knife down on the polished wood. Then I walk to the head of the table and stand behind Carm. His shoulders stiffen a bit, but he doesn't move. "Most of you are straightforward and call things how you see it." I place my hand on his shoulder before moving on to the man next to him and doing the same.

"Some of you are more ruthless than others and like to play with your food before you eat it." I get to my fat fellow Head, the one that disregarded me in the beginning until I told him I killed his mark. "We may be leaders in our area, but in this room, we are equal. Not one of us is any better than the other." I stop behind Wade and place my hand on his shoulder. He doesn't move and seems completely at ease. Cocky fucker. "We should protect each other and help each other because a win for one is a win for all." I squeeze his shoulder and the guy finally tenses. "You tried to have me killed, Wade."

"What?" He has the audacity to sound shocked as he remains frozen in his seat.

"You set me up to fight one of your guys. Who even knows if he was actually plotting your death?"

"This is absurd!" He tries to stand, but I squeeze the pressure point in his neck until he sits again with a pained sound escaping his mouth.

"You gave him a knife, and when he was almost beaten, he pulled that on me. He slashed me across the belly, and if he had been less than an inch closer, it would have splattered my entrails across that mat." Carm's face crumbles into a look of pain.

"I did not give him that knife," Wade says, sounding completely sincere as he looks up at my face.

"Yes, you did." Carm's voice rings out loud as he leans forward, his hands pressing against the top of the table. "My guard confessed to accepting payment from you to do so."

"Which guard?" Wade bellows. "Bring him in here so I may question him myself!" His eyes are wild as he glares at Carm, not backing down at all.

"He was taken care of. I do not house traitors," Carm smoothly replies as he sits back in his seat, his face smug.

"Convenient," Wade sneers, then sets his sights on me, his body stiff with ire. "How do you propose we correct this?"

"I propose a fight in the cage." I keep my face free of any emotion even though my lips fight to form a grin.

"Fine. I can't refuse unless I want to be portrayed as a liar. Tell me, Blur, what are the stakes?" His eyes remain clear and steady on mine, his jaw tensing with the effort to hold in his anger.

"Black Slaughter," I correct him, gesturing to my face with a smirk. "The stakes are to the death, Wade."

His face pales and he swings his gaze from me to Carm. "This can't be right, you can't murder a Head."

"Yet you tried just that," Carm grits out between his teeth as he folds his arms over his chest.

"I did not!" He finally stands and yells across the table, his fists connecting with the wooden top.

"I'll see you tomorrow night, Wade," I singsong as I walk back toward Trent and the door. "May the best man win."

I hear his voice behind me, begging Carm to make me reconsider. He sounds sincere, but I could too if I needed to be. My appearance as a Head probably irritated him, given my age and experience, and he figured I should be taught a lesson. Or better yet, maybe Carm was being taught a lesson because I was never meant to leave that cage.

I don't miss the wary looks from the others as I leave the room, closing the door slowly behind me. Good. I may be young and inexperienced at being a Head, but that doesn't make me any less capable of cleaving my own path in their organization.

VIN

Ember lays naked beside me, her hair fanning across the pillow and her fucking makeup all over the bed and me. I finger the pattern she tattooed under her left breast, an infinity symbol with our initials inside of it. It's an exact match for the one over my heart on my chest.

"He looked like he was telling the truth. Is my mind playing tricks on me?" she whispers as she looks at me. She looks torn and it breaks my heart, because as dark as Ember can be, she still walks the line of decency. She doesn't kill without reason and she makes sure every one of her victims are deserving of their fate.

"Do you think Carm's guard acted on his own?" I drag my hand over her breast, skimming along her throat before landing on her cheek, my fingers grazing her soft skin.

"I don't know." She shrugs and releases a long exhale. "Maybe if he was offered enough money?"

"Even knowing it would definitely come back on him?" I question as she groans, confliction clear in her expression. "If it were something I agreed to, I would ask for help to get out of here and never look back. Why would he stay?"

"And Trent?" she asks in a hushed voice. "He has no loyalty to me, but when he speaks to me, he seems like he truly cares."

I see her inner turmoil flashing through her features. This is hard shit, the most likely person to want her Head position is Wade, and obviously, he is getting what's coming to him, but I can see that Ember saw something to make her doubt that.

"If it wasn't Wade, then it was Trent," I tell her, knowing the admission is painful to hear. Carm wouldn't let anything happen to his sister if he could prevent it. "If there's something bothering you, then you need to get answers before you take a life undeserving of death."

"I know," she mutters, sounding tortured.

"Do what your gut tells you." I kiss her head and pull her against my chest.

Her enormous heart is pounding against mine, and I know as sadistic as Ember can be, she's agonizing over this decision. The boundary she laid out for herself from the very beginning was to only kill when it was absolutely the only answer, and she hasn't once deviated from that.

I suddenly feel her breathing even out and look down to see her heavy with sleep in my arms. So I match my breathing to hers and drift off as well.

I feel her rustle as she gets out of the bed. Since we're underground, I can't determine the time, but I have a feeling it's still night or early morning. Ember is creeping around, trying not to wake me, and I let her continue without alerting her that I'm awake. She pulls on a pair of sweats and swipes her hair up into a bun on the top of her head, then sneaks out the door. I throw the blankets off my body and scramble into my clothes, hurrying to open the door behind her.

I glimpse her turning the corner to my right and follow. A couple turns later, I see her talking to a guard outside of Carm's office. He permits her entry inside, and I blow out a breath of relief. She's probably going to talk shit out with him and figure out what he thinks about the whole situation. Now that I know she isn't putting herself in any immediate danger, I turn around and go back to our room. I may let Ember fight her way through life as I sit and watch, but I am watching, and if at any point I feel like her life's in jeopardy, I will step in and do whatever is necessary to protect her.

About an hour later, she comes back into the room. In her hands, she holds a file that she immediately pops into her bag, then I watch as she removes her clothes and crawls back into bed beside me.

"Everything okay?" I ask her.

"I had to talk to Carm," she reveals as she curls into my side, her head resting on my shoulder. "But he wasn't in his office. I found something though. I'll tell you about it tomorrow."

I nod and kiss her cheek as we fall back asleep.

Chapter Four

Ember

I don't get the chance to speak to Vin about Wade in the morning because Emmett comes through like a motherfucking tornado and demands our attention. We spend the day with everyone at Coney Island, and it brings back memories of my mother, and also memories of when Emmett and I took a trip to the island.

The day is fun, but all too soon, I have to prepare for my fight with Wade. I found a few interesting things in Carm's office, one of which was about Wade. They have linked him to a kidnapping ring on Long Island. Mostly snatching up teenage girls who come from broken homes, are runaways, or are homeless, then drugging them for a few days before selling them overseas. Am I surprised? Fuck no, this is nothing new. I knew the Head organization was a dirty one, and I have plans to gradually change that, but the fight today is killing two birds with one stone.

Wade inherited his position from his father—nepotism at its finest—and instead of cleaning up what his corrupted old man was doing, he kept capitalizing on the lower-income families in his area by pushing drugs to single moms and then taking their children to be sold in the sex trade or to sell more crack to other disadvantaged homes.

Whatever reservations I had about him yesterday have flown out the window, even if I'm still questioning if he had anything to do with the knife that almost gutted me like a fucking fish.

I'm warming up my muscles when Carm comes into the gym, his eyes narrowed as he approaches. "Hey. One of my guys said you came by the office last night?" He stands rigid, his shoulders tense and his mouth set in a firm line.

"Yeah." I stare into his eyes as they flick around the gym. "I forgot my knife in the meeting room yesterday. I can't sleep without it near me. Especially here. I figured you put it in your office."

"Yeah, I thought you'd have realized sooner that you forgot it." He relaxes and grins, his hands moving to his waist as he exhales.

"It's been fucking hectic." I scrub my hand down my face before standing.

"Just focus on the fight for now. Wade is trained, Ember. This one may be your toughest yet." He looks at me with worry in his eyes, and yet a part of me wonders if it's genuine. Immediately after the thought enters my mind, guilt floods me. Of course it's genuine. Carm has been working hard at being the big brother Emmett and I need.

"I figured. It has to be done, Carm. This fight will be watched by every Head member and I can't have them doubting my position. I need to eliminate anyone who even thinks they could take me or my family out."

"Fuck, you sound like him a lot sometimes," he confesses quietly, his face becoming pained. I don't make a remark because I do sound like the homicidal maniac who helped create us. It's rare that Carm mentions it though, so

I don't dare correct him. "He became really paranoid at the end, calling for anyone and everyone to be killed. Someone questioned him, he killed them. It was gruesome when he got out, like he knew while he was gone his hold had slipped. Then he asked us about Emberlise Craven and how well she was working for us." He looks at me with sad eyes. "I was the one that spoke so damn highly of you, the girl I had never set eyes on, who refused to meet me, and fought her battles in abandoned warehouses or empty parking lots. I had not a single clue who you were."

"It's not your fault." I shake my head, trying to relieve him of some of the guilt weighing him down.

"In a way, it is. His eyes brightened at my praise, and he just had to see you. I hunted you down, twisted Tommy's arm to tell me where you moved to. Raphael was eager to get to you. I told him the address and we were on the road almost immediately. I should've known it was something more. When we reached Toronto, he finally confessed to who you were and why we were picking you up." He shifts from one foot to the other, his face a mask of regret, and his eyes refusing to meet mine.

"Why was he picking me up? What was his endgame for me?" It's the last piece of the puzzle of my kidnapping that I've been stuck on. I killed for my father, I lost myself to a dark void, and then I committed atrocities for my freedom, yet I never did find out the true reason *why*.

"He wanted you to sit next to him. Be his second." His revelation has a gasp getting stuck in my throat, my eyes searching Carm's face.

"Your position." I clear my throat and narrow my eyes as he finally looks at me, his face hardening.

"Yeah," he agrees. I wait for more of an explanation, animosity, anything, but when I get nothing, I push a little more.

"And you were okay with that?" I blink through my shock as he lifts a shoulder.

"Of course not, and to be honest, I really didn't think you would live up to the hype." He smiles ruefully, the expression not quite meeting his eyes. "Even after you attacked our guards outside of your school the night we grabbed you, I still thought you were just a kid. A skilled fighter and talented as fuck, but just a kid. You proved me wrong while you were here. I decided I was going to help you, and if you were more suited for the position, then I would let it be." His confession feels off to me, almost as though he's telling me the things I'd want to hear. What he doesn't realize is, I don't want the Rampage, I never have.

Instead of taking his explanation and preening, I raise a brow and say, "And? Am I?"

"Yes," he answers reluctantly, yet honestly. "You would've ripped the Eastside Rampage apart and made it something better, eliminating anyone that was deemed a threat and do it all with ease and precision. The only thing against you? You're a woman and a fucking young one." Again, his praise doesn't quite hit the mark, and I don't know if it's because he wants to placate me or he's just naturally manipulative.

I nod anyway because he's correct. It's bad enough being young, but owning a pair of tits makes it difficult to order men around. Especially those who think their balls are the size of fucking soccer balls. "And now, Carm? How do you feel?"

"I feel like this would never be what you choose. You found someone you want to spend your life with, maybe start a family. If you were here, doing my job, your kids would be next in line, and I know you would want something better for them. Look, you wanted something better for your twin." He's right again, saying all the things I feel inside. This is not where I would raise a family, and if I did ever take over the Rampage, I would dismantle it in a hot minute.

"Emmett not being here,"—I study his face for any reaction as I continue to warm up—"how do you really feel about that?"

"I wanted him here with me. I didn't want him running off into the sunset with his—sorry—crazy-ass sister and thinking life was peaches, losing the abilities he took years to master, and becoming complacent in life. Instead, he has people he loves and is the happiest I have ever seen him. I'm jealous I couldn't provide the same, but I'm grateful to you." Sincerity shines from his eyes as he slips his hands into his pockets, rocking back on his heels.

"And me? What do you see when you look at me? Am I your sister or the best fighter you have?" I haven't had Carm as a brother from the day I was born like Emmett, so as much as I'm anticipating his answer, it wouldn't be devastating if he did see me as his best fighter.

"Both." He doesn't hesitate. "When we were in Spain, I went there knowing I cared about you because you were my sibling. It was innate, but that was it. I didn't want harm to come to you because of how important you had become to Emmett, and also because we shared blood." He shakes his head with a chuckle. "I wanted to kill you pretty much every day of that trip. Then, the last few days, I found myself fucking laughing at your antics, even though it was always at my expense. I saw you weren't just fearless, but you were multidimensional. You had depth so deep, I could drown in it, and you weren't just strong, you were soft too.

"So, yes, Ember, you are my best fighter. When I have you in that ring, no matter the type of fight, I am rolling in money. You know it too because I send you home with a sizable chunk of it, but when you are outside of that ring, you're my baby sister and I don't know what I would do if anything were to happen to you." His eyes fill with sincerity, showing a rare moment of vulnerability as I shift on my feet. I'm not used to Carm being like this, so it's hard to articulate exactly how I feel about him.

"Just know I would kill for you, Carm. You're my family, and from the day I knocked you out with that gun instead of shooting you, I knew you would be important to me. You're my big brother. You helped me with finding Vin and Travis, moved at my every whim, and were always the first to protect me. I love you," I profess as my chest squeezes with emotion.

His eyes fill with unshed tears and his cheeks turn pink as he hauls me in for an awkward hug. "I love you, little sis."

Once we pull apart, we're back to business as he runs through some drills with me and helps me tape my hands. Vin walks in with Travis and Emmett not too long after, both of them looking a little on edge.

"Where's Adri?" I look around them toward the door, waiting to see if she emerges from the hallway.

"She's watching the other fights happening before yours. I think she's trying to desensitize, maybe?" Travis smiles, the expression not quite meeting his eyes. He's worried about her because of the last fight, but I bet he's also working through his own trauma from it as well. "Trent is sitting with her."

I look quickly at Vin in question, my heart beginning to race with worry. *Do we trust Trent?* He nods once and I let myself relax. Vin wouldn't let anything happen to our family.

"Are you nervous?" Emmett asks, worry plain as day reflecting in his eyes.

"A bit," I admit with a shrug as I pick at the tape on my hand. "Mostly I just want this done because I have a lot of shit to get back to at home."

Carm and Emmett chuckle while Travis comes up beside me to pull me into his arms and tucks my head under his chin. I can feel the tension thrumming through his body, and I try to rub soothing circles into his back. I know he hates when I fight, and out of everyone, he is the most prone to overthinking.

"Tell me to whisk you away right now," he whispers into my hair as his heart pounds against my cheek.

"I have to show people what happens when they mess with us," I whisper back. "A moment of weakness would leave you all vulnerable."

"Okay," he replies, sounding sad as he squeezes me a little tighter.

"Look at it this way." I pull back and look up at him with a grin. "I'm going to enjoy kicking that scumbag's ass. Wade has had it coming from day one. I will not lose, Travis," I promise him as he searches my eyes for any sign of deceit.

"There's no option, Ember. You don't have a choice. You have to win." The tremor in his words and the way his jaw tenses has my heart cracking inside my chest. I hate this fear he has, though I feel powerless about how to erase it. Travis has been abandoned many times in his life by the people who were supposed to love him, so it's only natural for him to constantly be wary of the same thing from me.

I get on my tippy-toes and kiss his cheek. "I will never leave you," I vow to him as his body slowly relaxes.

He crushes me back against his chest, and I wrap my arms around his waist once more, soaking up his affection. Travis needs to feel loved, not just hear it.

"Hey, stop monopolizing my fiancée." Vin's raspy growl bursts our little bubble and we pull apart with a laugh.

"Fiancée?" Carm's voice has me turning to face him as he looks at Vin and then me, shock and confusion warring across his features.

"Yeah, bro, our baby sister is getting married." Emmett holds his hands to his chest as his eyes round with mock emotion.

"You don't know that you're older!" I stomp my foot as I glare at my twin, his wide grin only pissing me off further. "I can bet I am because you still act like a pubescent."

"What? I trim that shit. Manscape, baby!" He gyrates his hips, his lack of vocabulary glaringly clear.

"You're a fucking idiot." Carm slaps the back of his head and then faces Vin. "Congratulations,"—He holds his hand out to Vin—"brother."

Vin takes it and Carm drags him in for a hug. "In this family, we are touchy as fuck." He chuckles when Emmett jumps on the both of them, hugging them tighter.

This overpowering feeling courses through my chest as I look at each of them and sigh in contentment.

My family.

The energy in this place tonight is molten. I have no other way to describe it. It's moving slowly, but once it hits someone, they are completely enveloped by the rush. The fiery burn moves and fills the arena with a restless aura, making it hard to sit still. People line the aisles as my family paces the perimeter of the cage.

Molten lava.

When I admitted to Emmett that I was nervous, it wasn't about me fighting Wade. It was about having them here watching me again. I worry about Travis, who is so empathic, feeling everything I'm experiencing, and Adri, who is innocent to this side of my life. I may take some hits tonight, Wade is a trained Head so I'm prepared for that, but I worry they aren't.

I look at my reflection in the mirror, and the grin that climbs across my mouth and creeps into my eyes is fucking scary. This Black Slaughter makeup is no joke. I look demonic with my face makeup and I fucking feel like it too. I've let my anger simmer for days now, and after learning what I have recently, it's brimming over. I almost feel sorry for Wade. Almost. I told Carm that I wanted a portion of tonight's winnings to go to his wife and child. He agreed and will send a portion of his as well. Maybe I'm saving their lives by eliminating him, or not. Either way, it doesn't change anything.

After pulling on my sweater, I open the door to find Emmett and Carm waiting, their bodies tense and their faces stern. "How much longer?" I ask them, my eagerness to have this done obvious.

"They're bringing him out now," Emmett hushes and closes the door.

The crowd inside the arena falls quiet as I strain to hear anything. They are all probably watching Wade being escorted to the cage, knowing he's Blur's opponent. Only tonight, I'm not Blur. I'm not fighting to the death to settle a score. I'm fighting to protect my family and myself from a threat. Tonight, I'm Black Slaughter.

A slow chant for Blur begins and quickly escalates, making me grin because I know they've shut Wade into the cage. I've given my new name to the MC along with new music. Blur would come out to "Bodies" by Drowning Pool, but Black Slaughter needs her own identity.

"Welcome back!" the MC booms over the mic. "Tonight, we have your favorite fighter in the building!" Chants for Blur grow louder. "Tonight, she's not Blur." The crowd falls silent as gasps fill the air. "Tonight... she is Black Slaughter!"

Goose bumps break out over my skin as adrenaline courses through me. Black Slaughter is standing inside this room, her lust for blood growing hot inside me. She will do anything to protect her family. I can be the monster needed and then rein it in on command. I can do this without losing myself.

I really hope I can do this without losing myself.

Skillet's "Monster" melody begins over the speakers and the door in front of me opens. I look into two sets of eyes. One so dark they look black, and another like the Caribbean Ocean, but both shining with pride. They turn and lead me toward the aisle, my heart beating to the bass of the music. As I pass, people either gasp at my appearance or try to touch me while I step out of reach of their hands. I'm already on edge, I don't need strangers pushing me into losing it before I get inside the ring.

By the time I get to the cage, Skillet's screaming about feeling like a monster. *Ditto, dude.* I look through the chain links and see Wade in nothing but a pair of track pants, his wide, toned chest and stomach on display. He's leaning against the side of the cage as he casually waits for me to get this going.

The cage door closes behind me and I throw my sweater to the side, keeping an eye on my opponent. We already know he likes to play dirty.

"Black Slaughter!" Wade calls out to me, but I ignore him like I do all the others and concentrate on regulating my heartbeat and breathing. "I didn't do it. I didn't plant a knife on the man that conspired to kill me. If I didn't do it, that leaves something you don't want to even fathom, right? That means someone real close to you is betraying you and trying to kill you."

I don't let his words affect me because that's what he wants so he can finish what he started months ago. I shake out my arms and legs, keeping my muscles warm as I narrow my eyes on him.

"I won't take it easy on you, but if at any point you want to tap out and end this, I will oblige. I don't want to kill you. I fucking respect you." He's looking at me earnestly as he pushes off the cage, his eyes begging me to believe him.

His words don't invoke the usual rage I feel when I'm about to fight. It's there at the base of my stomach, but it's not bubbling its way to the surface. Not that I need it. Regardless of the shit spewing from his mouth, he has to die for what happened to me. Everyone watching needs to see the consequence of fucking with me and mine.

I barely hear the MC calling the match to start as I begin running at him. His eyes widen, but then a smile spreads across his face. Once I'm in reach, his arms come out to grab me, but I quickly sidestep and punch him on his right elbow. Imagine knocking your funny bone... now imagine that pain times ten. He yelps and jumps back out of my way.

My disadvantage here tonight is that Wade has occasionally seen me fight, and although I try to keep each fight unpredictable, I do have moves I rely on more with men who are bigger than me. This time, I know I'll have to switch it up. Where I usually play levelheaded and dodge in the beginning, I'll now have to flip and try to catch him off guard.

I snap my leg out for a roundhouse kick and he looks triumphant as he grabs and holds my foot. Perfect. Using the momentum and the strength of him holding my one leg, I swing my other leg off the floor and kick him on the side of his head. We both hit the mat with a loud *thud*, but I'm already on my feet while he gets up to his knees. So far, he really hasn't tried to hit me or act on the offensive and I need to change that up.

He jumps to his feet, and I swiftly kick out again, catching him in the stomach this time. He bends over, and I quickly slam my knee up and into his face, hearing the distinct *crack* of his nose.

"That's it!" he screams as he stands to his full height, his nose dripping blood. "I was taking it easy on you, but that ends now."

Wade may know some of my moves. He may have watched me and learned for just this moment, but he doesn't know exactly what blood does to me during a fight. I watch transfixed as it runs over his lips and drips off his chin, the crimson color so bright against his white skin. Time to take this match to the next level.

He flies toward me, and I dodge both of his hands as they reach to grab me before the heel of my hand shoots out and hits him under his chin, driving his bottom teeth into his top lip. Again, he spits more blood onto the mat. I bounce on the balls of my feet, trying to contain the surge of adrenaline rushing through my body. I want to pound his face so fucking badly, but I need to keep a level head. He's not worn down enough, and if I lose my cool, he could get a crucial hit in.

"Black Slaughter!" He laughs, his teeth covered in blood, giving him a manic look. "This is absurd. I don't want to kill you."

Then he's coming at me again, his bare feet making loud, slapping sounds against the mat. I move out of the way of his fist, but I'm not fast enough because he clips me on my left cheek. I stumble, and before I can right myself, he punches the back of my head. Hitting the mat face down, my hands breaking my fall, I flip quickly onto my back to find Wade nearly on top of me. This is a dangerous position to be in when fighting a man of his size.

I kick his left knee and he drops onto it, his hand flying out to grab my neck, but I quickly jerk it to the side. Using my core strength, I lift my upper body and headbutt him in his already broken nose. The impact does some damage to me too as a throbbing starts on my forehead. He falls back, both hands clutching his flattened nose as he rolls across the mat, trying to get away from me.

I stagger to my feet and try to blink through the fog creeping along the edges of my vision. The motherfucker hit me good. I can feel the tight ball on the back of my head. He's on his hand and knees, one hand still clutching his shattered nose. I prowl toward him and quickly jump back when he tries to grab at me. Then I skip behind him and kick him on the back of his neck. He falls forward again and tries to drag himself toward the cage door. I take advantage and stomp down on his left ankle. The crack is satisfying, but his scream of pain is euphoric. Fucking music to my ears.

I grab that ankle and grin as he screams some more before dragging him back into the center of the ring. Then I drop his ankle and chuckle when the bounce makes him moan in pain. Straddling his back and reaching down to grab a handful of his hair, I lift his upper body, making his back bend in an uncomfortable position.

"It wasn't me," he says as he struggles to breathe. "You need to talk to your brother."

"Desperate words coming from a dead man." No matter how much my stomach twists at his confession, I remind myself he's still scum and deserves to die.

"I know I'm dead. I'm not getting out of this. I'm telling you so this doesn't happen to you again."

I don't let his words sink in. At this point, it's dragging out the inevitable. My arm comes around his neck, almost like a sleeper hold, and the other rests against the side of his head.

"I'll make sure your family is okay," I promise him seconds before breaking his neck. He falls with a dull *thud* to the mat, his life shut out forever.

So why do I still feel like this isn't over?

CHAPTER FIVE

"Daddy!" Rebecca giggles as she runs out of her closet and into her bedroom. "I need new pajamas. These are getting too small."

"That's because my big girl is growing," Jack croons as his salacious eyes skim over his young daughter.

My insides twist with a mixture of terror and disgust as I watch them both through the ajar door, my breath trapped inside my chest for fear of being caught. She sits on the bed, her hands resting in her lap as she looks at him expectantly.

"Did you brush your hair?" he asks her while taking a piece and holding it to his nose. His eyes roll shut as a rumble moves through his chest, the sight making my body tremble.

"Not yet." She jumps off the bed to grab her brush, her movements quick and obedient.

Her birthday is tomorrow and she'll be eleven years old. I fear every day as her body slowly becomes that of a woman's. What will he do to her then? What does he do to her now when I am not around? I want to ask her but I'm afraid he's brainwashed her or she would be too concerned with the consequences of telling me.

"You can't even lift your arms in that shirt." Jack chuckles as he leans back on the bed. "Take it off to brush your hair, then you can put it back on." I bite my bottom lip to stop myself from crying out, knowing I'm a coward for not interrupting this to save her.

"But I'll be naked." Rebecca turns to look at him with a pout, her tiny shoulders stiffening.

"I'm your daddy," Jack says soothingly as he gives her a soft smile. "I've seen you naked plenty of times."

"Okay." It's almost reassuring that she looks uncomfortable. It means she can sense this is wrong.

She pulls her top off and places it on the vanity top, my heart breaking at her compliance. Fear skates through her bright blue eyes—identical to his—as she stares into the mirror and brushes her hair.

"Lots of tangles," Jack remarks as he sits forward on the edge of the bed, watching her closely. The look of complete possession in his eyes has my heart stalling.

"I think I got them all," she murmurs after a few minutes, her voice quivering as goose bumps appear along her arms.

"Keep going," he demands, and I watch as she visibly swallows.

I want to go in there to help her, but I am nobody in this house... just a woman. If I attempt to stop this, he will not hesitate to kill me and bury my body in the backyard. Then what could I do? I just have to wait for the perfect moment to act on the plan I have put together. Something that will hopefully save both of the little girls in this house.

"Turn around and face Daddy as you put that shirt

back on," Jack rasps, his tone saturated with lust.

Rebecca does as he says, and I sigh in relief once the shirt is on, covering her once more. She plods to her bed and looks at her father while she climbs up and under the covers. There's a slight furrow between her brows as she watches him stand up. I hope she's beginning to understand that this isn't a normal situation between a father and daughter.

"Okay, my big girl. Time to sleep. Tomorrow, I will come pick you up from school." He reaches down and brushes his knuckles along her cheek, the touch seemingly innocent, but it's filled with ominous intent.

"Okay, Daddy." She turns away from him and lifts the blanket up over her shoulder.

I step away from the door and hurry down the corridor. One day soon, I will gather my courage to save them and put an end to this once and for all.

Chapter Six

The drive home is quiet. Em hasn't spoken much since the fight last night and I can tell something is eating away at her because it's not like her to be this quiet. Her face is pensive and that adorable little crease she gets between her eyebrows alludes to the fact that she's troubled.

"Em." She blinks out of her thoughts at the sound of my voice and turns to look at me. "Tell me what you found in Carm's office."

"I found a file on Wade. He was into some fucked-up shit, as most of the Heads are, but he went a step further. Kidnapping young girls for sex trafficking, drugging them, and assaulting them. He has a fucking family. A wife and a young son. Why? What made him want to do that stuff?" I can hear the disbelief in her tone, her words infused with sadness as her eyes slowly blink to stave off the tears. "It looked like Carm was investigating him, so maybe my fight tonight was serving a purpose for him too." I can't tell if she's upset about being left in the dark or being used by her brother to take out the trash.

"The same thing that coerces everyone... money," I tell her truthfully, my eyes flicking from the road to her face. "You should talk to Carm about it."

"There has to be more, like there's something sadistic inside of people like that." Her hands press against her chest. "I have it too." Her admission jars me and I ease my foot off the gas as I give her a shocked expression.

"No, you don't." She rolls her eyes and drops her hands, making frustration rise within me.

"Yes, Vin, I do." She looks out of the passenger window. "I *want* to kill people. I *like* to kill them. I enjoy knowing I'm handing out a different sort of punishment, something absolutely permanent. It's wrong. No matter what these people do, it's wrong that I want to kill them."

"Em—" I start as she shakes her head, not wanting to hear reason.

"Stop," she cuts me off as I stop at a red light. Then she turns to look at me, her eyes filled with conviction. "I know you love me and I'm so grateful you see the good in me, however small it is, but I am my father. Everyone says it, and even if they didn't, I would still think it. Trent, Carm, and the Heads all think I am exactly like him."

"However small it is?!" I can't help it, my voice rises a few octaves as I break eye contact with her and clear the intersection. "Your kindness outshines anything else for us. Who gives a fuck about what they think? You took in a long-lost twin. You didn't even know him, but you gave him a home and a family. Despite him living with his brother, it still wasn't home for him in New York. You took in my brother, who was so broken, and you were a major part in piecing him back together. Adri, who went through high school lonely and sad until you came along. And me, Em! Me! The guy who couldn't stand to touch a girl in public for fear of forming a bond, a guy who couldn't muster up any feelings of love outside of his mother. I hated my brother, and you showed me how to love him! You did all of that." I pull over to the side of the road and turn on my hazards so I can really take a look at her.

She turns toward me, tears streaming down her face. Ember isn't a crier, and I don't enjoy seeing her do it.

"If anyone else says you are like your father again, I will have them in that cage, whether it be Carm, Trent, or even Emmett himself. I'm not going to listen to it anymore," I vow as my knuckles whiten with my grip on the wheel. I'll kill anyone who makes her feel an iota less than what she truly is.

A small chuckle escapes her as she swipes the moisture from her cheeks. Her eyes still shine with tears, but now they hold a hint of humor.

"You would fight Emmett?" she asks, her mouth curving upward.

"Yes," I answer. "No hesitation. You will always come first, Em. While you look after all of us, I will always look after you."

"Like following me to Carm's office?" She narrows her gaze on me, but humor remains in the depths of her ocean blues.

I roll my eyes. Of course she knows I was there the entire time. "Especially when you put yourself in dangerous situations."

"I love you, Vincent Greene."

"I love you, Ember soon-to-be Greene."

She throws her pretty little head back and lets loose a laugh, a real one. I wasn't kidding. If one more person compares her to her piece of shit dad again, I'll fucking lose it.

"I found something else in Carm's office too. I just need to read through it some more and process it before I talk about it," she murmurs as I ease back onto the road.

"Bad?" I ask her.

"I'm not sure.

We end up getting home before the others, and I carry a sleeping Ember into the house and up to her room. I haven't officially moved into this house yet, despite spending six out of seven nights here. I hate the thought of my mom being alone, so I try to see her as much as I can and stay with her at home at least one night a week.

My mom works long hours at the restaurant, and it hasn't been a big deal that I stay here most of the time. I just know once I say I'm moving out, she'll get all sappy about it. Kind of like when I asked for Nana's ring. She was surprised, and at first, she tried to talk me out of it. Not because she doesn't like Em, but because she still feels we're too young to take this step. I didn't take it personally because I knew where she was coming from. Her first love turned out to be her worst. Thankfully, she and Em have patched everything up and Em visits my mom once a week too. Are they as close as I'd like? No, but it's getting there. My mom is having a hard time relinquishing the title of the woman most loved by me to Em.

Speaking of, my phone vibrates as *Ma* flashes across the screen. I throw a blanket over Em and kiss her cheek before I step out into the hall to answer the call.

"Hey, Ma," I whisper, not wanting to wake Em up.

"Hi, baby. Just making sure you got in okay," she says, her tone sounding relieved to hear my voice.

"Yeah, just got in. How was your weekend?" I lean against the wall of the hallway.

"The restaurant has been steadily getting busier,"

she replies with a sigh. She's been tired and trying to find extra help, but it's slim pickings here in our small town.

"Did you hire anyone yet?"

"Actually, Adrianna came by and asked if I had something open. I told her to come in on Monday." Adrianna has been privy to my concerns about my mother being too busy, and appreciation courses through me at her offer.

"That's good. Probably wants to pass the time before college."

"It was really sweet of her. God knows she doesn't need the money." Ma snorts as I smile. It's no secret that the Hintons are one of, if not the wealthiest family in Whitsborough.

"Hey, Ma? Can you tell me a bit more about Jack and Rebecca's relationship? Were they close?"

"They were close, yes." She pauses, probably caught off guard by the sudden change in conversation. "But she was always worried about upsetting him or disappointing him. Rebecca never dated because she didn't want to upset her father. He was strict about boys. That's why I figured she ran because he wouldn't let her be with Ray."

I hum in response. I bet he didn't approve of guys because he wanted to be the only one touching her. The thought makes me feel sick.

"Why the questions?" she asks.

"Em went by the storage unit and found some of their belongings. I just wanted to know," I explain without going into too much detail.

"He was a really serious and stern man. The neighborhood kids and teenagers stayed away from his property unless invited by Rebecca or Debby. I was there often because I was best friends with both her and Debby, but no boys were allowed, and if he caught one on the property... Well, let's just say he had a favorite rifle."

"Sounds intense," I mutter. He probably didn't allow boys there because he wanted his older daughter for himself. "I'll be there later. Just waiting for everyone else to get home."

"Okay, son, see you soon."

I hang up the phone and head back into Em's room. She's still out, recovering from the physical drain her body has gone through this weekend. Her words still replay in my head about being compared to her father and I'm once again bubbling with anger. I think I'm like mine too though. It's there in how I don't convey emotions well and I also have a darkness that has settled inside me. If anyone ever comes for Em, I will obliterate them. This woman will carry my children and be my wife until we grow old and die together. There's no other scenario I will accept.

The security app pings on my phone, letting me know a car is turning into the driveway. I notice it's the Mercedes and head downstairs to meet them. Travis is the first to enter, his tawny hair tousled on top of his head and his green eyes looking tired.

"Bro," he groans and shakes his head. "I need like twenty-four hours of sleep."

"Em does too." I clap a hand to his shoulder as he walks by, his head hanging with exhaustion.

"Hey," Emmett says as he strides into the house, his eyes looking bleary from the long drive. "Where's Ember?"

"She's sleeping. I thought the four of us could have a quick meeting before I leave to check on my mom," I suggest as Adri steps into the foyer, her hair a mess and the side of her face reddened from sleep.

"Is everything okay?" she asks, her expression filled with apprehension, because a meeting for us means something or someone needs dealing with in some nefarious way.

"Yeah, I just want to go over a few things."

They follow me into the kitchen, and Travis pulls out a beer for each of us. Once we're all seated at the large table, I begin.

"Ember has a lot on her plate. She wants to roll up on Judge Watkins this week, and she wants to check in with Andrew. I was thinking we might pair up and each take something off her agenda." I take a sip from my beer as they look at me expectantly.

"Like what?" Travis finally asks as he takes a swig of his beer.

"Two of us need to continue to go through Rebecca's things. Now, no offense, Emmett, but I was thinking you shouldn't do it. Sometimes looking at shit like that as a family member will cloud your judgment." I wouldn't stop him if he really wanted to find out what happened to his mother, but I would have to pair him with someone who could look at things objectively.

"You're right," he agrees, his jaw hardening with anger.

"So I was thinking Travis and Adri could work on that." I look at both of them as they gaze at each other. Travis' trauma stems from his family, and I would completely understand if he wasn't feeling up to digging through another dysfunctional one.

"Cool." Travis nods, his voice quiet. I'm relieved when he agrees because he has the most analytical brain besides Em in this group and I don't think she'll be able to read it without anger clouding her judgment. He would catch something the rest of us would potentially miss.

"What about you and me?" Emmett asks, his finger swinging between us.

"Shay." Emmett's mouth begins to curl upward, the sight eerily reminding me of Em.

"Wait, maybe I should talk to Shay," Adri interjects as she looks from Emmett's expression to me. "She sees me as a friend.”

“Knowing Shay, she would try to take advantage of that. Besides, I think Emmett and I can convince her to be a little more forthcoming,” I explain to her.

“Makes sense,” she murmurs, her shoulders sinking a little. “You’re not going to hurt her, right?”

“No,” Emmett assures her.

“Not if she complies,” I answer at the same time.

Emmett grins and slaps his hand to the table. “Yes! I vote for waterboarding!”

“Emmett!” Adri hisses at him, pinching the skin on his arm. “She could be a victim too.”

“Or she wants people to believe that. Maybe she and Marlana both have created an elaborate story. I wouldn’t put it past them,” I tell her.

“Oh.” Her eyes widen. “Do you think they’re still up to something?”

“Only one way to find out.” I shrug.

Chapter Seven

Ember

Emmett and Vin leave the house to go speak to Shay at the gym while I stay behind with a major case of FOMO. When he told me his plan, I will admit I was relieved, but it still would've been nice to watch the bitch squirm a little. With so much on my plate right now, I'm beginning to feel like I will never get to accomplish everything. Travis and Adri have taken every tote we have of my mother's and grandfather's things and set up a spot in the kitchen. Again, I am beyond grateful for that. Vin is right, they'll have a more observant eye.

My job today is to go over everything I've collected on Judge Watkins in the last six months. I head off to my dad's old office, now mine, to set in stone what I plan to do to take him down. Walking through the door brings me some comfort knowing Dad used to spend a lot of time here. When I sit in his big leather chair and pull up close to his desk, I feel very close to him. I miss his sarcastic humor and the way he would draw me out of any gloomy mood.

Pushing aside all emotions, I open up the folders on the desk and get to work.

Judge Joseph Watkins, Ontario's provincial judge, has been on the job for nineteen years. Tomorrow is his last day before he retires and moves to his cottage in the Kawarthas. Lavish, I'm sure. He has been acclaimed in his position and people speak highly of him, calling him fair.

I know differently.

Judge Watkins has set free rapists, murderers, child abusers, and drug dealers with rap sheets as long as the river Nile. How? He sets up evidence to be 'lost' with Whitsborough's police chief, Moore, and the Toronto police chief. He has a few paid lawyers under his belt and has friends in the Federal court. His pockets are fat and swollen with the money of very evil people, and one of those people was Robert Greene.

I found out after exhaustive research that Robert was DNA tested for the multiple rape victims who came forward to the police. His test results came back negative thanks to the work of Moore and Watkins. Dream team of motherfuckers.

Judge Watkins' final court session of his career ends at four in the afternoon tomorrow. Vin and I will be in Toronto to watch the proceedings. He has no wife or kids, and I am relieved because I hate the prospect of dealing with the families of my victims. Our plan is to make the whole thing look like an accident, which fucking sucks because I would love nothing more than to sink my blade into him repeatedly, but I don't have the Toronto police in my pocket.

After that, I need to spring a surprise visit to Andrew Cox, Whitsborough's elementary school principal, who is also corrupt as hell. He made a promise to me a few weeks ago that he would resign as principal and live a life free of child pornography as long as I didn't kill him. I'm hoping to find some shit so I can kill him because keeping him alive makes me antsy. Two in one day, that will be a record.

A knock on the office door interrupts my thoughts and then I hear Travis say through the slab, "E, you need to eat. You've been at it for hours now." I look at the clock on the wall and see that he's right. I've been in here for four hours, which has become my norm lately.

I get up and open the door to find him looking a little concerned. "Any word from Vin or Emmett?"

"Yeah. Emmett says they're waiting for her shift to end. Should be soon, but they want to watch her to see if anyone comes by while she works." Knowing who comes and goes at the gym while Shay is working is a good idea. There's not much we know about her affiliates and I don't really trust her to be honest about it.

"Cool." I close the office door and follow him to the kitchen. "I just hope she makes it easy for them. I'm tired of trying to dig for needles in haystacks."

"Same. If Emmett can't charm it out of her, then I'm sure Vin can scare it out," he replies casually as we enter the kitchen.

Adri is standing at the stove, her dark maroon hair piled on top of her head. She's dressed in a pair of too-big sweatpants and an oversized T-shirt, probably something she raided from her boyfriends' drawers.

"True," I agree with Travis as I approach Adri and give her a hug from behind, resting my chin on her shoulder. "Please tell me you didn't cook. I'm actually hungry."

"Fuck off," she retorts with a chuckle, shrugging me off her. "Travis made this. I'm just stirring it."

I look into the pot and find a delicious-looking beef stew. My stomach begins to growl with hunger as I move away from Adri and grab some bowls out of the cabinet. We sit at the table and begin eating while I'm lost in my thoughts of our plan to kill off the judge. I only blink out of my trance when Travis calls out to me.

"Shit, sorry." I shake my head and give him an apologetic look. "What's up?"

"We gather your grandfather was definitely abusing your mother. All the signs are there in her journals." His face looks sad, and I know it's because this is so close to what he endured as a child. "She also wrote about running away with him."

"With her father?" I clarify as I try to understand what my mother's thought process was. Why would she want to run away with her father if he was abusing her?

"Yeah, just him and her." He nods, the crinkle between his brows showing he's as confused as I am about it.

"So he wasn't doing the same to Aunt Debby, just my mother?" I flick through my memories of conversations with my aunt and I'm sure she never once confessed to her father being inappropriate with her or my mother.

"I can't be sure yet, but I think it was just your mother." He scratches his chin.

From my recollection, Aunt Debby only ever spoke about how strict her parents were, or more so her father. She rarely spoke about the car accident that took her parents' lives, and at the time, I didn't know much about this town to question it. After my father confessed to having them killed, I chalked up the *accident* to his doing, eliminating the two people who stood in his way from being with the woman he wanted. Now that I know more, some things aren't lining up.

"What about the crash that killed them?" I ask as I drop my spoon into my barely-touched stew. "Are we sure that one of the bodies found was my grandfather?"

"Nothing I found is official." Travis rubs his cheek. "I'll take a trip down to the police station and demand the reports from that night. They should be public records now and it's worth looking into."

"At least this is before Moore and his cronies," I muse. "Hopefully the reports are an actual account of what happened."

"We have a few more totes to go through," Adri cuts in as she lifts her glass of water to her mouth. "They belong to your grandfather's office. Maybe we'll find some answers in those." She swallows down the water and places the glass back on the table, her face filled with contemplation. I've noticed she's been looking at me with more sympathy lately and I know it's because of what she's finding in those totes.

"Thank you for all your help. There's no one else I would trust to do this." I give them a smile before we resume eating.

VIN

We sit in the Mercedes and wait for Shay to finish her shift. We took this car since my Hummer is pretty well-known around here, hoping to catch her off guard. She hasn't done much today except scroll on her phone and greet people as they come in, but her phone is her main time consumer. As it always was. That device is always within her reach.

"She doesn't seem to be thrilled about whatever the fuck it is she's looking at," Emmett states, his eyes on Shay behind the counter. Thankfully the car windows are heavily tinted because we decided to park right in front so we could see her every move.

"You're right," I agree as the furrow between her brows grows deeper and the nervous look she keeps making becomes more frequent the longer we sit here.

"What the fuck is this girl messed up in?" he murmurs as he runs his fingers along the growth on his chin.

"We're going to find out today," I vow as I crack my knuckles.

"I hope it doesn't add more to our plates. We already have so much shit to do," Emmett grumbles as he leans forward to get a better look at Shay. I will say that she's not very observant if she hasn't come to check out the car parked in front of the gym for the last few hours.

"Keeps things interesting though." I chuckle and then laugh harder as he shoots me a scowl. "That face can't intimidate me. It belongs to the girl I'm going to marry. You look so adorable." I reach over and pat his cheek.

"I'm getting plastic surgery," he groans as he slaps a hand to his forehead.

"Your loss." I flick his ear as he swats me away. "That face is gorgeous."

"Fuck, that's true." He rubs his chin again and throws me a grin.

I hit his chest before pointing out the windshield. "She's getting her shit. Looks like her shift is done."

"I'm ready," he says as he rubs his hands together and squirms in his seat. I have to hand it to him, for a guy who can barely sit still, he did great with me this morning. I didn't think he'd last this long to be honest.

Shay steps out of the gym and shades her eyes with her hands as her head turns from left to right, as if she's looking for someone. I put the car in drive and pull up beside her as Emmett pulls his baseball cap down over his face and lowers the passenger window.

"Get in," he tells her gruffly, making her take a few steps back as fear coats her features.

"What?" she asks, a slight tremor in her voice. "Who are you?"

I lean across the center console and look out at her. "Shay, we need to chat." Her shoulders relax as she takes a deep breath, her hand pressed against her chest. Then she gives me a narrowed look as she approaches the car.

"Fuck, Vin," she breathes out on an exhale. Emmett hops out of the car and into the backseat, leaving the passenger seat free for Shay. She climbs in and we pull out of the gym parking lot, making me wonder why she came so willingly.

"Where are you taking me?" I can see her shooting me looks as I drive, her hands clutching her purse tightly.

"Just to the park. That way we can sit and chill," I explain as she turns her head toward the window, her right knee bouncing.

She remains quiet as we drive to the park I once took Travis to. Her nervous energy soon thickens the air inside the car as she casts nervous glances around her. That's good. It won't take much for me to convince her to tell us everything she knows.

Emmett leans up from the backseat, placing his head between us. "Can I give you some advice?" He turns to face Shay and she tips her head to look at him before nodding. "Good. Tell us what you know. Help us and we'll make sure you're good."

I see the angle he's working here, good cop to my bad, and fuck him, but I think he's onto something here. With his big-ass, green-blue eyes and thick black lashes, he might just suck her in.

She nods again, and he flops himself back against the seat, our eyes meeting in the rearview as he winks. Little bastard. I pull into the park and we all get out of the car, Shay following us to one of the benches, but I notice she keeps looking behind her.

"What's up?" I ask, and her head snaps around to look at me.

"N–nothing," she stutters and drops her head to her shoulders when I raise a brow at her. "Someone has been watching me."

"What?" Her statement has me looking around our surroundings, searching for anyone standing nearby. "Why?"

"Because, Vin, I know some shit, and when I tried to inform Ember last time, I got in trouble," she whispers, her eyes becoming the size of saucers as fear gathers in their depths.

"You're going to tell *us* now, and I promise, we will protect you," Emmett stresses, and I watch as Shay's eyes roll into her head.

"Oh, yeah?" She turns and looks at him, her tone

becoming skeptical as her voice raises. "How will you protect me?"

"We'll figure it out. We're not fucking liars," I growl as she turns back to face me, her mouth tight with tension as her jaw clenches.

"What do you want to know anyway?" We sit on the bench, placing Shay between us as she continues to clutch her purse in her lap, her crossed leg swinging with agitation.

"It's about Coach Halbert—" Emmett begins, but Shay cuts him off.

"You need to look beyond that." Her voice is small as her eyes dart around, never completely landing on either of us.

"Then tell us." I lean forward, placing my elbows on my knees as her eyes finally meet mine.

She trembles a bit as her eyes fill with tears. "It's who's connected to Halbert."

"Okay..." I draw out as she huffs.

"Marlana's mom," she mutters as she quickly looks over her shoulder. "She used to be a—an escort."

"A prostitute?" Emmett cuts in, leaning forward as well, his mouth hanging open.

"Sure." She shrugs as that foot of hers keeps swinging and her knuckles whiten around the strap of her purse. "She used to be friends with Halbert."

"And?" I press her, leaning in a little closer.

"She had some high-end clientele around here. Rich folks. I saw her once, in a car at the mall parking lot... with your dad." Her confession has my head reeling. I thought I couldn't be surprised anymore with the shit my father was capable of, but I was fucking wrong.

"And?" I wave her on, feeling a little impatient with

how slowly she's revealing things.

"I told Marlana..." Her head drops against her chest as she inhales. "I didn't know she was a prostitute until then. Marlana confessed Robert was her mother's number one customer."

"Fuck," Emmett growls and gets up to pace. "Everyone is connected here." It's true. Whitsborough has always been a tight-knit town, but it's looking more and more like a fucking jigsaw puzzle.

"I only met Marlana's mother once, and she seemed alright. I didn't get escort vibes," I murmur as I scratch my chin. "What's her name again?"

"Tonya," Shay says under her breath as she once again glances over her shoulder.

"Sounds familiar." While I try to place the name, Emmett looks like he's seen a ghost as he stares into Shay's face.

"Tonya? That's her name?" He bends to look at her, his hands on his knees. His skin is pale and his eyes wide as his chest heaves with each labored breath.

"Yes." Shay's reply is full of surety as she nods her head.

"What happened after that?" I draw Shay's attention back to me as Emmett continues to pace, his hands tangled in his hair. It's obvious he's already pieced something together, but I need to hear the rest of what Shay has to say before I get him back to the house to find out.

"Marlana told her what I saw." Her chin shakes and a tear drops to her cheek. "A week later, I was raped in the locker room at school by Halbert. He told me to keep my mouth shut or he would make the raping a regular thing. I was scared, so I kept my mouth shut, but then Marlana started blackmailing me. She has a copy of that rape and the way she filmed it made it look consensual, but I promise you it wasn't!" Her voice becomes frantic as her foot swings rapidly back and forth, and tears begin slipping down her cheeks in rivulets, creating tracks through her makeup.

"I believe you." I place my hand on her shoulder, hoping to calm her down. "This is what's going to happen. I'm giving you my number and you are to call or text me if you hear anything from Marlana. Even if you feel like something bad is going to happen. I will pick you up and bring you to Ember's. She'll protect you."

"She hates me," she moans and shakes her head. "Besides, what can Ember do?"

"No, she just takes a while to trust." Emmett stops pacing to speak to her as I nod in agreement. "Ember is a Craven, you know she has pull around here."

Shay wipes the tears from her cheeks and relaxes, her foot finally back on solid ground. "Okay."

After we drop Shay off at her house, we sit on her street and wait to see if we notice anyone familiar lurking around. Being in Ember's Mercedes makes it easier to blend in.

"Tonya," Emmett breaks the silence, his voice infused with shaking rage. "That was the name of the prostitute your father had for Travis."

"What?" I snap my head around in shock.

"Yeah." He scrubs his hand down his face and lets out a heavy breath, the anger leaving his voice. "The one he forced him to fuck."

"Maybe Tonya needs to be paid a visit too." Another name to the ever-growing list.

"Any idea who Marlana's father is?" I know why he's asking because I had the same thought at the park, although it was fleeting.

I laugh and throw my head back. "It'd be funny if it were my father. That's what you're thinking, right? Add incest to the pot." I shake my head and chuckle. "Her father lives in Toronto, and trust me, I know it's her father. She looks exactly like him."

He nudges my shoulder and points out the windshield, directing my attention to a familiar car driving toward us. We slide down a bit in our seats and watch as a recognizable purple head passes by us.

"They are definitely watching her," Emmett says under his breath.

"Yeah." It's evident that Shay was telling the truth, and now it looks like we have another problem on our hands.

Chapter Eight

I don't know if I'm more excited about learning Shay's secret or the prospect of killing Marlana and her dirty whore of a mother. Scratch that, obviously it's killing Marlana and her mother, and knowing what her mother did to Travis just gave them a gruesome end.

"Em." Vin's voice breaks through my thoughts of blood and purple hair.

"Hmm?" I blink out of my thoughts as everyone comes back into focus.

"What should we do about Shay?"

"I don't trust her," I growl, "but I don't want anything to happen to her either. Maybe we should hit up Marlana's house by the end of the week." I scan everyone's faces around the kitchen table, and they all agree with a nod of their heads. Trust doesn't come easy to us, and I may be a murderer, but none of us are monsters.

My gaze lands on Travis, noting he's been looking a little down lately. He's come a long way and has been stronger and not so susceptible to depression, but I don't want him to ever get to the place he once was.

I get up from my seat at the table and lean toward him, his brows coming together as he looks at me. "Travis, can I show you something in the office?"

He stands from the table to follow me as the others continue their conversation. Then I lock us inside the office and sit at the desk while he sits on the sofa across from me.

"How would you like me to deal with Marlana's mother?" I know what I *want* to do, but I also know it has to be his decision.

"I'm not sure." He looks torn as he shifts in his seat, his eyes on the floor. "She was a victim too, right? My father told her to do what she did, forcing me to do what he would to her."

"I don't know about *victim*." I shake my head as my fist hits the top of my desk, anger scorching through me at the thought of what he endured at the hands of disgusting adults. "It didn't sound as though she hated taking part in the rape of a boy, because that's what it was."

"I know. He threatened me, saying he'd kill her if I didn't. I'm sure he said the same to her." He drops his head to his chest and runs his hand through his hair. "Maybe we should find out more information before we decide anything?"

"With your situation aside," I interject gently as his eyes meet mine. "Halbert raped Shay because Marlana told her mother what Shay saw. That's something we can't ignore. We also can't ignore the fact that Marlana filmed it and then continued to blackmail Shay for years. Remember the party? She blackmailed Shay to release the video of Vin and me."

"Right." He releases a breath and shrugs his shoulders. "I know they're not good people. I just don't want to be the one that decides their fate."

"No problem." I clap my hands and fall back into my

chair. "I would love to be the one that does. I just wanted to make sure you were okay." Relief coats his features as he relaxes with my offer.

"I'm fine. Just sad that I grew up around some of the most despicable people. I can't believe how fucked-up this little town is." I'm just as dumbfounded as he is. As idyllic as Whitsborough is, every inch of the place is teeming with pests that need extinguishing.

"We're going to fix it," I assure him, knowing the brunt of that mission rests on my shoulders, but for my family, it's worth it.

"I know." He stands from his seat and gives me a tentative smile. "I'm going to continue on your grandfather's things. Thanks, E."

I nod as he leaves the office, his steps seeming a little lighter than when he first came in here. I can only hope I've relieved a bit of his burden even if it means I've taken on more.

Vin and I sit at the back of the courtroom watching the latest sentencing Judge Watkins hands down to a first-time drug offender.

"Twelve years." He hits the gavel, and I want to scream as I watch a young black man being hauled away. The systemic racism in North America is so blatant in people's faces and yet all of us turn a blind eye. Easier than dealing with the repercussions of fighting against the most corrupt system. I seal his name into my memory—Rodney Jones— and vow to do something about that unfair sentence.

"Piece of shit," Vin grinds out, his jaw clenched tight as he watches the Judge get up from his seat.

"We're going to hand him a sentence too, baby." I pat his knee reassuringly. The thought of enacting our own judgment has me giddy with excitement.

Judge Watkins is a severely overweight man and he literally waddles out the fucking door, his gut hanging down low. I also know he has a terrible peanut allergy, and after a few weeks of watching him and studying his daily activities, I found the perfect way to get rid of him.

He always orders his lunch—through his very young and attractive secretary—from the deli across the street. Corned beef on rye, no sauce, and a side of horseradish. It took a few days of reconnaissance to learn the routine, but it was so damn worth it. Once the order is placed, they have someone from the deli run it over. Today, I'll pick up his lunch and add one ingredient to it, then drop it off with his secretary.

Hanging back, I watch as the secretary exits the courtroom and rushes off to her office down the hall. "Five minutes, then we head to the deli across the street," I tell Vin, and he responds with a curt nod.

He's always quiet when I'm on a job because he hates the possibility of danger or getting caught, but he refuses to let me do it alone. Regardless, I would much rather have him with me than not. No one else on this planet loves me more than him, so I can count on him protecting me at all costs.

"Five minutes," Vin says as he stands from our seat in the last row, and I get up to follow him out.

Once we're outside, I see the deli across the street and head over there on foot while Vin turns the corner to walk back to our vehicle. It's better I do this alone because the secretary has only picked up the food once in the two weeks, a few other times she sent one of her interns. I've been watching, and it would look suspicious if I went in with Vin.

The bell chimes and the two friendly faces behind the counter look at me with a smile.

"I'm here for Judge Watkins' lunch," I announce as I walk to the counter.

"Are you new?" the lady asks as she rolls the sandwich into its wrapping.

"No. His secretary just got called into an important meeting and asked me to come by. She wouldn't be there for the drop-off," I explain sweetly as I keep a smile on my face. "Could you not wrap that?" I point to the sandwich. "I'm supposed to check it."

The woman smiles and nods, her face softening at my request. I guess I passed the test. The secretary did the same thing when she picked up last week and I happened to be inside the store looking over the menu. I take the foam container and place it on the table, my back to them, and open it up, seemingly to check that the sandwich is plain. What they don't see is me pulling out a small vial of peanut oil from my jacket sleeve and pouring it between the many folds of meat inside the sandwich. Thankfully, Watkins likes double the meat and double the side of horseradish. He shouldn't taste the oil at all.

"Thank you!" I tell them as I cover it back up. "Have a great day."

"You too!" they say in unison as I leave the store.

I cross back to the courthouse and walk in through the front. The officer at the door sees the deli bag and waves me forward. To them, I'm just the delivery person. I make my way to the secretary's office and knock lightly on her partially opened door.

"Hi!" she says as she gets up. "Thank you so much."

"No problem." I wait as she opens the sandwich, sees that it's plain, and closes it back up.

Then she hands me a ten-dollar bill as a tip. "Have a great day."

"Thanks, you too." Slipping the money into my

pocket, I leave her office before exiting the courthouse.

I round the same corner Vin did earlier and head to the McDonald's beside the parking garage, slipping in between the crowds and sliding into the washroom. After locking myself inside a stall, I remove the platinum-blonde, lace front wig Adri put on me and meticulously wash off the makeup with the baby wipes in my massive purse. When I'm done, I fluff my hair and stuff the wig and wipes into my purse, then leave the building. Vin is waiting for me out front in Adri's parents' Lexus SUV. She told us it's rarely used and would blend in better than any of our other vehicles. She was right.

"Everything good?" Vin asks as I get in.

"Yeah." I grin, sitting back while we get onto the highway leading back to Whitsborough.

"Judge Watkins has been pronounced dead this evening in his chambers at the downtown Toronto courthouse. Cause of death is still unknown, but it looks to be natural causes. The police currently do not suspect foul play. Judge Joseph Watkins was in his nineteenth year as a judge and today was his final day before his retirement. We will update you as more information is released." The attractive news anchor continues on about some other event happening, and I tune her out as I look at the others in the room.

"Everything was smooth, right?" Emmett asks me, concern flashing in his eyes. "It won't come back to us?"

"We're good." I get up, my attention already switching to my next appointment. "I need to prepare for my visit to Andrew."

I dress in a black, knit jersey dress and pile my waves up on top of my head in a messy bun. Leaving my face void of makeup, I throw on a pair of Adidas sneakers.

"Ready?" Vin asks as his eyes sweep over me appreciatively. Mine does the same over him in his dark jeans, white V-neck, and leather jacket.

"Yeah." I nod and follow him outside to the Hummer.

The ride to Andrew's is quiet. Vin is letting me brood without interruption because he knows how I get in these situations. I'm relieved to watch the corrupted tumble from their pedestals, but with every death, the weight on my soul increases. With every life I end, their essence seeps into me, and the evil always outweighs the good. My brother is right when he says not everyone can handle killing, because sometimes the weight becomes too much.

"He's home alone?" Vin breaks through my thoughts as we pull up to Andrew's house.

"Yes." I take a deep breath and get out of the Hummer. "The kids are at swimming lessons with their mother."

He takes hold of my hand as we walk up to the front door. I can hear the TV inside and it's playing the news about Judge Watkins. I ring the doorbell and soon after, I hear the shuffling of Andrew's feet as he nears the door.

When he opens it, I watch as the blood drains from his face, leaving him pale and sweating.

"Judge Watkins—"

"Hello, Andrew," I cut him off and force him back inside his home. "Long time no see."

"Judge Watkins is—"

"Yes, yes." I wave him off. "The fucker is dead. Why are you so freaked out?"

"D—did you d—do it?" he finally stutters out, and I flash him my award-winning smile.

"Show me the proof of your resignation while Vin takes a peek at your computer." I snap my fingers at him.

He jerks forward, and we follow him into a small office, then he points to his computer before handing me a folder. I already know his computer is clean and has been for the last few weeks because I have enough spyware on there to detect a sneeze from another room. I also already know what's in the folder because I sometimes pay him and his family late-night visits while they all sleep peacefully in their beds. It's the only way I can keep tabs on his 'progress,' regardless of how much sleep I lose.

Vin sits and powers up the desktop. He knows as well as I do that there's nothing to be found, but fear is a potent ally, and one I plan to keep. As soon as I lose that, I go back to just being a teenage girl who knows how to fight really well. The girl I was when I first came to Whitsborough.

I open the folder and see his formal resignation inside and a printed copy of the school board's regret over his sudden departure. I hand it back to him and flash him another smile, which earns me a feeble exhale.

"Relax, Andrew." I shake my head at him. "I'm just Ember today."

"You're never just Ember," he squeaks.

Vin's deep chuckle attracts my attention, and I look over at him. "Clean," he says to me with a nod.

"Good!" I clap my hands like the psycho I am. "Andrew, you did a good job."

"Wait…" Vin interrupts, and I turn slowly to look at him once more. We've rehearsed this, so I know exactly what it is he's about to say, but Andrew looks just about ready to pass out. "There's an email on here from Chief Moore."

"Yes." Andrew nods profusely, his Adam's apple bobbing on a thick swallow. "That folder has the printed version. I even put your name on it." He's a blubbering mess, but he's right. I know he had no intention of keeping it from me.

"What does it say?" I ask Vin, keeping my eyes on

Andrew.

"Some heavy shit." He lets out a low whistle.

"Read it."

"'Andrew, Black Slaughter is becoming a serious problem for us. I know she's been by to see you and I need you to give me everything you got on her. Everything! I plan on getting rid of this problem by the end of summer.'"

"Sounds like he wants to kill me, huh?" I watch as Andrew's eyes widen and sweat breaks out along his brows. "What did Andrew reply with, Vin?"

"'I have nothing. She's threatened me with resigning and to clear my computer or else I die. That's all I have,'" Vin reads.

"Hmmm." I rub my chin in thought. "I think you should meet up with Chief Moore. We'll give you some bullshit to tell him about me. I want you to get me as much information as you can."

"Okay." He dips his head eagerly. "Whatever you need."

"There's a good boy, Andrew. Vin, I didn't even have to pull the knife out once." I look at Vin with mock-surprise as my man smirks, his dimple appearing in his left cheek.

"He's learning." Vin's deep voice is laced with approval. "Looks like some people can change." He leans back in the chair and holds up his hands with a look of shock.

"I'll need that information by the end of the week," I tell Andrew with a firm pat to his cheek, and the way he flinches satisfies something deep inside me.

"No problem." He swallows hard and averts his gaze to the floor.

Vin gets up from the desk and walks around before stopping in front of Andrew. "Don't fuck this up." His voice sounds scarily sexy, and I may have just soaked a perfectly clean thong.

We leave Andrew's after he promises to call Moore and set up a meeting. I want to know how this guy plans on killing me so I can hit him first, but a hundred times worse.

"Pull over," I tell Vin when we're about five minutes from the house.

"What? Why?" He looks at me with his eyebrow raised.

"I want to ride your dick before we get home, without having to wait until the kids are asleep," I snarl back at him.

He chuckles and pulls the Hummer over to the side of the road where the trees are thick and traffic is almost nonexistent. I reach under my dress to grab my panties when his hand curls around my chin and forces me to look at him. His thumb sweeps over my bottom lip, pulling until they fall apart with a small *pop*.

"Leave them on and hike that dress up around your waist," he growls, then drags my face to his so he can ravish my mouth.

This version of Vin is my favorite. The one who demands and works my body like an instrument in which he's the only one who knows how to play. His tongue ring flicks against my tongue, and I moan at the feeling. Then his teeth sinks into the plush cushion of my lower lip before he finally releases and pulls away. I look at his lap and see he's already undone his jeans and belt, and just the thought of having him in my mouth makes my saliva pool in anticipation.

"Pull those down," I demand, my husky voice deep with arousal.

He does as I ask and drops his jeans around his feet. His black silk boxers are magnificently tented, the fabric unable to hold down the awakened beast inside. I skim my hand over him inside his boxers and smile at his intake of breath. When I reach his tip, I can feel the ring through it, and my underwear becomes unbearably wet. He's so fucking wide and so fucking long. I'm always amazed when he fits so snugly inside me.

He lifts his hips and pulls the silk down just enough to have his cock spring out, then I'm bent over with him down my throat before his ass can even sit back on the seat. I have to slacken my jaw just to fit him inside, and I moan when the head presses against my throat. Since I've been with Vin, my gag reflex has leveled up. That bitch gives me no trouble when I slurp him halfway down my throat now.

I swallow around him, and he moans, digging his fingers into my hair before abruptly lifting me off his dick.

"Give me that pussy or I'm going to coat that pretty throat with my cum," he rasps with a smirk on his mouth. Asshole.

"Fucking weirdo," I mutter as I climb over him, loving the idea.

Straddling his waist, I press myself against him, rubbing my soaked panties along his velvety skin. We both moan at the contact, and he reaches forward to drag my dress down and away from my breasts. He slides his tongue out and flicks the tongue ring over my hardened nipple as the sensation travels down and pools into heat in my lower belly. I grind against him harder while gripping his short curls. Then I rip his V-neck down the center until I can see the tattoo he got for us and tip my head forward to kiss it.

"Babe," he groans, his head hitting the seat rest. "That's the third shirt this week."

"Shut up," I snap before giving him a sharp slap to the chest. "I'll buy you more."

He chuckles as his fingers lightly travel over my ass crack and down toward my panty-covered pussy. Then he grabs ahold of the thin strap and rips it off my body before bringing the fabric up to his nose to inhale deeply.

"That's my favorite fucking scent." He sounds like a

starving man sitting in front of an open buffet.

"Pussy juice." I snicker as he tosses my underwear into the backseat.

"Eau de pussy." He chuckles again and lifts me to impale me in one thrust.

The first thing I feel is pain. It's sharp, but it's quick. He's so large there's no way I wouldn't feel the sting, but just as soon as it starts, it's done, and the pleasure of him spreading me wide and being so deep washes over me.

Then he pops his seat back and rests his hands on my hips. "Ride your daddy."

His words always ramp up my arousal, and I can feel how fucking wet I am as my juices slick against him, soaking my thighs, his balls, and his lower stomach. His piercing hits that certain spot inside me that makes me see stars, and I ride him faster and harder. I can feel the pressure building and I know I'm about to make the both of us extremely fucking messy.

"Vin, fuck," I pant and clench around him.

"Is my baby going to rain on her daddy?" he says into my mouth, and that's all it takes for the gush of wetness to flow and soak us both as I scream his name.

He grips my hips harder and thrusts up into me, chasing his own orgasm. Not too long after, he's groaning against my neck as he slowly pumps his release into me.

"I'm gonna have to tell the kids I pissed myself." He snorts and I laugh against his chest.

Chapter Nine

"My parents called me today," Adri declares as we all sit in the family room. "They'll be home tomorrow night."

After we got home and had a much-needed shower, Adri called us all here for a meeting. I could tell she was anxious and looking really uncomfortable, and now I know why. We haven't dug up anything further on her parents because we've been busy with other, more pressing shit.

"Maybe it's time you introduce me to them," Em suggests as she wraps an arm around Adri's shoulders.

"Are you gonna… you know?" Adri asks slowly as she turns to face her.

"Kill them?" Em clarifies, and Adri nods with her eyes wide. "Despite popular belief, I don't just kill anybody. No, I won't be killing them, but we will have a very honest conversation."

"Okay." Her whole body relaxes, and it almost makes me want to laugh. Em has effectively scared the shit out of us all with how unpredictable her stabbing is.

"I want to head out and see Carm for a few days," Emmett says from his position on Adri's other side, dragging our eyes to him. "I feel like he's been really stressed about shit lately."

"Oh yeah? Why?" Ember asks as she sits forward on the couch. I remember her telling me she had more from Carm's office but needed time to go through it. What does she know?

"Not sure, but the last few times we talked, he sounded off." Emmett shrugs. He's trying not to look too worried, but I can see the concern in his eyes and the way he's picking at his fingernails.

"I'll come with you," I offer. He needs someone to be with him in New York and I want to see what I can find out about Carm as well. Maybe get a brief insight into what's been going down in New York while we've been cleaning up over here.

"Thanks, bro." Emmett smiles briefly before it disappears. He's definitely worried.

"But my parents will be here." Adri looks at him strangely, her mouth set in a firm line.

"And? What? You want to introduce them to our throuple?" He lifts a brow as a grin creeps over his mouth. "They know Travis. It wouldn't be such a leap to know you two are together."

"But..." Adri drops her head. "I shouldn't have to hide who I love." Their relationship will always be a difficult one to explain and I feel for her. My relationship with Ember doesn't have the same obstacles as hers, but I can still imagine the strain she's feeling.

"You don't," I tell her. "There are just some people who will never understand."

"I'm not upset about it," Emmett reassures her as he lifts her up and onto his lap.

She nods and snuggles her face into his neck while Travis smiles at them from his seat beside me on the couch across from theirs. He has the same look I get when I look at Em, like they're his entire universe. It also makes me feel good to know my brother finally has his head straight after years of fucked-up shit. I still curse myself for never seeing it, for being so clouded by my anger and not being able to see the signs of his abuse. Only adding to it.

I don't know if I can ever forgive myself for how badly I treated him, though I try to make it up to him by being the family he's never had. He's even become close to my mother, calling her Ma and doing all the same things for her that I do. She loves him and loves the fact that she has another son in Travis. Her motherly love is something he has been missing his whole life.

"You're in deep thought," Travis remarks as his eyes meet mine.

"Look after Ma while I'm gone." Reaching over, I clasp a hand on his shoulder.

"Of course." He nods, giving me a genuine look.

"When you get back, we'll pop in for a visit with Marlana and her precious mother," Em tells me with that devilish smirk of hers. I know this confrontation has been years in the making and I can't muster up an ounce of concern for Marlana after what she put us through. "Then we'll have a lengthy conversation with Shay."

"What if all this never ends?" Adri whines from her spot on Emmett's lap, her face filled with despair. "Always someone to investigate or spy on or kill."

"Hopefully that won't be the case soon. I plan on ridding this fucking town of every cockroach," Em growls. "Stop whining anyway. I haven't asked you to kill one person." The smirk lining her mouth gives away her teasing.

"What?" Adri sits up in Emmett's lap as his chest shakes with suppressed laughter, her face filled with distress.

"Will you have me kill someone?"

"Fuck, no!" Em laughs. "Can you fucking see it?" She looks at all of us and we laugh, even Adri, whose agitated demeanor melts away.

"We could ask her to cook someone something... anything. Some of her concoctions could seriously kill," Emmett deadpans, his face losing all mirth.

Adri slaps his chest, and Em falls back on the sofa, laughing. "Remember Vin's party when we made those Ex-Lax brownies?" Em asks her. "And I explained to people they tasted weird because you baked them?"

"Best thing ever was watching Marlana and Danny almost shit themselves." They both snort and fall into fits of laughter.

"I remember that." Travis chuckles. "Hey, what's going on with Danny?" He directs the question to me.

"Last I heard, his father shipped him off to a relative in Louisiana." It's been a while since I've reached out to my ex-best friend, but in all honesty, Danny was headed down a path I didn't want to take.

"We should've looked him up while we were there," Em adds, and I shrug my shoulders. A few months ago, Ember suggested we all go on a family vacation, somewhere that wasn't New York and where we could eat good food. Adri suggested New Orleans and it served its purpose. It was the calm before the storm of what we would face here in Whitsborough.

"Nah, we only went to New Orleans for a week. It was an overdue family vacation. I wanted it to be about the five of us and not involve Danny and whatever drama he could find," I explain as Travis grunts in agreement.

"How do you propose we approach Adri's parents?" Travis asks Em, changing the subject back. "They are snobby as all hell."

"They are," Adri agrees without hesitation. Her parents are absent, leaving their daughter to raise herself for most of her life. It's clear they never wanted children and only adopted Adri to fulfill a family line.

"Tell them you're the granddaughter of Jack Craven," I suggest, and the room falls quiet. Jack Craven was a dominating force here in Whitsborough until my father stepped into his shoes.

"They liked him?" Em asks, her nose crinkled in disgust.

"I don't know if anyone actually liked him, but they feared him. He was powerful and fucking mean." I grin and scratch my chin. "People still talk about him and the shit he did."

"What did he do?" Emmett angles his face around Adri to get a better look at me.

"I remember my father once telling a story at a town hall meeting. Our family was donating to the hospital and building a wing." Travis waves it off and continues, "During his speech, he spoke about the importance of good health care and the quick admittance from the ER. He joked, *'Because some of us here remember being on the wrong end of Jack's rifle or between the jaws of his dogs.'* People laughed, but a lot of the men around my father's age mumbled and nodded."

"He was an avid hunter," I reveal as I lean forward, resting my elbows on my knees. "My mother told me he had animal heads all over his house. He had dogs trained for tracking and hunting. Sometimes he unleashed them onto whoever decided to stupidly enter his land without permission."

"He sounded psychotic," Emmett grumbles, then buries his face in Adri's hair. A part of me wonders if he and Em feel somewhat disgusted to be related to the despicable man, if somehow they feel like they have tainted blood.

"Or someone with something to hide," Em says, deep in thought.

"He was also a drunk, I heard," Adri adds as she squirms off Emmett's lap before plopping onto the cushion beside him. "Everyone who grew up in Whitsborough knew of Jack Craven. They had that enormous property just on the edge of town, and I remember my parents saying he was a regular at a few bars in town."

"What about my grandmother?" Em inquires, her voice soft as she looks over Emmett to Adri.

"Not much about her," Travis answers before Adri has a chance. "She was quiet, and I would assume with a husband like Jack, she just stayed out of the way."

"Ma said she was really sweet to them, always baking and bringing them snacks," I tell her, hoping to give her some relief that not everyone in her family were monsters.

"I went by that house they lived in. The family that lives there now knew my grandparents and apparently didn't want to rent at first. According to them, Aunt Debby dropped the price because no one else showed interest. They are living there practically for free and told me they would move if I raised the price," Em mutters as she crosses her arms over her chest and leans back against the couch cushions. "I was confused at the time since I didn't know what I know now about my grandfather, but it seems his reputation is still lingering around."

"We need to dig deeper into Jack Craven." Emmett shifts on the couch, his face a mask of frustration.

"And our grandmother, who sounded like she may have been complicit in what he was doing to at least one of her daughters." Em clenches her jaw as her arms tighten across her chest.

I also need to dig deeper into my mother and Nana too. What brought them to this town and why did they stay? It couldn't have been easy being women of color in a town of prominent white men whose privilege leaked from their very pores. It never bothered me before, but the more I find out about the seedy underbelly of Whitsborough, the more I'm confused about how they came to be a part of this place.

Em reclines on the Mercedes with her arms crossed and her face apprehensive. "Make sure you call as soon as you get there."

I cage her in against the car and press my torso to hers. "Sure." Then I bend down to lick her bottom lip and suck it into my mouth as she wraps her arms around my waist.

"I hate you going there with Talia on the loose." Her voice is strained with worry as she exhales a shaky breath against my chest.

"We'll be with Carm."

"Yeah," she mutters, not sounding entirely convinced.

"Hey, what is it?" I grip her chin and force her to look at me.

"Just watch your back and please watch Emmett's too. He sees that place as home and his guard will be down." Her eyes are filled with pleading.

"Okay, baby." I kiss her lightly. "I'll look after the baby brother," I say loud enough for the fucker who's walking toward us.

"Did you find out about another sibling?" Emmett asks as he leans over me to kiss his sister's temple. "Because I only know about a baby sister." He dodges Em's fist and chuckles as he slips into the driver's seat.

"Don't worry." I kiss her again. "I won't let anything happen. I'm prepared." I have my gun with me and it's not leaving my side the entire time we're there.

"I love you," she whispers against my mouth.

"I love you too, wife." I kiss her deeper and grin when she moans and grips my ass in her small hands.

"Be safe," she says as I pull back.

"You too, Black Slaughter."

Her eyes light up when I say that name, and she turns to smack her hand against the windshield. "Shithead! Behave yourself!" she yells to Emmett.

He blows her a kiss and then flashes her the middle finger. I chuckle at them both and slap Em's ass as she walks back to the house.

"Bro!" Travis calls out from the front doorway. "Stay safe."

I nod and throw up my deuces before getting into the car.

"The audacity of you two... little brother my ass," Emmett grumbles as he pulls out of the driveway.

"I'm gonna nap. I was up all night fucking your big sister. Wake me up when you need a break," I mumble as I pull my cap down over my eyes.

He curses under his breath as I chuckle.

Chapter Ten

Pulling into Adri's driveway in Shelby, I raise my eyebrow at her when I see a large stretch limo in front of me. "Yeah." She rolls her eyes. "They're extra."

I snicker as we both exit the car and walk up to the front door. "Just you and me? Or is Travis going to show?"

"Travis and my parents have never really gotten along. They think he's ungrateful of his lineage and should be more prominent in the community." She waves her hand around as her face fills with disdain.

"So... what you're really saying is that they're going to adore me." I snicker, and she joins in.

"They are going to absolutely hate you, and I can't fucking wait," she squeals before opening her front door.

"Adrianna?" a woman calls out, her voice making me picture a genteel lady from the eighteen hundreds.

"Yes, Mother!" Adrianna calls back with a huff.

"We are in the receiving room!" a man's voice rings

out, much louder and stronger than the woman's.

"Receiving room?" I give her a questioning look.

"That's what the snobby folks call it, dear." She raises her hand and puts on a haughty attitude.

I snort and follow close behind her. I've been in Adri's house a few times, but we never linger. This place is cold and lacks the warmth only a family can provide. We walk into what I would consider the den or family room and Adri makes the proper introductions.

"Mother, Father, this is Emberlise Craven. Ember, this is Georgina and Abe Hinton." Adri's mother has pale blonde hair that hangs just above her ass and skin the same color. She's tall and willowy with big, round, green eyes. Her father is about the same height as her mother, but he's the opposite in appearance. Where she is pale and light-haired, he's olive-skinned and black-haired. He's robust, and his dark eyes hold a glimmer of humor as he watches us. I can see how they passed off Adri as their own. If I didn't know any better, I would assume she got her looks from her father.

"Nice to meet you." I choose the polite path, tossing them the ball on how they decide to proceed.

"Craven?" The mother's eyes widen as she takes another sweep of my appearance. I'm wearing a cream-colored blouse and a gray pair of slacks. I swept my hair up into a tight bun and didn't bother with much makeup, leaving me feeling exposed.

"How are you related to the Cravens?" her father asks as he sucks back half the amber liquid in his tumbler.

"Rebecca Craven was my mother."

"Oh! Yes, we heard something about this, right, Abe? Twins apparently," Georgina says, her voice a mere whisper as her face relaxes.

"Right, the scandal." He chuckles and pours the rest of the liquid down his greedy throat.

Not sure what it is, but I suddenly get the urge to wrap both of my hands around his turkey-like neck and watch him fight for his next breath. Adri clears her throat, her brow lifting as if she can read my thoughts, and motions for me to take a seat beside her on a fancy settee across from her parents, the cream of the fabric covering matching my blouse. We sit, and I look at her parents with interest.

"When are you guys planning to leave again?" Adri asks, breaking the heavy silence and sounding hopeful.

"Oh, we'll discuss family matters later." Her mother gives her a pointed look.

"No need. I already know about your absent parenting technique." I look at Adri with a wink as she smothers a grin. "She turned out great because of it, by the way."

"I beg your pardon?" her father booms and stands up, looking thoroughly offended and outraged.

"What?" I widen my eyes and feign innocence. "Did I say something wrong?"

"We suggest you leave now." Her mother's tone is filled with dismissal as she waves her hand like I'm a speck of dust.

"Not happening." I snicker and sit back further in my seat before crossing my legs.

"The disrespect will not be tolerated here, young lady." Her father sits back down and leans forward. "Women should never conduct themselves in an inappropriate manner."

Yep, he's on the brink of dying and Adri must sense it because she intervenes. "I think you will both want to hear what Ember says."

"Adrianna, we have warned you against befriending such people." Her mother looks at me with disdain. She's next.

"It's about my adoption," she stresses, and they both fall deathly silent, shock saturating their features.

"Finally." I exhale dramatically. "Let's drop the act."

"You told her." Her father looks at me with narrowed eyes.

"No, actually, Robert Greene did." I grin at them both.

Her mother visibly swallows and her hands shake as she crosses them in her lap. "Why would Greene tell you that? What else did he tell you?"

"Quite a bit... before he sadly took his own life." I know the smile on my face looks menacing because both of them pale and look at each other. "I just want to know more information about how you adopted Adri. That's it."

"What information? We went through an agency," Georgina retorts, but the tremble in her voice betrays her lie.

"Jennifer Talia," I interject, and then I watch as they both exchange looks.

"We signed an NDA, even if we wanted to talk to you—which we don't—we couldn't say a darned thing." Her father throws me a smirk, looking so proud of himself as he quickly switches from being nervous to looking smug.

"An NDA won't stop me from slipping my knife out and playing cut and paste with your fucking faces," I growl, letting them finally see me for who I am as I lean forward.

"Oh, God!" Her mother's face gets a nice sheen of sweat on it as she buries herself back into her seat, trying desperately to move farther away from me. "She could be as looney as her grandfather."

"Look." Her coward of a father folds as that smug look slips away and concern etches into his features. "They set us up with Jennifer through Robert. We didn't converse so much with her. We just explained we needed a baby and we were willing to pay."

"Do you know where she got Adrianna from?" I press, hoping to not only give my friend more information but also get more dirt on Talia's dealings.

"We only know it was in New York. One of the seedier places," her mother shakily replies.

"Why mess with her birthdate?"

"Because we wanted her to have a completely new life. We kept her back from school for a year, and Robert provided us with a new birth certificate." Her father clears his throat.

"Good ole Robert, huh?" I rub my hand over my mouth. "Upstanding citizen. I'm going to need to see that NDA."

"He wasn't our friend," her father spits out. "He was an atrocious person, but we knew he had the ties we needed."

Her mother gets up from the couch to exit the room. A few minutes later, she returns with a brown envelope.

"Good riddance," her mother utters and takes a deep breath as she hands me the envelope.

"We just wanted an heir. We're not parents. We chose to have this life, and we made sure Adrianna had everything she needed," Abe explains. "We couldn't look weak, and our family line needed to continue."

"It's water under the bridge at this point." Adri stands, her face resigned as she comes to terms with her parents' lack of empathy. "I have a family now anyway."

"We will fly back out tomorrow." Her father nods at her. Then he looks at me as I stand up beside her and inclines his head. "When we heard about what happened to Robert, we were happy to hear it. You can pass that along to anyone who may have been involved."

"Like?" I ask him with my brow raised.

"Like a certain female known to be taking out the trash." His throat bobbles like a real fucking turkey.

"We were poor parents," Adri's mother chimes in. "But we knew you were well cared for, and unfortunately, we know no different. We were raised the same. I'm happy you found... people."

I guess that's as close as Adri is going to get to an apology.

"Just keep that bank account stocked," Adri retorts as she gives them the gun salute and exits the room.

I snort and cover my mouth with my hand. "I got her from here on out."

They both dip their heads, and I walk out of the *receiving room* and into the foyer, where Adri is waiting by the door with a big smile on her face.

"What?" I ask her.

"I feel like I'm free." She shrugs and we leave the house as relief flows through me. "Sorry we didn't get much information."

"I got this." I wave the NDA in the air. "We'll see if it can get us any closer to that bitch."

VIN

Dinner in the compound is different from anything I've experienced. They have a few chefs who cook a spread every day and it's a free-for-all. Then there's a large dining area that seats a hundred people at least, and that's where people congregate. It's impersonal, and nothing about this setup screams family. It's like a work break room, only much bigger. This is no place to raise children.

"Silvio made the baked salmon today," Emmett says as he sits beside me. "You better get it while it's still there."

"Is this how it was when you were a kid? First come, first serve?" I ask as I watch him shovel food into his mouth.

"Yep," he replies around a mouthful.

"Where does your brother eat?" I scan the room, searching for Carm among the crowd.

"Usually in his office."

"I'm done." I push my plate away and stand up. "I'll see you later. I'm gonna go chill."

He just nods as he continues to stuff his face. I chuckle and ruffle his hair, then make my way out of the dining hall and head toward Carm's office. When I get to the large double doors, two guards are there. Once they recognize me, they wave me by and continue their conversation about baseball.

Opening the door, I peer in at a very disheveled-looking Carm. His hair is a mess of black waves on his head, his dress shirt is rumpled and untucked, and his eyes have serious dark circles beneath them.

"Bro, when was the last time you slept?" His head snaps up at the sound of my voice and his shoulders relax when he sees me.

"Yesterday?" It's a question.

"What's going on?" I press as I sit across from him.

"I misplaced important information and if it gets into the wrong hands, then I might as well shoot myself in the face." Stress lays heavy on his face and along his bent shoulders as he sits behind his desk, drawers open and papers scattered.

"Whoa." I chuckle. "Nothing is ever worth that. When was the last time you saw it?" Probably the last time Em and I were here and she snuck off in the middle of the night to Carm's office.

"Fuck, about a month after my father... passed away." Murdered... by his own daughter, he means.

"Okay, where did you have it placed?"

"In this locked drawer. No one can get in there." He shakes his head, as if the thought of anyone getting in there is impossible, but I bet Em can. If it was something pertaining to her mother or Jennifer Talia, she has it.

"Did you leave it unlocked at some point?"

"No, I barely use it," he growls with frustration. "Trent is the only other key holder, and he swears he hasn't been in there."

"Does he know about this item?" I ask him.

"Nobody does." His eyes bore into mine, and I find honesty in their depths.

"Cameras?"

"Not this corridor. The... uh... holding rooms and interrogation rooms are along here. Plus, this office does not need to be monitored." His face falls into his hands as his fingers slip into his hair, tightening around the strands. Whatever it is, it must've been of importance.

"Shit, maybe it does though, right?"

"Yeah, you're right. It looks that way." He scrubs his hand down his tired face. "How's my brother? We should hang out tonight."

"Stuffing his face with salmon." I shake my head and he laughs.

"He's doing okay there with you guys? He's happy?" The concern for his brother is clear on his face. I guess it would be hard to let the baby brother you took care of move to a different country.

"Yeah, man. He's happy."

"He told me he's thinking of joining the police academy." Carm barks out a laugh. "His big brother is one of the largest gangsters in New York and he wants to be a cop."

"He hasn't said that to me, but mind you, our fucking plates have been stacked lately and I haven't had the chance to speak to him about his future." He looks amused about Emmett's choice of career, almost like he believes that won't happen.

"Yeah, good work on the judge." He nods as his eyes droop.

"Did Em tell you about that?" I don't remember her telling me she filled Carm in on her latest hit and something isn't sitting right with me.

"Either her or Emmett." He waves his hand like it's no big deal.

"You should get some rest," I tell him as I stand up. "You look like shit."

"Thanks." He barks out another laugh as I open his office door. "Vin," he calls out, and I turn to look at him. His face falls a bit as sadness bleeds into his eyes. "Thanks for watching them." I nod before closing his office door, leaving him to deal with his own problems as I stow all the information I've learned away for now.

Chapter Eleven

Ember

"Says here your mother was a crack addict, and no father was present at birth. You showed signs of drug dependence." The papers in my hands crinkle as I flip to the next page.

"Is it true?" Adri looks worried from her seat across from me at the kitchen table. Her hair is a mess of tangles around her face from constantly tugging on it and she has tired bags beneath her eyes, the purple color more pronounced on her makeup-free face. She's been agonizing over these papers for a day and they're taking a toll on her.

"Even if it is, you're fine now," I assure her as I skim over the next page. "But again, I don't know if they doctored this paperwork to fit the narrative."

"So this could all be lies just to steal babies?" Her eyes widen as her fingers once again sink into her hair to tug on the strands. "They're targeting single mothers without support and coercing them to give up their babies?"

"That's what I'm thinking, but it's all speculation right now." Frustration builds inside me as more information unfolds. How can I handle all of this and continue to keep my sanity? "The age looks correct though, you are definitely a year older." I chuckle at her exasperated expression.

"Emmett will have a field day with that," she grumbles, and I almost feel sorry for her until I remember she's the one who fell in love with him.

"Ember, why are you doing all this?" She spreads her arms out wide, her tone filled with irritation. "Why not let this town rot and move somewhere else?"

"It's my legacy." It's hard to explain to someone my motives when I'm mostly running on emotions. Whitsborough is my seed, the place where my family roots were grown, and I refuse to chop down the tree now. "This place is where I'm meant to raise my family. It's my right as a Craven."

My phone chimes with an incoming message, distracting me from my conversation with Adri.

Principal Perv: It's done. We're meeting tomorrow.

Me: Where?

Principal Perv: Behind the elementary school.

Interesting. Why would Moore want to meet him there? It's summer, but then again, they always hold summer camp there.

Me: What time?

Principal Perv: 2:30 pm.

Huh… just before summer camp lets out.

Me: Let me know as soon as it's done. I want details.

He doesn't reply, but the message says read. He better be of some fucking use to me, or I will enjoy carving out his intestines and tying him up with them.

"Is that Vin?" Adri interrupts my thoughts of blood and human entrails.

"No, it's Principal Perv telling me he's meeting up with Moore tomorrow," I clarify as I place my phone back on the table.

"Ember, I don't like the thought of someone planning your murder." Adri's eyes well up with tears. "None of this is worth it if you are dead." Her face crumples with despair, and I reach across the table to grab her hand.

"It'll be worth it for your children, my future nieces and nephews. It'll be worth it for all those children being abused and unable to get the help they need. Trust me, Adri, I will do everything I can to avoid being killed, but our endgame is to eradicate the corrupt." She links her fingers through mine and squeezes, making my chest grow heavy with sadness. I don't want to see anyone in my family unhappy, and that's why I'll continue to fight, knowing the greater good will be worth my blood.

She shakes her head and lowers her eyes to our clasped hands. "What about my parents?"

"To be honest, I don't think they are bad people. I think they needed a baby quickly. Sometimes the adoption process can be lengthy, and yes, they bent the law, but they didn't hurt anyone. Plus, they are away most of the time, so I'm not too fixated on them." As much as Adri is at odds with her parents, the relief lining her face and shoulders tells me she still cares about them.

"What did we find out from those papers?" She points to the file in front of me, and I release her hand to spread them out.

"Nothing referring directly to Talia here, but there is a name of an adoption agency in New York. I'm going to send it to Carm and ask him to look into it for me," I explain to her. "The boys will be back tomorrow."

"Yeah." She smiles, the first one she's had since we've opened the file. "This house feels weird without Emmett."

"Quieter, less chaotic?" I lift my brow as I look at her.

"No." Her eyes shine with adoration as she laughs. "More boring and all business."

I shake my head and laugh with her because she's right. Emmett has a way of walking into a room and making the most miserable human being crack a smile. His energy is contagious, and you just want to be on his level to experience life the way he does. That's what he gives me that none of the others can, my life in prismatic technicolor.

"I'm going to go give Carm a call. I put some menus on the table. Pick whichever you want for dinner." I stand from the table and point toward the counter at the menus piled in the corner.

"Okay." Adri nods and gets up to go to the counter.

I head to my office with the file and stand in the doorway. Sometimes I keep a firm lock on the memories of my adoptive parents, telling myself I'll grieve them when my mission is complete, but some days, like today, they slip free and I can almost imagine them here. Dad would be at his desk, pouring over auctions for cars or finding someone's dream vehicle. *I miss you, Dad.* Uncle Scott will always be my dad in my eyes. I only wish I had more time with him to experience it. Aunt Debby was a great follow-up mom to the one who gave birth to me, and I miss her terribly too. There was just so little time with them, and all I can do is hope they are proud of me. Not for murdering and torturing, that's just fucked, but for finding out what happened to my mother and trying to clean up the town they loved.

I sit at the desk and dial Carm's number on my cell phone, listening as the dial tone purrs in my ear.

"Big bro services, how can I kill someone today?" he answers, making me snicker.

"Is this a new business venture?"

"Well, with siblings like you two, it should be," he retorts with humor in his voice.

"Emmett isn't behaving, I gather?"

"He is. Seems your boy, Vin, keeps him in line."

"Vin can be intense." I snort.

"He's a good man that loves you both." He sounds almost sad.

"Everything okay over there, Carm?" I ask him as my stomach grows tight with tension.

"Yeah, little sis, things are fine. I'm tired, that's all. Are you okay?"

"I'm good. I came across some new information about Jennifer Talia."

"What?" He suddenly sounds wide awake. "What information?" I swallow the growl of frustration sitting in my throat as I inhale a deep breath. He should've already found this, it wasn't difficult.

"Remember my friend, Adri?" When he grunts his affirmation, I continue, "Her parents adopted her with help from Robert. She was born in New York, and I spoke to her parents and they knew Talia was the one that set it up."

"Okay. We already know she has an adoption scam going on."

"I know the name of the company," I tell him.

"Oh. That *is* new," he mutters. "What's the name?"

"Love the Tots. Heard of them?"

"No." His answer is quick, making me suspicious. "But I'll look into it."

"Okay. Thanks, bro."

I hang up the phone and can't help the uneasy feeling that starts spreading over me. It's always the same. As soon as I get in range of Talia, something goes wrong. When we were in Spain, Carm did a lot of the legwork with his men, but on one of those days, Vin and I went to breakfast at a little café not too far from where we were staying. We sat outside on the patio and when the waiter came with our food, he greeted the table behind us.

"Ahhh! Jennifer Talia!" he exclaimed. I couldn't see anything since they were directly behind me, but Vin could. I can't explain what happened next. Maybe she knew what Vin looked like or maybe the bitch just had a sixth sense, but she left in a hurry, and by the time we reached the entrance of the café, she was long gone.

I knew after that I would have to come home. If she found out we were there and that we were tracking her. It only made sense that she would flee, and I couldn't leave my family here vulnerable.

"You look deep in thought." Travis' voice brings me back to the present, and I look up from my darkened phone screen to find him leaning in the doorway.

"We found some information on the adoption agency used for Adri," I reply, filling him in. "So I called Carm to find out more since it's in New York."

"Cool." He steps into the office and stands at the other side of my desk. "But we're doing our own investigation, right?" He looks at me expectantly, like he already knows the answer but needs to hear me say it as he rests his hands on the desk.

"Of course." I tap the folder on the desk. Even though I asked Carm to investigate, I don't expect much from him lately. My call was more of a kick in the ass for his slacking.

"On it." He reaches out for the envelope.

"Thanks, Trav." I hand it to him and exhale the stress brewing inside my chest.

Then I clear my head of all adoption agencies and thoughts of Talia as Travis leaves my office with the file in his hands, because I need to plan how my confrontation with Marlana and her prostitute mother will go down.

Chapter Twelve

"Aren't you going to wear your Black Slaughter makeup?" Vin asks from the bed as he watches me dress.

"I want to, but I need Marlana to see my face and know it's me." I look over at him with a grin. "How do you feel about what we're going to do to your ex-girlfriend and her mother?"

"First off,"—he sits up with a growl—"you were my first and only girlfriend, who is now my fiancée. Second, I don't give a shit. She and her mother have caused me and my family enough pain."

"You mad?" I tip my head to the side as my pussy clenches with need. He's the sexiest when he gets fired up.

"You're trying to set me off and you're not going to like it when I fucking snap. Don't ever play like I had a single important relationship in my life before you." His eyes blaze with anger, and I know he will make good on his promise if I push him too far. So I let it go because he shouldn't have to fight with his fiancée after driving eight hours to get home.

"Tell me what you found out in New York." I continue to dress while I smile at him, letting him know I'm done with the teasing.

He lies back and relaxes. "Not much. Carm looks tired and ragged. Not from running the Rampage though, because I see Trent doing most of that. Carm was gone a lot, Em. His little brother went there to see him and probably only set eyes on him twice."

"So what is he up to?" I walk into my closet to grab a black hoodie.

"What do you have him working on?" he asks, his voice clear as I pull the sweater on.

"I didn't ask him to do anything until yesterday. I asked him to look up the adoption agency that was used for Adrianna. It's located there in New York." I come back out of the closet to find a confused expression on his face.

"Maybe he's still trying to track down Talia for you since Spain was such a fucking bust." Vin sits up, his brows drawn together and his finger tracing the design on my bedspread.

"Yeah, maybe." His head snaps up at the uncertainty in my voice.

"Do you think he's into something else?"

"I'm more worried about him. Maybe he's so exhausted because he feels alone and his entire family is in another country. That would drain anyone." It's an excuse to cover my suspicions about Carm, one I'm not ready to reveal yet. I sit on the bed beside him and he wraps an arm around my shoulders.

"True," he agrees. Then I get up from the bed and open the top drawer of my dresser to grab my knife.

Once I'm ready with my knife and the rope in my hoodie pocket, we leave the house and head out to Vin's Hummer. I watch as he adjusts the gun in the back of his waistband before humming my approval.

"Were you guys seriously leaving to do indescribable acts of terror and torture without a farewell?" Emmett says from the open garage, making me turn with exasperation at the sound of his voice.

"You know it," I deadpan and get into the Hummer. He walks over to the passenger side and taps on the window, which I lower with a roll of my eyes because I'm expecting him to say something silly or sarcastic. "What do you want?"

"Be careful, and call me when you're done." The serious tone of his voice and the pleading expression on his face has me swallowing my retort. He's falling into the brother role with me more nowadays, so his recent concern for me is nice even though it can be overbearing.

"Okay," I say instead as he brushes a hand through his hair.

"Still haven't heard from Andrew?" he asks as his eyes search mine, worry shining in their depths.

"No." I shake my head. "I'll go by his house when we're done with Marlana."

"Let me know if you need me to meet you there." He narrows his eyes like he knows I'll try to dissuade him.

"Okay." His features relax, taking me at my word. Our trust has cemented over time too and we're truly like family now.

"Love you." He leans in and kisses my cheek then looks around me to Vin. "You too, bro." Vin blows him a kiss, and I chuckle at their camaraderie. It's nice they get along as well as they do because it would be a pain to have to constantly break up arguments.

We're on our way to Marlana's when Vin breaks the silence. "Why is Andrew ghosting us?" He's worried about it, and frankly, so am I.

"If I find out he's up to something, I will make him wish we killed him many times over."

Marlana's house comes into view, and I can feel the anticipation wash over me. I tried to move on and leave her alone. She was nothing to me anyway. She made my first few months here in Whitsborough annoying—I let it go. She taped me having sex with my boyfriend and tried to distribute it—I let it go. But learning about Travis, and then the shit she pulled on Shay, I can no longer let it go.

"Let's get this done," Vin growls as he gets out of the car. We're parked on the street, a few houses up from hers so we don't alert them that we're here.

Vin rings the doorbell when we walk up to the door. "We'll be lucky if her drunk-of-a-mother is even awake."

"I won't mind waking her." I shrug.

Marlana, and her eggplant hair, opens the door, and her eyes nearly bulge out of her head. Her first reaction is to slam it in our faces, but Vin is quick and blocks her attempt with his boot.

"Anal Ram!" I put on an exaggerated pout. "Don't you want to see some old friends from high school?"

"You are not my friends," she spits out as we push ourselves inside.

"You're right," I snarl into her face as I shut the door. "We're not friends, and when I leave here today, everyone will know it."

Vin grabs her by her biceps and forces her into her kitchen. "Where's your whore mother?" he grinds out at her.

"Sleeping." She struggles in his arms as anger saturates her words. "She works nights."

"I bet she does." I chuckle and throw Vin the rope I have in my sweater.

He forces her onto a kitchen chair and uses the rope

to secure her. While she's fighting and screaming at Vin, I grab a dirty kitchen towel hanging from her kitchen sink and use it to stuff her mouth.

"I'll go find her mother." Vin leaves the kitchen, and I'm alone with the bitch herself.

She glares at me with tears flowing down her cheeks, the dirty towel stuffed so far down her throat that it's probably difficult to breathe.

I bend down in front of her and smile widely. "Do you know why we're here?" She shakes her head as her tears run faster. "You tried to tell Emmett about Shay, remember that?" Her eyes widen and her spine straightens in the chair. "Now I know why you did that. You were trying to scare her into working with you by telling Emmett her darkest secret."

She tries to refuse, but my hand flies out and slaps her across her face. Her head whips to the side as she sobs, the sound choked by the towel in her mouth.

"Yes!" I move in closer as her face fills with fear. "You were blackmailing her the same way you tried to blackmail me, but hers was different. She was being raped in that video and you knew that." I slap her again. "You knew that because you made it happen." She's trying to talk around her gag and still profusely shaking her head, still trying to deny everything she's been a part of. "You did. When she told you what she saw your mother doing, you set your plan in motion and then taped it for insurance."

Her head slumps forward with resignation as Vin brings in a disheveled, older version of Marlana. He throws her down in the chair next to her daughter, and I watch as she attempts to stay upright, not really taking in her surroundings.

"Is she drunk?" I ask Vin.

"No, I found a needle and some other shit on the bed beside her. She's a fucking junkie."

Tonya's bleached blonde hair is severely damaged

and standing straight on her head in a frizzy mess, her face still has remnants of makeup that look at least a few days old, and her skin is an unnatural orange color.

Her head keeps falling forward, and each time she's barely able to pull it back up. I slap her too for good measure and watch as she literally flies off the chair with a yell and hits the floor. Her cheap, faux silk robe flies open, and we all get a view of her unkempt lady bits.

I gag and point at her. "Please tie her to the chair too." I retch again. "I don't want to see that again."

Vin heartily laughs as he picks up the junkie and slams her back onto the chair, her eyes finally looking around the room as she grunts with pain. Between my slap and Vin's jostling, she seems to have sobered up some.

"Vincccent." Tonya's eyes widen and then they narrow on him with a blatant look of lust. "Gossshh, you filled out."

"Ew." I heave when she spreads her legs, her robe falling open. "Hurry and tie her up. Tie those legs together too."

Vin is still chuckling as he wraps the rope from his sweater pocket around her and secures it tight.

"What'sss going on?" she slurs and looks at me. "Who are you?" She still has yet to notice her daughter, who is sitting right next to her. I shake my head at her with disgust, not bothering to answer because we have more pressing matters to talk about.

"What kind of deal did you have with Robert Greene and Coach Halbert?" I question her.

She's lucid enough to answer. "I ffucked them bothh for a price." Then she grins like it's something to be proud of.

Marlana squirms, making noises behind her gag, and her mother dearest finally sees that we tied her offspring to a chair next to her. She gives her a confused look as she groans.

"See your daughter?" I ask her, grabbing a handful of Marlana's hair and tugging her head back as she growls through the towel. "I will hurt her if you don't answer my questions honestly and quickly. Understand?"

"Yess." Tonya nods her head as it lolls around. The drugs have either numbed her to what's truly happening or she's just not scared.

"Good." I release the god-awful cabbage head and wipe my hand on my pants. "Now, what was your deal with Robert Greene and Halbert?"

"I wass both Robert'ss and Halbert'ss esscort, and when thhey called me, I would have to go. I alsso brought them other ladiess to enjoy."

"Now we're getting somewhere." I crouch down in front of her and Marlana screams at her mother through her gag. "Were these ladies willing?"

Her eyes roll around for a bit before she looks at her daughter. She's probably wondering how much we know. "Uh..."

"Let me remind you,"—I pull the knife from my pocket—"I will not hesitate to hurt your filthy bitch of a daughter." She pulls her head back as her eyes scan the blade, her mouth forming a thin line.

"Okay." She licks her dry, chapped lips and bobs her head. "No, they didn't alwayss know what I wass bringing them into."

"Were they all of age?"

"Yes." She nods. "I only brought them women."

"What about Shay?" I raise a brow at her. "Wasn't she just a young girl when you stuck Halbert on her?"

Her eyes widen and she twists her head to face

Marlana. "You told them?" She suddenly sounds sober as anger fills her tone.

Marlana rolls her eyes before tipping her head back.

"She didn't actually." I twirl my knife in my hand. "But she was blackmailing her with the actual video of the rape. Did you know that?"

Her mouth clamps shut, and she continues to look at her daughter, her body rigid and trembling. I can't tell if it's from fear or anger.

"No answer?" I make sure the excitement I feel about hurting her daughter is clear with the gleeful expression on my face.

I stand up, grab Marlana's ugly-ass hair again, and slice through it with my knife really close to the scalp. Then I hold up the sizable chunk and throw it at her mother's face. Marlana is screaming through the towel, her face a crying, snotty mess as her mother gasps and tries to struggle against the rope holding her.

"Still no answer?" I say to her as I grab her daughter's chin to tip her head back. As soon as the tip of my blade touches Marlana's throat, Tonya finally opens her mouth.

"Yes! I knew! I knew!"

"Why would you be bothered that a high school girl knew you were a prostitute?" I ask her.

"I didn't care. It was Robert that told me to make sure it stayed quiet. He didn't want anyone finding out he was fucking whores. He told me to make sure no one ever found out. I could've killed her. She got off easy."

"Well, lady, now you've done it." Vin chuckles from his seat at the kitchen table, his mouth sounding full of food. I turn to look and find him chewing, his humor-filled eyes watching me. Is he eating a fucking apple?

"Easy?" I turn back to Tonya and hiss at her. "You

think rape is easy, huh?" This time, I have her coarse, frizzy hair in my grip, and I pull her head back. My knife rests against her jugular and I press it into her skin.

"It's better than being dead," Tonya pants as she tries to stay still, her self-preservation finally kicking in.

"Is that why it was so easy for you to rape Travis when he was just a child?"

Marlana's head twists around and she's staring at her mother with shock in her eyes. It could be an act, but to me, it looks genuine. Marlana didn't know what her mother did to Travis. I'm relieved by that, but it's miniscule. Marlana is still guilty of doing terrible things.

"I had no choice," she whispers, her eyes shining with terror as her throat works on a swallow.

"We all have choices in life." I bring my face closer to hers. "You enjoyed what you did to him." She doesn't answer or try to dispute me. In her defense, I'm not asking, I'm making a statement. "So I have a problem with that. I also have a problem with your daughter and her amateur porn filming ambitions, but today, the focus is on you. You have to pay for what you've done, the damage you inflicted on other women, what you did to that young boy, and how you raised your daughter to believe rape and extortion are *easy*." I flip my knife in my hand and then, with it gripped tight, I stab it into Tonya's thigh.

Marlana looks at her mother's leg with fear and begins to frantically shake her head while her mother stares down at the knife embedded in her thigh with wide eyes, her body trembling with pain. Though I have a feeling the drugs she shot into her system are dulling her reaction and controlling the panic, preventing her from being afraid of us.

Vin throws the eaten apple core over Marlana's head and it lands in her lap while I roll my eyes and give him a pointed look. He shrugs his shoulders and leans in his chair, licking his plump lips as he watches me.

Tonya whines as more blood pours out of her thigh, her face still a mask of shock. She'll probably die if we don't get her to the hospital.

Shame.

Marlana cries again, and I bend down, forcing her to look at me. "Your mother, Robert Greene, and Coach Halbert were part of a rape ring here in Whitsborough. I'm going with my gut here and choosing to believe you didn't know. This will be your one chance to prove to me you can follow rules and that you are capable of change. One fuck up and I will gut you. Now, pay close attention to what I do to people who fuck with my family."

I turn back to Tonya, who looks a little pale under her fake orange skin. She screams as I rip my knife out of her thigh, making me chuckle. Then I cut the rope from around her body, and she slumps forward, putting her hands on the wound.

"Tonya, this is my town now. I decide who stays and who goes." I yank her up by her hair and start pushing my knife into her gaping mouth. "You have to go. No child predators or rapists can stay." She stays still, completely petrified of the knife I've inserted in her mouth. One quick move and she knows the serrated edge will rip open her cheeks. I look up over her head to find Vin with a look of complete rapture on his face. His expression takes my breath away as I shove the knife and hilt into her mouth, severing her spine.

Then I tear my eyes away from Vin's and look down into Tonya's lifeless orbs before throwing her body to the floor as Vin gets up and stalks toward me. My stomach coils with need as my heart begins to pound inside my chest. Marlana's muffled screams do nothing but heighten the moment.

"You have some blood on you." He stands in front of me as his thumb wipes along my cheek, and I don't know why, but those words set me off into a frenzy.

I rip his shirt right down the center and unbuckle his belt. He doesn't stop me, just watches with a sinful smirk. Then I lick his infinity tattoo, and he groans, tipping his head back.

Marlana grows still, her eyes wide on us as tears run down her cheeks. I pull down his pants, leaving his boxers in place before pushing him onto Tonya's chair. He looks down at her body in front of him, staring wide-eyed at the ceiling, my knife still protruding from her mouth.

I take off my leggings and then straddle him in the chair as I look over at Marlana. "Remember this cock?" I ask as I pull him out of his boxers. She looks—of course she does. This cock is memorable. Who wouldn't want a final look? "Remember this." I pull my panties to the side and sink down onto him. "His big-ass cock disappearing into my eager and wet pussy."

She whimpers as I ride the fuck out of my fiancé over her mother's dead body. The blood on my hands transfers to his neck and face as I grind my pussy hard into him, and he leans back a bit, working himself deeper.

"You're getting blood on me, baby," he growls as he pumps up into me. "Filthy whore's blood."

"Fuck." I lean forward and bite his lip before drawing it into my mouth, clamping down once more as I near my orgasm. This one is going to be explosive. I pull away and release it with a *pop*, then grab his chin and smear more blood across his one-day-old scruff. The sight of the blood does it for me and I'm coming so hard around him, clenching him tight.

"Shit," he moans at the feeling of me sucking him inside.

Then he releases a raspy groan when he finally comes deep inside me, his cock jerking and pulsing. I finally look over to Marlana, whose head is hanging down, chin to chest as she cries softly now.

I stand up off of Vin and he adjusts himself back inside his boxers before he grabs my face and presses a bruising kiss to my mouth. Once we're both dressed, I take the gag out of Marlana's mouth.

"You two are the most disgusting people I have ever met," she grinds out, sucking in mouthfuls of air.

"Nope." I point to her mother. "She is, but fuck it." I bend down until I'm in her face. "I'll gladly take second place."

"Why did you kill her?" She whimpers and cries as her body quakes with fear.

"She helped ruin so many people's lives. You are on the fast track to doing the same. Consider this your one and only chance to turn your life around without her polluting it. Change, do good, and be someone worth living here. Or else I will be back, and after seeing everything I am capable of, I would suggest you heed this warning." I stand upright once more and go to the sink to wash my hands. "I'm going to untie you, and when we leave, you will call Chief Moore over here. Tell him everything, exactly what we did and why we did it. The most important thing you tell him is *who* did it."

I nod to Vin and he unties her. Once she's free, she stands and rushes to her mother, gathering her head into her lap as her cries fill the room. Most people would look at her and feel pity that she's now parentless because I took away her decrepit mother and her father isn't in the picture, but I see it like I saved her from a shit parent and I'm giving her a chance to make herself better. Some kids are better off orphaned than with parents who would lead them into a life of corrupt depravity.

"Sorry, gonna need this back," I say quietly before pulling the knife from Tonya's mouth. "Call Moore as soon as we leave."

"Yeah," she murmurs, refusing to look at us. "Just leave."

Vin grabs my hand and pulls me out of the house and straight to the Hummer. Once we're inside, he pulls the seat belt across my chest and leans in to place a sweet kiss on my lips.

"Let's find out what happened to Andrew," he suggests as he starts the vehicle and pulls away from Marlana's house.

I hope I never have to come back here again.

VIN

Once I've washed up and Ember is showering off the blood from her skin, the notification on our phones ping at the same time. A car is coming up the driveway. It's black and nondescript, very much like an undercover police car or maybe something the chief would drive. I guess Marlana did what was asked of her.

"Em!" I call into the shower. "We have company."

"Oh, goodie!" I hear her mock-squeal, and I chuckle as I close the door.

Then I head downstairs to find Emmett, Adri, and Travis standing on the front porch, forming a line. We may be fucked-up and completely dysfunctional, but we don't let anything happen to our own.

"This is the fastest I've ever seen the police work!" Emmett sneers as Moore steps out from the vehicle.

"So you know why I'm here?" Moore's eyes brighten like he's caught us.

"Yeah," Emmett replies while leaning against the doorframe. "I just reported my cat missing an hour ago."

Travis coughs on a laugh and I cover my mouth to hide my smile.

"What are you doing here, Moore?" Adri demands, her voice commanding and strong as she steps forward and crosses her arms over her chest. Out of all of us, Adri's surname is the most powerful. The money her family owns alone is leaps and bounds over anyone else's. Her family put the most money into the creation of Whitsborough.

"I just came from a fellow student of yours' home. We found her mother murdered, and she claims it was

Ember Craven."

"Interesting." Travis leans against the brick wall. "Warrant?"

"Warrant? I'm not searching or investigating anything. I just thought she and I could have a conversation," Moore placates with his hands out.

"You mean you want to talk to all of us," I correct him as I step forward into his view.

"Ah! Vincent Greene. Yes, I will speak with all of you." He nods eagerly.

"Oh, for goodness' sake, guys!" Ember exclaims from behind us. I turn to find her standing there with her hair wet and wearing a robe. "Let him in. This is just plain rude. Do we have cakes and cookies?" she prattles as she walks toward the kitchen.

"Fucking psycho females," Emmett mutters as he walks by me and into the house.

Adri and Travis stand close to my back as I wait for Moore to come into the house. He eyes me from head to toe and I meet his gaze with a stern one of my own.

"Don't try anything, Moore," I warn him.

"Wouldn't dream of it, Greene," he retorts. "I've seen what happens to the people who do."

I follow closely behind him and into the kitchen. Em is making coffee and humming at the counter while Emmett and the others are seated at the table, watching her with interest. Everything Em does is premeditated, and I can only assume all of this is as well.

Moore and I sit at the table and wait for Em to finish her show. Once she has her coffee and a muffin, she offers some to the rest of us. We all politely decline, and she shrugs as she pulls up a chair.

"Your loss," she moans over a bite of muffin. "What

can I do for you, Chief?"

"We received a call today from Marlana. You know her, I presume?" He's relaxed as he sits slouched in the chair, not even bothering to pretend to take notes.

"Oh, yes!" Em nods emphatically. "Such a great person."

I once again cover my mouth to push back the chuckle that wants to escape. Even Moore can see through her obvious façade.

"Her mother was murdered today." Moore leans on the table.

"The prostitute?" Em asks innocently.

"Escort," he corrects her. "Surely her profession shouldn't dictate whether or not she lives?"

"No, that is determined by someone's actions," Em provides around another bite of muffin.

"What could she have done to have this tragedy happen to her?" he presses.

"You're the cop, Moore. Investigate." She waves him off. "I'm not trained in such things, but if I were you, I would start with her daughter. I bet she has a mountain of information, not about how her mother was killed, but what led to that conclusion."

"I will certainly take that into account. Is there any reason Marlana would accuse you of killing her mother?"

"Again, I can't help you with that, but I'm sure with your superior investigative skills, you will connect all the dots," Em says with a glint of anger in her eyes.

"Well, it seems that's all I will get at this time." He stands and looks at each of us. "Thanks for your time."

I stand and walk him out as everyone else stays quietly sitting at the kitchen table. Once we get to the front door, he turns and looks at me. "Be available for questioning," he warns as he slips his sunglasses over his eyes.

I shrug and watch as he walks to his car. Looking at him as anything other than an extortionist and a fraud is difficult. He covered up some of the most heinous crimes against children and women, all to keep his pockets fat. There will never be an ounce of respect in me for that man.

"We need to take a trip to Andrew's," Em's voice sounds from behind me, jarring me for a second.

"Yeah, I have a feeling he's avoiding us."

"Do you think Moore threatened him?" She looks up at me as I turn to face her.

"Maybe?" Annoyance flits over her face with the thought of Andrew fearing the police chief more than her.

"I'm going to get dressed." She saunters up the stairs as I debate whether or not I should follow her and have a quick fuck.

My conscience wins out, knowing that Andrew is an important piece of the puzzle to keeping Ember from being killed.

"The house is dark," I whisper to Ember as we try to peer through the window in Andrew's front door. "The wife's car is in the driveway, but not Andrew's."

"Do you think he skipped town? Without his wife and kids?" Her brows drop over her eyes as she stares at the house menacingly.

"Nah." I shake my head, remembering how scared Andrew was with us. There's no way he'd bring more of Em's wrath if he could avoid it.. Something must've happened. "I don't think he'd do that. Where was he meeting Moore?"

"Behind the elementary school."

We get back in the vehicle and I pull out onto the street to drive toward the school. Maybe something there will give us a clue about what happened. I turn down the residential street that winds around behind the school, and right away we see Andrew's car parked on the side.

"Fuck," Ember snaps under her breath as we park a few car lengths behind him. She grabs her knife in her hand, and I do the same with the gun from my waistband.

I have a bad feeling about this as we both get out of the Hummer and stride toward Andrew's car. "Don't touch anything," I warn her as I walk up the driver's side and she walks up the passenger side.

Then I look in the driver's side, finding it empty, save for a lot of blood. It's sprayed all over the windshield and the center console. I look farther in and see Andrew's slumped form sitting in the passenger's seat.

"Fuck," Ember breathes out. "He made it look like a fucking suicide. The entrance shot is on the left side. How much do you want to bet Andrew is right-handed?"

"It won't matter either way." I scrub my hand down my face. "We could get the trajectory of the bullet and do an analysis of the gunpowder residue, but it will always be ruled a suicide. That's the power Moore has."

"Motherfucker!" she growls and kicks at the car tire.

"Don't touch anything," I remind her and back up, ambling toward the Hummer. "Let's go. We don't want witnesses linking us to this."

"Fuck!" Ember bellows as soon as we're in the Hummer and pulling out onto the street. "I needed him!"

"I know, babe." I try to keep her calm, even though my insides are churning. "We'll figure it out."

She sits quietly, seething, as I take us back toward

home.

"Take me to the station," she demands, her voice low and filled with ire.

I whip my head to look at her. "What?"

"I need to have a word with our police chief."

"Em, I don't think—"

"Vin!" she screams into the car. "I won't lose track of what I promised I'd do. What I'm doing in memory of my mother and my parents."

"It's dangerous!" I scream back as we drive through an intersection.

"Do you really think he'll kill me in a station full of cops and civilians? That may be the best place to engage him. Then I'm going home and planning on how to hit him where it hurts. I still have a name on that list."

"Wilson McKay." I've memorized that list and have been mentally ticking off each name.

She stays quiet as I reroute and take us to the police station. I know what she's saying is true. Moore would never kill her in the police station, but he could arrest her and hold her for forty-eight hours.

"Stop worrying," she says, her voice low. "I can feel your fucking anxiety."

I rein it in as I pull into the police station's parking lot. "I'm coming in there with you."

She nods and hops out of the Hummer just as I round the front, adjusting the gun in my waistband and following close behind her. It's late evening, but Em has the chief's schedule memorized, and we wouldn't be here if he wasn't. She storms in through the front doors and the two cops sitting at the desk stand abruptly.

"I need to see Moore," Em snarls. "Tell him it's

Ember Craven." They look at her like she's a pest when she lets out a yell, "Now!"

One cop has the common sense to listen to her and picks up the phone to make the call. The other cop is still looking at her like a buzzing fly, annoying and persistent.

Then he looks over at me and I raise a brow, planting a look of utter boredom on my face. Cops around here are antsy and fucking trigger-happy. I don't need him to find an excuse to draw his gun.

"Follow me," the cop directs as he hangs up the phone. He gives Em a curious look as he rounds the desk and leads us down a corridor, but the other cop is looking at her like she's unhinged and could combust.

Same, bro.

We get to a corner office and the cop knocks on the door. "Miss Craven is here for you, Sir."

"Show them in," the smug bastard says, knowing I'd be here too. I can't help the ripple of apprehension that slides through me. Did he plan this? Does he know Em's next move before she makes it? Em doesn't wait for the cop to open the door. Instead, she pushes by him and throws the door open herself.

"Miss Craven and Mr. Greene," he coos as he sits behind his large desk. "What can I do for you?"

Em lays her hands on his desk and leans into his face. "I found your message, you son of a bitch." Then she literally growls, her teeth clenched tight.

"Message?" He looks from her to me and grins.

"One day, Moore, it'll come down to me and you. Believe me when I say I can't fucking wait." Em matches him with an evil grin of her own.

"Is that a threat?" Moore's face transforms into a mask of mocking shock.

"You can fucking bet your criminal ass it is." She snickers and stands back up. "It'll be the most fun I've had since taking out my daddy."

Moore drops his mask and stands up from his desk, hatred and rage taking its place. "You are in way over your head, little girl."

"We'll see," she retorts and turns to leave the office.

Moore looks at me and I flash him a smile. "Guess I'll be seeing you around, pig."

157

Chapter Thirteen

A prominent man was found in an apparent suicide in Whitsborough and not one thing was mentioned about it in the papers or the news. I would say that's strange, but I know it's not. They built this town on magnificent cover-ups and forged truths, its pillars erected on the backs of rapists and murderers, and I can't wait to watch it all crumble. I want to dance in the destruction as the dust settles, then rebuild with sincerity and love. In today's world, it's hard to imagine such a place, but if one person can make a difference, imagine what my whole family can accomplish.

"McKay will be at the town hall meeting tonight," Travis informs me as he walks into the office. "Just a heads-up, he was close to my father and Halbert. Also, your mother."

"Maybe I can use that to get close to him," I murmur.

"You definitely could," Travis agrees. "I spoke to Sharla last week about your mother. I just wanted some insight about her and what she was like. Sharla told me she was a spitfire, E, just like you, and she had more admirers than she had enemies. One of those admirers? Wilson McKay."

"No way," I breathe out in wonder. "That will totally work for us."

"Sharla says they dated briefly in high school, but her father chased him off."

"I want to see their gravesites," Emmett says as he appears in the office doorway. "Our grandparents."

"Why?" I ask him.

"Because regardless of what happened, I want to see it. I need to see it." He looks adamant and I get it, our blood family is dwindling, and we've buried more than are alive. If I'm honest, I'm kind of curious too.

"Okay," I give in. "This weekend, if I have enough time to do a class, we'll visit after." Keeping up with the classes has been tough and I've missed some weeks, but overall, it's therapeutic and I try to get there as often as I can.

"Then we'll visit the family crypt to pay our respects," Emmett adds, his shoulders relaxing with relief.

"That's a good idea," Travis agrees, sharing a look with Emmett.

Then they leave my office with their heads close together and talking low. I don't have the time to figure them out right now. If they are cooking up something, then I'll just have to trust that they know what they're doing.

Tonight, Adri is helping Sharla out by closing the restaurant. That way, Sharla can come with us to the town meeting. I want McKay to be completely at ease while he speaks to us, and maybe if he sees a familiar face, he will be.

I go over the documents I have set out in front of me. I plan on offering the Fire Chief a sizable donation to the Whitsborough Fire Department, hoping it'll soften him enough that I'll be able to get him alone at a later date. He knows exactly who I am, and hopefully, money can pull the blinders over his eyes. It does for pretty much everyone else in this town.

"We need more Neighborhood Watch in our community. The other night, a group of teenagers were walking the streets and drinking!"

"Looks like she could use a bottle of something herself," Sharla mumbles while a townswoman hollers from her seat, and I snort into my hand.

"That is definitely something we can look into," the mayor mutters, looking like she's half asleep. "Next up, we have Fire Chief McKay with some very important tips on how to keep your home safe."

Whitsborough's asshole number... Fuck, I lost count. Anyway, another asshole walks his ass up to the center podium and taps the mic like a fucking loser. We just had Busybody Betty up there screeching. The fucking thing works fine, dipshit.

"How about not being a nasty-ass piece of shit who loves kiddy porn?" Vin grumbles, and I elbow him.

Sharla doesn't know about the underworkings of Whitsborough, or if she does, she doesn't know we know about it. I definitely do not want her knowing we know. *That's a fucking mouthful.* The Chief drones on about fire detectors and not smoking while extremely tired—thanks for that Coach Halbert. Finally, the Mayor joins him at the podium and cuts the very painful speech short.

"I was informed about an hour before this meeting of something amazing." She sounds like Emmett when he's forced to study for school, bored and witless. "We have a fairly new citizen to Whitsborough, but her family name goes all the way back to the founding of the town. She would like to donate one hundred thousand dollars to the Fire Hall Restoration Project and another one hundred thousand for a new truck."

The crowd begins to clap as many faces look around the hall curiously. The mayor squints out at the crowd, and I want to roll my eyes in utter disdain. Her uselessness knows no fucking bounds. I stand up and give my best impression of the Queen's wave.

"There she is." The bitch's robotic tone grates on my frayed last nerve. "Amber Craven."

"It's Ember!" Vin yells out, obviously annoyed to shit.

"Sorry, yes. Ember Craven." She waves off her error, and I kind of want to watch her bleed for that.

"Craven?" McKay's eyebrows shoot up. Now I want to do a happy dance with the recognition in his eyes. "Thank you, Miss Craven." *Aw, whataya know? The perv has manners.*

I nod my head and sit back in my seat. "It's really great what you're doing, Ember." Sharla pats my knee.

She's been eyeing the ring on my finger the whole time we've been here, and I know she's not one-hundred-percent on board. Yes, I love the woman because she birthed my soul and raised him until I found him, but she wants us to wait. A long time. Vin won't hear it and I don't entertain it. If this is what he and I want, then there's nothing and no one on this planet that will stop us.

Once the hall clears out and everyone moves outside for refreshments, I make my way over to McKay. When he sees me up close, his eyes widen further.

"You look a lot like her." He shakes his head in awe before moving his eyes from me to Sharla. "Hello, Sharla."

"Hey, Will." She smiles at him. "Ember is planning to

build a family here with my son, Vincent. So making it safe is her number one priority." She doesn't know how accurate her words are.

"I believe I've heard about Ember around town." Yep, I bet he and Moore have talked at great lengths.

"I'm sure you did." I grin at him. "My aunt and uncle were also big contributors, so I wanted to continue that in their names."

"Yes, Debra and Scott." His turkey neck moves as he nods. "They were good people."

"How are the restorations going?" I ask him, sounding extremely interested.

"Great."

"I would love to come by and see the progress." I blink at him innocently. "Oh! And when the truck comes. Right, baby?" I look at Vin.

"Yep." Vin pops his P.

"Uh, yeah, sure, come by anytime." McKay shifts from foot to foot.

"Great!" I clap. "We should get home. Helping clean up this town is exhausting." I grin at him.

His thick swallow gives me all the information I need. McKay does indeed know who I am.

"It was nice seeing you again, Will." Sharla places her hand on his arm.

"Yes, it brings back some old memories." His eyes haven't left mine. Eyes that belonged to the girl he dated so long ago.

I nod at him and slowly walk away between Sharla and Vin, but I glance back when we get to the hall's entrance and see him already on his cell phone. *That's right, tell Moore I was here.*

Vin and I drop Sharla off back home and we watch as she walks up to the front door. I don't like that she lives alone but she won't hear anything about it. She refuses to move and refuses to date anyone. I mean, I get it. Robert fucked her over, but come on, I would look at that as a fucking blessing. She could've been in Travis' mom's shoes. Both of them, the one who birthed him and the other who called herself Mom.

"You want to stay with her tonight?" I ask Vin as he turns to look at me.

"She's fine," he replies, but I can see the worry in his eyes. "McKay tomorrow night?"

"Yeah." I shift in my seat as my mind thinks about the next mission. "McKay will be on duty."

"So Marlana's now?" He puts the Hummer into reverse and slowly backs out of his driveway as Sharla raises her hand in farewell at the front door.

"Andrew's first. I just want to put this in the mailbox." I hold up a thick envelope.

"That's good of you, Em." He smiles as he drives us toward Andrew's house.

"His family didn't deserve to lose him this way, made to believe it was a suicide." The envelope is filled with one hundred thousand dollars for Andrew's family. Without his income, I fear they may lose the house. Even though it's not my problem to think of, I have more money than I will ever spend, and if I can help a family avoid the hard life I had as a poor child in a single-parent household, then I'll sleep just a bit easier at night.

When we pull up outside of his house, I notice a few lights on upstairs and hope they don't see me placing this in their mailbox. I wouldn't even know how to explain what the fuck I'm doing.

Vin waits in the Hummer while I walk up Andrew's driveway. He was a piece of shit. The things he did in life were deplorable, but I want to believe he was changing, and his family doesn't deserve his fallout.

I drop the unmarked envelope in the mailbox and hurry back to Vin. When I get back in the Hummer and do up my seat belt, I look up to the second story. There's a lady standing there in the window watching us.

"Sorry," I whisper as we pull away.

Marlana's house may look deserted, but I know differently because it has looked this way every time we've come by. She just hasn't left the house in days, and fuck, who knows, maybe she's gotten into her mama's stash of narcs. As much as I wanted to kill the purple-headed toad, I think she can serve a purpose. Really, I'm just hoping she can change her life around.

"Rock, paper, scissors?" I hold my fist out to Vin.

"We're both going in, Em," he huffs with a roll of his eyes.

"Fine, I'll let you try for best two out of three." I flutter my eyelashes at him as he leans over and kisses my cheek.

"C'mon." He chuckles while getting out of the Hummer.

I grumble about his brutish ways and follow him up the path to Anal Ram's house. He tries the front door, and unsurprisingly, it swings open. Maybe she's become the town escort now.

"It smells like a trash dump in here," Vin groans, covering his nose with his hand.

"If we find another dead body, I'm out. I just want to eat some sushi and go to bed." The house is dark and the smell is disgusting, but I've smelled worse at Trav's house when his mother went on a rampage.

"How can you think of food right now? It literally smells like shit in here." Vin kicks aside a bag of trash as I shrug my shoulders.

"I'm hungry. I haven't had dinner yet." I pout and follow him farther into the house.

We get to the kitchen, where the floor is still covered in Tonya's dried blood. That would contribute to the stench. Then we head down a hallway toward Marlana's bedroom, the floor covered with dirty laundry and old takeout bags. It's fucking gross.

"Anal Ram!" I yell out, and Vin snorts. "This place is a fucking dump. Where are you?"

"Go away." A faint voice floats toward us, the tone sounding like a kicked dog.

"I want to, trust me, but we have some business to get into." I bypass another pile of clothes, the smell of dirty laundry and rotting food growing stronger the closer we get to her room.

"Fuck you," she says louder, putting some grit into her voice.

I get it. No matter how much I hate the bitch, I killed her mother. I wouldn't be too happy to see me either, but too fucking bad. She either pulls it together and does as I ask, or I kill her too for being a waste of fresh oxygen. Not that there's much of it in this house.

I kick in her door while Vin leans against the wall. Her room smells like a literal asshole, and I gag into my shirtsleeve. She has rotting food everywhere and the air in here is thick and humid, like she didn't bother to even open a window.

"Just kill me," she moans from under her covers, the mound moving slightly as I walk into the room.

"Where would the fun be in that?" I rip the blanket off of her, finding her hair a matted mess on her head and her skin sickly as she groans and throws an arm over her eyes.

"My mom is dead. What's the point?" Her voice cracks as she tries to hold in her emotion.

I bend down and look into her gray pallor face. "My mother was murdered too, only she didn't rape boys and help build a sex trafficking ring... but I digress." I hear Vin chuckle from the hallway. "What I'm trying to say is you can either wallow in here and just kill yourself, or you can get up and make something better of your life."

"Why do you care?" She drops her arm and glares at me, her anger potent in her eyes.

"Oh, fuck." I cackle as I stand straight, looking her dead in the eyes. "Don't mistake this for kindness. I hate you and would love to watch you swing from a rafter, but I don't want to kill more than I have to. Don't make me have to kill you."

"What do you want?" She slowly sits up, her aggravation giving away to despondency.

"I want you to shower." I pinch my nose and take a step back. "And then we need to have a long conversation. Clean this place up and I'll be back to see you in a few days."

I leave her and her stinky fucking self to join Vin back out in the hallway.

"Can you believe you used to fuck that?" I ask him, thumbing back at Marlana's room.

"Em." His voice holds a hint of caution. He hates when I bring up his past with other chicks, but I love to get him riled up.

"Honestly though, remember when her hair was like vagina pink? You fucked that." I don't get much of a warning before he grabs me around the waist and throws me over his shoulder. "Vin!" I squeal. "All the germs!"

He whacks me hard on the ass and mumbles something under his breath as I grin to myself. Mission accomplished.

Chapter Fourteen

"What's the deal with Marlana? What are we going to do with her?" Emmett asks while we sit around the table eating breakfast.

"I was actually going to talk to Carm about finding her something with the Rampage." I bite into my bagel with cream cheese as the room falls quiet.

"Seriously?" Vin finally asks, his face a mask of confusion. "Didn't you just tell her to turn her life around?"

"She doesn't have to be a gangbanger to be useful. I just thought getting her out of Whitsborough would be beneficial to all of us," I explain as Vin continues to look at me with creased brows.

"Not everyone in the Rampage is a criminal. They have accountants and chefs. I'm sure Carm would find something for her." Emmett nods as he bites into his bagel. "And I think it's a good idea to get her out of this place."

"Yeah, I can see your point," Vin agrees and continues to eat.

Last night, when we got home from Marlana's, he was still a little irked with me and took it out on my pretty little vagina. I can barely sit this morning. I shift a bit in my seat to distribute the pain and catch Vin watching me with a smug look on his face. He chokes on his coffee and starts fisting his chest when I narrow my eyes at him and flip him off.

"What's going on down here?" Adrianna comes into the kitchen with her mouth wide open on a yawn.

"Girl, that esophagus is large. I can see why the boys rave about it," I say around a mouthful of bagel.

"E!" Travis chastises from across the table, his tone filled with humor.

"Fucking right." Adrianna winks at me before sitting down beside me.

I lean over and kiss her cheek, then fill a plate with a bagel and some fruit for her. Adrianna is the sister I never had. The bond we share is strong and unbreakable. My life is hectic and filled with rage and blood, death and gore, but she brings me equilibrium and balances out my crazy with her calm energy. There's absolutely no one who can replace Adri and what she does for me. I would lay down my life for hers in a heartbeat.

"What is the Black Slaughter going to do next?" she asks me as she stabs a strawberry.

"Kill Wilson McKay." I grin at her.

"He was always a creep when we were kids." She shudders and looks over at Travis. "Remember how he used to show up at the playground with popsicles and follow the kids around?"

"Did he have a lost puppy in a nondescript white van too?" I ask.

"Fuck, did the founding families all have a meeting and decide to only let in pervs?" Emmett growls as he drops his fork to his plate in frustration.

The room goes silent after that as we fall into deep thought. I love this town because my roots are deep here. I feel obligated to do what I can for it and make the future a brighter one for our children. For that alone, I would risk everything.

"E," Travis breaks the silence. "Emmett and I are going to take a trip out to the storage unit today. Is that cool?"

"Yeah." I shrug as I stuff the rest of my bagel into my mouth. "Let me know if you find anything worthwhile."

Once I can get away, I hide out in my office and go over the files I found in Carm's office again. I can't tell if what I'm reading is the complete truth since there's no way to fact-check it. Government files are tricky like that.

Speaking of, I decide to call him while I have this plan for Marlana fresh in my head.

"Little sister, what can I do for you?" He's tired, his voice sounding like he hasn't slept in days.

"Hey, Carm. I have a girl here who's troubled with no family and in need of some strict life regimens. Can you take her?" It's another favor I'm asking of him and it causes my stomach to coil with guilt.

"Are you speaking about yourself?" He snickers, his tone laced with humor.

"Har, har, har." I roll my eyes as his laughter increases.

"Does she have classic daddy issues and needs regular spankings?"

"Ew." I gag audibly, grinning when his bellowing laugh greets my ear again. "Stop, you're not allowed to fuck her because I hate her, but I want to help her become something better... make sense?"

"Not even a little, crazy girl," he replies once his laughter dies down.

"Okay, thank you. I'll tell her to get her shit together." I smile as he huffs into the phone.

"Fine. Send her here, we'll straighten her out," he reluctantly relents.

"I also have a few pictures I want to send you and see if you recognize them at all. They might have had some affiliation with the Rampage at some point."

"Sure," he says as he exhales loudly.

"Thank you, big brother. Love you," I tell him sweetly as he snorts. I can see his eye roll through the phone.

"Love you. I will speak to you soon."

We hang up, and I stare at my phone. Carm is the perfect older brother, protective but soft for his baby sister. He gives me everything I ask for and chases behind me to clean up my messes. Our relationship started out strained, but I like where we've ended up.

The photos of my grandparents are spread out on the desk as I hover my phone over the photos and take a series of pictures to send to Carm. I hope we catch a break and find out what really happened to them.

Me: These are the photos. I need to know if you recognize the people in these pictures.

He doesn't respond and I go back to looking over the file. I'm at war with myself over the information it provides. I want to be completely unbiased while reading it, but that's just impossible. Carm is my big brother. If what I'm reading is true, then everything I thought I knew will be out the window.

"There will be firefighters inside all day and night," Vin remarks as he looks over my Black Slaughter face while we sit in his Hummer. We're parked outside the fire hall as the sun sets. "How do you plan to get him alone?"

"That's why you're here." I grin at him.

"I knew it," he mutters, and I roll my eyes.

"I've scoped the place out and there's an easily accessible entrance in the back used by the contractors when they're working. It's right beside his truck, which makes everything simple. I'll need to use that entrance, and after seeing the building plans from our city's website, I know where his office is." I rub my hands together and smile. "I just need you to meander up to the front and strike up a conversation about the construction and whatnot."

"Sounds easy enough, but what if they don't want to fucking talk to me?"

"Baby, you're an actor," I deadpan. "Act some shit out."

"That pussy will be destroyed tonight," he growls as he gets out.

I squeal as the insatiable bitch throbs at his words. Looks like sitting will be impossible tomorrow too.

Vin walks around the fire hall to the front, and then I hop out of the Hummer. I scouted the cameras a few nights ago and noticed the back only has one aimed toward the door. It's an old-style camera, as big as a fucking brick and sticks out of the wall. I strategically placed four large stones in the hedges for tonight. I've always had good aim and all I really have to do is hit it until it swings away from the door, or even better, take it out completely.

My first rock nicks the edge of the camera, causing

it to bend and point closer to the door. The next one does the trick and the camera stem snaps, leaving it swinging against the wall. I hurry over to the door and turn the knob. It's locked, but it's one of those old-school, knobs only locks, and the fucking thing is ancient. Besides, no one wants to break into a fire station filled with firefighters day and night. Except for me, I want to do just that.

The third rock is gripped in my hand, and I slam it down onto the knob and breathe a sigh of relief as the thing just pops off, leaving the door to swing outward. The corridor inside is empty and I can hear a TV on somewhere. I send a quick text to Vin, letting him know I'm in before heading off in the direction of the chief's office. I can't be sure the chief went outside to talk to him and I also can't be sure there aren't others chilling around here, so I take my time and slowly peruse the offices until I come upon the one with his nameplate on the door. It's empty, and luckily his laptop sits on top of his desk. Beside it is a nice-looking, customized Zippo with his name on it. So naturally, I pocket that.

Then I slip into the attached bathroom and wait. A few minutes later, my phone vibrates.

Vin: He's coming back now. I'll meet you at the spot.

My stomach swirls with anticipation as the excitement of watching this man die has my blood simmering. After McKay is done, my concentration will be solely on Moore and how to get him alone to be tortured.

The office door shuts and he groans as he sits in his chair. I wait a little while, collect my bearings, and prepare my mind for what's coming. Yes, killing is easy. I'm not bothered by watching someone die at my hand when I know they're deserving. It's the weight of what I've done afterward. Carrying the dead with you is heavy lifting and something I'll endure until the day I die.

Snores filter through into the bathroom moments later, and I roll my eyes at this man's audacity. He's in here sleeping while his men are trying to stay alert for their night shifts. This is as opportune time as any, so I slip out of the bathroom and dash into the office. He has his legs propped up on the desk and his hands are crossed over his stomach.

I head over to him and lean against the desk right beside his chair. Yes, this would be so easy if I decided to just slit his throat while he slept, but that's not the plan.

Thrumming my fingers along his desk, I wait for him to rouse. He sleeps lightly because, at the soft sound of my fingers, he bolts upright in his chair. Must be helpful when he has to pretend to be awake at a moment's notice.

His eyes meet mine and they widen with surprise, but then dim with reservation. McKay knew I was coming for him, and he either accepted his fate or feels he can get out of it. I'm excited about finding out which one it is.

"I knew you'd show up sooner rather than later," he states calmly as he lowers his feet from his desk and sits straight. I don't answer him as I continue to thrum my fingers on his desk. His eyes watch the movement as his body stiffens with tension. "How are you going to try this?" he asks boldly, his eyebrow arching. Try this? This man doesn't know a damn thing. I don't *try* anything once I decide to kill someone. It's done. Except for Carlos, I'll always regret not hanging that fucker by his neck.

"Wilson," I croon serenely as I look him directly in the eyes. "I appreciate what you did with the Halbert situation. That cover-up was well done."

"It was that or have everything blown up for the public's viewing pleasure."

"And we wouldn't want that, would we?" I taunt him. "Nobody should ever find out that Fire Chief Wilson McKay watches their little boys and girls, brings them treats at the park, and invites them to look for his lost puppy."

"Lost puppy?" He looks at me with confusion.

"Listen." I walk around his desk and stand in front of him. "I'm going to be straight with you. I know the shit you're doing, I know your preference for young children, and I know you are corrupt as fuck. You took money to cover up Halbert's horrific death."

"You're the one who killed him." He looks at me with wide eyes.

"Yes, I did that. I cut off the one thing that controlled him and you covered that up. As long as the money is right, you will deceive anyone. As long as the money is right, you will hurt children or watch them be hurt." My words serve to shake him up as he begins to turn red.

"I don't take part in anything to do with children. Yes, if the money is right, I will fib on cause of death or fire." He leans on the desk and looks me in the eyes. "I was part of the department when your grandparent's car was found completely burned."

I know this already, and I was hoping he would bring it up. "Oh?"

"Funny one, that." He leans back in his seat, his anger melting away. "To me, it looked like arson through and through, but for some reason, the Fire Chief marked it as an engine combustion."

"There should be some official report about it around here, huh?"

"Let's say there is." He pinches the hair on his chin. "Would that make you disappear?"

"No," I answer honestly. "I live here. I'm not going anywhere."

"Would you back off of me?" he counters.

"No, but I would give you a chance to make things right."

"How so?"

"By telling me about the corruption in the force and with Moore. By leading me in the direction I need to go to clean out the rot in Whitsborough. And then, you yourself would have to change."

He gets up from his chair, and I slip my hand into my hoodie pocket to run my fingers along my knife before following him down the hall and into an old filing room.

"You came just in time. They will destroy a lot of these closed cases in a few days." He looks back at me like I'm so lucky. Fuck off, I knew this already. "Here we go." He pulls out an old banker's box and hands it to me. It's light, and I grin as I think about how much information is in here. Obviously, bypassing all lies.

I follow him back out into the hallway and place the box by the exit door, then proceed back into his office, closing the door behind me.

"Moore is tricky and no real friend of mine," he declares as he sits back down. It's funny how fast they turn on their friends when their lives are on the line. "He was always in with the likes of Halbert and Greene. Those parties they held, the meetings in the basement of the town hall, they just weren't my thing. I don't know what you heard, but I'm not into children and I don't rape women."

Right.

"I went because it was better than being viewed as against them. They would come here—much like yourself—and threaten me, or worse." He continues, "I did whatever it took to keep them off my back."

"Did you recruit children?"

"They asked me to, but I never fulfilled my end of that bargain."

Yeah, right.

"Did you take part in the rapes at all?" I ask him.

"Only when Tonya provided her prostitute friends, and they were always willing."

Liar, liar.

"Halbert and Greene were the sick ones, Moore and Cox like to watch, and I showed up to keep my position."

Pants on fire.

"I see." I tap my chin.

"How can we keep this relationship going? Do you want me to tell you when Moore has a cover-up? We don't have any more meetings since you killed most of the members."

Boo hoo.

I go back to leaning in front of him against his desk. He's searching my face—most likely trying to see the features under the makeup—to see what I'm deciding, and I can't keep this farce up any longer.

"You have your mother's exact eye color. She was beautiful, and I was always a little in love with her until she became rebellious."

"Rebellious?"

"You know,"—he waves his hand around—"she became a little freer with whom she slept with."

Oh, he means raped. She became a little more raped. By his friends, no less.

"Mmm." I nod along.

"Debra was the quieter one, she had always been with Scott, but your mother was a spitfire. She was always getting into some sort of trouble, a wild one."

"Those wild ones." I *tsk* as I shake my head.

"Trouble finds them." He bobs his head.

I want his to be a bloody death, one that I could get my regular high from, but I know I can't. Moore is on my tail and he's ready to jump me for even the smallest infraction.

"I'll see you around, McKay." I head to the office door, but then stop to look back at him. "Thanks for being so honest."

"You bet." He grins like the slime he is.

On my way out, I grab the box and lay it just outside the door, then I make my way over to McKay's truck and douse it with the gas Vin left here for me. I hear him walking up and he helps me throw the gas all over too.

"What's in the box?" he questions as he tosses the empty gas tank into the back of the truck.

"Official papers on my grandparents' death. McKay was nice enough to give them in exchange for his life."

"Interesting."

After the truck is thoroughly saturated, we go back to the SUV and drop off the banker's box to wait for McKay to leave the fire hall. His first mistake? Parking his newer model truck in the back alone with no other vehicles around. All the other firefighters park in the designated area to the side of the building. Second? Trusting that I would let him live after the blood of his friends have soaked my hands.

"After this, it's onto Moore and then Talia," I murmur to Vin.

"Then I can marry you in peace and put some babies in you."

"You're serious about this marriage thing." I look at him. We're young, and I guess I always thought marriage would happen when we were at least thirty. Not that I wouldn't marry Vin tomorrow if that's what he wanted.

"As a heart attack." His face shows his love as he looks into mine.

"I'd kiss you, but I don't want to mess up your face with this makeup," I whisper.

"Later." He grins.

I nod and look back at the truck that reeks of gasoline. I wait around the corner of the building for the man himself to get the fuck out here. I want to get home and read what's in that box, then I need to call Carm.

The door finally squeaks open, and I watch as he looks down at the broken knob with a shake of his head. The beep of him unlocking the truck sounds as he saunters up to it like he doesn't have a single worry in the world. Like he lives a life of good intentions. I watch him as he stops in front of the driver's side door and smells the gasoline.

"What the hell?" I hear him mutter before he looks around.

I bet the gas smells fucking strong and his heart is beating out of his chest as he tries to figure out what is going on. The thought brings a smile to my face and my heart jumps in response. This is my favorite part of the hunt, the pounce and kill. The feeling of achievement when I watch a devious life being expunged and sent to Hell.

I'll see you there, McKay.

He opens the truck door to smell inside, and I run up behind him, grabbing a handful of hair on the back of his head to slam him against the side of his truck. The crunch of cartilage and his grunt of pain washes over me, and I feel that familiar swirl of red, fiery anger move inside me.

With his head still firmly in my grasp, I give him a good shove into the cab of his truck and tuck his legs in before closing the door. Vin opens the passenger side door and clocks him once more with his fist, effectively knocking him out.

We both back away from the truck and I flip open the fancy Zippo. Seems fitting. I flick the flint and stare into the fire's orange-yellow depths, then I fling it over and into the bed of the truck. It instantly ignites, and we stand there, transfixed by the towering flames. We walk backwards toward the Hummer a few moments before the gas tank explodes, causing the bed of the truck to buckle and the windows to shatter. The cab is an inferno of flame and the heat radiating from the truck can be seen stretching higher than the fire hall.

We get to the Hummer just as the firefighters burst through the back door. They scramble around the truck trying to see inside, but the flames are too much. I watch as a few come out with a hose, but I know McKay is long gone by now.

"Trouble doesn't just find the wild ones, it hunts the evil ones too," I whisper.

Chapter Fifteen

I've showered twice, but the stench of gasoline and smoke is embedded in my skin. There has been no report on the news about McKay, and we suspect maybe Moore is suppressing it for now. He wouldn't want the town reacting in hysterics with the overwhelming death toll this year, especially to their *upstanding* citizens.

I'm on my way to my house to finally speak to Ma about what brought my grandfather and Nana Germaine to Whitsborough so long ago. Since learning about the fucked-up people here, I need to find out if they knew what was going on and what made them stay here.

Adri is closing the restaurant for my mother tonight, and I can't express how thankful I am to her for easing the load. I feared my mother would work herself into the ground over this restaurant because she had nothing else in her life besides me. Another thing we need to talk about.

Soon I will be moving in with Em permanently. We're engaged, and I want to build a life with her. My mother needs to understand that, even though we may be young, we are two halves of an old soul.

I pull into the driveway and see her red Mini Cooper sitting there. We purchased this house after Ma came back from Toronto with me. Before that, we lived in a small, two-bedroom townhome with Nana Germaine until she passed away before I turned a year old.

Sitting in the Hummer, I watch the house for a bit, thinking about how I'll broach this subject with Ma. She's always been a little closed mouth about Nana and never gives me much detail. I have no memories of the woman, but I know she was married briefly to Ma's dad until he died in a hunting accident when Ma was five.

I get out of the Hummer and notice the lawn's been cut, and cringe when I remember it was supposed to be my turn to do it. I remind myself to thank Travis when I get back to Em's.

When I open the front door, the smell of mac and cheese wafts under my nose, making me groan. My favorite dish.

"Ma!"

"Kitchen!" she yells back.

I get to the kitchen and find her sitting at the table with a glass of wine, her cell phone illuminating her face. Standing behind her, I look over her shoulder to find her reading a news article.

"Mac and cheese?" I ask her as I drag in a long breath, the cheesy scent making my mouth water. "Did you know I was coming?"

"No." She chuckles and sets her glass on the table. "I was going to bring it by when it was done though."

I take a seat at the table beside her. "Can we talk?"

"Sure, son." She nods, then puts her phone down, looking back at me expectantly.

"I want to know more about Nana Germaine and why she came to Whitsborough."

"Oh?" Her brows raise as her body stiffens with surprise. "Why?"

"Just curious. Seeing her ring on Em's finger reminds me I know next to nothing about how our family came to be here." It's not the complete truth because I don't want to worry my mother with how much I know about Whitsborough. If she's ignorant to the fact that this town was built and run by corrupted men, then that's how I want her to stay. I would protect her from it all, especially with Em by my side.

"Mother and Father moved here to Whitsborough when I was three years old. Originally, we were from North Carolina, but according to Mother, it wasn't safe where we were living." She gets this far-off look in her eyes. "Mother was a maid to a wealthy family there, and it was all she knew, so she applied for that here in Whitsborough too. Father was a good groundskeeper and a notable marksman with hunting rifles."

"Why didn't you ever tell me about this stuff before?" I question as she shakes her head softly, her mouth turning downward.

"Because there is a bit of a scandal related to your grandparents, and I didn't want you to feel ashamed," she explains as she picks up her wineglass and takes a sip.

"I want to know everything, Ma," I tell her sternly as I lean forward.

She nods her head and continues, "They found a family here in Whitsborough, Canada. A quiet little town and far enough away from the troubles they had in North Carolina. They were a prominent family here with a large estate and my parents were thrilled to start over... With the Cravens." Her eyes meet mine as she visibly swallows, the apprehension clear throughout her features.

My heart stops and I look at her wide-eyed with shock. "Ember's family?"

"Yes, her grandparents, Jack and Laurann Craven. Jack was an avid hunter and he bonded with my father right away. Laurann was quieter and stayed to herself, so Mother was mostly there to cook and clean. One day, Father and Jack were out hunting, and Jack came back to tell us there was a terrible accident. Another hunter shot Father and he died instantly."

"What?" I feel like I've been physically hit in the face as my head snaps back and my mouth hangs open. "Who did it? Were they put in jail?"

"No one fessed up to it and it was a different time back then. Nobody was charged, but there were rumors. Some believed it was Jack himself, trying to get rid of my father because he knew too much." She exhales a heavy breath as she places her glass back on the table to run her hand over her short hair.

"About what?" My phone vibrates in my pocket, but I ignore it. It's probably Em and she'll understand when I explain everything later.

"I don't know," she admits as she throws both hands up with frustration. "Mother never talked about it, and whenever I asked, she would shut me up. She was different after that. I wasn't allowed up at the main house too often and if I wanted to play with Rebecca and Debra, they would have to come down to the cottage. Mother and I moved off the property when I was twelve and lived in our townhome until she passed away around the time you were nearly a year old."

"How did Nana die?" Her eyes well up as her hands rest against the table top, her lips tightening as she tries to hold back her emotions.

"That's another scandal." She releases a breath and stares down at her hands before looking back up to me. "As you know, Nana died in a car crash when you were a baby."

"Yeah." My phone goes off again, the vibrations running down my leg. Em is probably having a moment of needing to know where I am, past trauma of me being taken will do that. I'll call her in a few minutes.

"Jack and Laurann also died in that car and there was a lot of speculation about the cause of the accident at the time." I am completely speechless as she gives me a grim look, unable to form words even if I tried. "Some believe it wasn't an accident at all and that the car was set on fire and meant to kill everyone inside."

"Why was Nana in that car with them?" I ask quietly, my heart racing.

"She still worked for them, and they were all going into town for lunch. This was a weekly thing, and they did it every Friday without fail. Same time, same place."

"So whoever killed them knew their schedule," I mutter.

"There's no evidence they were killed, son," Ma implores as her face fills with fear. "The fire chief and police chief at the time ruled it an accident. Yes, I was skeptical at first, but I had to let it go or it would consume me. I was already in a difficult situation at the time with raising you as a single mother, and Debra needed me because Rebecca had run away from home the year before. We needed each other." Her words are rushed as she tries to persuade me to leave it alone, and I know it's because she fears what could happen to me if I dig too deep.

My phone goes off again and I continue to ignore it. I need to find out every single thing before I speak to Em.

"It's easy for things to be covered up in this town," I explain to her as her eyes shut and she takes a deep breath.

"I know." She runs her hand over her short red hair and looks at me again. "I'm just one person and I was afraid to rock the boat."

"You have no idea the amount of things one person

can do when they put their mind to it." Thoughts of Em flood my mind.

"I'm not that person," she huffs and rests her cheek in her hand. "And I don't want you to meddle with it. Leave it alone." Her eyes are filled with a mixture of fear and exhaustion.

"Ma,"—I lean over the table—"you are that person. You dealt with my scum of a father, raised me alone and under scrutiny, and now you have a very successful restaurant. You are that person."

"Thank you," she replies with a genuine smile on her face.

The timer rings for the oven and she gets up to pull out the mac and cheese. If she won't dig any further into this car accident, then I will. Even if it scares her to learn the truth. Em and I have the means, and the power, to find the information we need.

I walk into the house with the tray of mac and cheese and find everyone seated around the kitchen table.

"Do you not check your phone?" Em snarls, and I cringe. I fucking forgot to check it before I left.

"Sorry, babe," I shrug and give her a bashful look. "I was having a little talk with Ma."

"She's okay?" The anger is forgotten and true concern shines in her eyes.

"Yeah." I hold up the tray. "She sent mac and cheese. I also have a story to tell you all."

"We found some shit we need to talk to you about too," Travis adds.

I sit at the table and Emmett opens the tray, eating

it straight from the dish, so we all join in, doing the same.

"What did you talk about?" Em asks around a mouthful of food.

"About my Nana and Grandpa." I gaze up into Em's wide eyes. "Your grandparents too."

They look at each other and then Travis says, "We want to talk to you about that. We opened the file containing the car accident report involving E's grandparents."

"I know all about it." I lean back in my seat and lick the cheese from my fork. "Nana was there too. She worked for them, and they were going for their weekly lunch."

"That's the connection." Em's shoulders deflate with relief. "I read the official report and saw she was the third victim in the car. I was worried she was there against her will."

"There are some weird circumstances concerning our grandparents. I wish Debra and Scott were here to fill in the blanks," I explain as I run my hand over my face. Debra and Scott wouldn't have lied or made the situation seem better than it was. If they suspected foul play, I'm sure they would've looked into it further, which leaves me to believe that the police did a good job covering up a crime or it truly was an accident. My gut is going with the first option.

"Like what?" Adri asks as she stabs her fork into the tray.

"The circumstance around my grandfather's death is one. There was a hunting trip and Jack Craven returned to say my grandfather was accidentally shot and killed."

"What?" Em gasps as her fork drops from her hand to land on the table.

"Yeah. No one questioned it either. It was reported as an accident and the file was closed. End of story."

Em gets up from the table and brings the box we

got from McKay over. "There are a few redacted reports in here and some pictures of recovered teeth that match dental records. So we can confirm they are all actually dead and this wasn't a cover-up orchestrated by my grandfather," Em says as she hands me some photos. "The car was burned completely to the frame, which really makes no sense without an accelerant." McKay's truck comes to mind. His truck looked the same when they finally put the fire out because Em and I used quite a bit of gasoline.

"It really looks like someone tried to cover up the fact that they were murdered, but if Raphael really did it, then why would they cover it up? He wasn't a resident of Whitsborough," Travis muses, his brows crinkled together in thought.

"Because this little town doesn't handle scandals so well," Adri chimes in. "They would all rather bury their heads than deal with anything like that. Look at my parents. They rarely come home."

She has a point.

"Plus, if our grandfather was as fucked-up as everyone is saying, then I can't really see them trying to investigate too much. More of a good riddance attitude," Emmett adds as he continues to dig into the mac and cheese.

"That's also true," I agree as I tap the fork against my mouth. "The question is, do we want to blow this shit wide open?"

"Do *you* want to? This involves your nana," Em stresses as she reaches for my hand.

"I would like to know why she had to die," I admit.

"We'll find out then." She lifts the paper and waves it around. "The prior fire chief is someone by the name of John O'Conner."

"He passed away a few years ago," Travis informs us. He's truly a great asset to have around because our father practically ran this town, so he knows everyone. "Remember they had that parade after he died?" he asks Adri.

"Oh, yeah." She nods.

Em continues to read the paper. "The prior police chief was Carl Halbert... Wait..."

"Shit! How did I forget that?" Travis slaps his hand to his head. "Coach Halbert's father was chief of police at one time."

"Explains why things were covered up and swept under the rug with the rapes our father committed," I growl as I lock eyes with Travis.

"I don't know how much he'll remember," Travis declares with a smile on his face. "But he's alive in a nursing home."

"We'll pay him a visit." Em grins conspiratorially and it makes my heart skip with apprehension as my dick hardens.

"You're not going to scare the shit out of an old man, are you?" Emmett questions Em, his mouth filled with food and his spoon suspended in front of his face.

"I'm not above making him shit his geriatric diapers if that's what needs to happen." She cackles and Adri joins in.

"Coach used to make the team do charity games to donate to the nursing home," Travis tells us as he scoops up a spoonful of mac and cheese.

"Em, you stay here and relax. It's been a long day and you need to rest." I smile at her, hoping she takes me up on the offer. Setting her loose in an old age home could be catastrophic. "I think Travis and I can deal with this one tomorrow."

"Yeah." Travis nods.

"Okay," Em says around a mouthful of mac and cheese, looking a lot like her twin.

"Adri and I will check in on Marlana tomorrow," Emmett adds with a roll of his eyes. "Make sure she showers and eats something."

"I'll even smack her around a bit if I have to," Adri comments with a grin. It's scary how much Em is rubbing off on her.

"Anything interesting in the storage unit?" I turn to Travis and Emmett.

"Nah." Emmett shakes his head. "I brought back some books though. These are classics and worth a lot. It would look good in our library."

"Cool." Em nods.

"Okay, little one." I stand up from the table and bend down to scoop Em into my arms. "Bedtime."

"You still smell like burning McKay. It's making me hungry." She chuckles as she inhales along my neck.

"That's just gross." Emmett screws up his face.

We both laugh as I carry her up the stairs and into her room—soon to be our room—and lay her on the bed.

"I'm sorry for what my family has done to yours," she whispers, her voice pained.

"Don't apologize for things out of your control, and we really don't know what happened." I try to soothe her pain as I brush her hair off her forehead.

Her mind is tortured by the past, and when something bothers my girl, she doesn't let it go until she's rectified it to her liking. I wish I could convince her more, make sure she knows this isn't her burden to bear, and that no matter what, I can see her soul's worth.

I crawl up her body and settle between her legs, pulling her face to mine. "I love you, Emberlise Craven." Then I kiss her nose.

"You called me Emberlise," she breathes out as her face shines with surprise.

"Because I'm being serious, baby. I need you to be able to tell the difference," I echo the words I told her so long ago.

Her wide smile lets me know she remembers when I first said those words. Even then, I knew I was in love with her, and it's only grown stronger with each day that passes. If anything happens to her, and god forbid I lose her, I will be right behind her. There's nothing in this life for me without her.

I kiss her gently, her soft lips molding against mine perfectly as my tongue swipes along her mouth. Her lips open on a sigh as I deepen the kiss and run my tongue ring along her tongue, swallowing up her moan.

Then I run my hand up her thigh and under her shirt, slowly lifting it as I go. Pulling away from her mouth, I take just long enough to get rid of her shirt before I'm fused right back to her.

She isn't wearing a bra, and I groan at the fabric of my shirt separating her body from mine, so I pull back and rip my shirt off in record time, then I'm pressing myself against her. She feels like silk running along my bare skin, smells like citrus, crisp like a summer day, and tastes like the sweetest ambrosia, designed just for me.

I break our kiss once more and run my nose down her throat, breathing in her essence and letting it nestle deep inside me. Then I graze my mouth along her collarbone before settling over her beating heart, the rhythm like a language only I understand.

Sucking one of her nipples into my mouth, I flick the hardened peak with my piercing while pinching the other between my finger and thumb, and her breathy moans and gasps have my cock rock-hard and ready.

Thrusting it into her center, I grin when her moans

increase. She presses up and into my cock, rubbing herself along its hardness. It jerks in response, and I groan as my sweats create friction against my sensitive skin.

I want to feel her wetness and I want her glistening pussy in my mouth so I can taste her. Trailing my mouth down over her stomach, I dip my tongue into her belly button and nibble on the flesh.

"Why aren't you pounding that big cock inside of me yet?" she demands, and I laugh at her frustration.

"It's not going to be one of those nights, Em." I lick over her hip bone. "This is going to be slow and sweet."

"Why?" she groans as she lifts her hips closer to my mouth.

"Because sometimes you need to take your time and truly enjoy what you have. I want you to know I worship you, and even when I'm not here, I want you to remember how much you mean to me."

"Where are you going?" Her voice holds a touch of panic.

"Nowhere." I chuckle as I drag her shorts and panties down her legs. "I'm just saying sometimes you need to stop and smell the roses."

I don't hear her reply because I've literally nosed-dived into her pink, glistening folds. With the first swipe of my tongue, her essence explodes in my mouth, and I moan at the sweet tang of it as I slip my tongue deep inside her.

"Yes, Vin," she gasps as her hands fist the bedsheets.

I suck her clit into my mouth and slip two fingers inside her as she writhes on the bed, clenching around me. My baby is ready to detonate, and I don't want to miss one drop of her cum.

I pump into her faster and suck harder on her clit, feeling her juices run down my chin. "Vin, I'm going to..."

Her body tenses and she lets out a low whine as her pussy clamps down on my fingers. Her body trembles with the force of her orgasm, and I chuck off my pants before I make my way back up her body.

She is breathing heavily and her body is lax when I grab her thighs to spread her wider. I line my head up with her entrance and stare into her eyes as I slowly push myself inside. Feeling her stretch around my cock is the sexiest thing, and it takes everything in me not to slam myself into her.

Her back arches when I'm fully seated inside her, and her walls clench around me tightly. I stay there and lean down to kiss her softly. She's looking at me with questions in her eyes as I continue to kiss my way up her cheek and press my face against her neck. I move slowly, just feeling her warmth and savoring her like this. She's completely vulnerable and soft.

"Vin," she growls. "Harder."

"Soon," I whisper in her ear.

I continue my lazy strokes and reach up to thread my fingers into her long, thick hair. She sucks her bottom lip into her mouth and bites down as she watches me closely. This is intimate, personal, and solidifying the bond I've always felt with my girl.

This isn't our usual. I can't think of a time when we've just made love. Nothing more and nothing less. Just us and the love we share. Her hands glide up between us and she grabs both of her tits, squeezing as she moans.

This woman is testing my control right now, and I'm close to failing. Her hips lift and we both groan as I hit her at a different angle, her juices running down her thighs and gathering against my balls.

"I love you," she breathes out, and those three words send me into a frenzy.

I pull out of her and chuckle when she growls with

frustration as I flip her over onto her belly and lift her hips. Then I'm slamming into her full force. This is our usual. Hard, wet, and intense.

"That's... all... I... had... to... say?" Each word is punctuated by a thrust.

"Maybe." I grin as I slip two fingers into her ass. "Now rain on your daddy."

It doesn't take much after that. Em has always been reactive to my words. She screams as she throws her head back, and she does indeed rain on me.

Her release runs down my legs as I really pound into her. The sounds of wet flesh slapping and her pussy sucking me in has me falling over the edge with one final hard thrust. My fingers are still lodged in her ass and my dick is deep in her pussy as I drape myself over her back.

"I love you too. Always remember that," I tell her.

Chapter Sixteen

"Did you call her? Is she packed?" I mumble as I wait in the Hummer for the rest of them to come out of the house.

"Yes, Mr. Grumpy-pants," Emmett mocks me as he throws a bag in the back. "I don't want to be doing this either. Like, why the fuck do we have to ride with her and the girls get to ride in Shelby?"

"Because you suck at poker, babe." Travis hops up and into the passenger seat.

"I didn't know Ember was a fucking cheater!" he whines.

"We still don't know that she is," I say to him as he gets in the backseat.

"She ain't no fucking Rainman," Emmett mutters as we pull out of the driveway and make our way over to Marlana's.

"Let's just get this done with. I know sitting in a car with Marlana for eight hours will be torture, but we've dealt with worse," I assure Emmett as he continues to grumble under his breath.

"Like being kidnapped and beaten for info," Travis chimes in, giving me the side-eye.

"Or like carrying your brother's body into the hospital emergency," I counter as I stop at a red light and raise my brow at him.

"Being a guinea pig for Adri's cooking," Emmett adds, and we all burst out laughing.

"Sparring with E when she's pissed," Travis continues as I move through the intersection with a snort.

"Finding out your father's a rapist," I growl.

"Oh, that's a good one." Travis nods. "I think you win this round."

"Hearing your twin sister scream disgusting things in the middle of the night?" Emmett interjects as I snap my fingers.

"You win." I nod at him as Travis laughs.

"Travis, you have to sit back here with Marlana. I can't guarantee I won't kill her. Ember and I share the psychotic gene, you know." Emmett grins smugly as I turn onto Marlana's street.

"Sure, I'll sit back there." Travis shrugs. "But I'm not convinced your sister is psychotic. I think she's the most levelheaded out of us all."

Travis has a bond with Em that even I can't penetrate. Normal boyfriends would find that threatening, but not me. What they are and do for each other goes way beyond the connection between a man and a woman. If I believe Em and I are soul mates—and I do—then I believe Travis and her share the same soul material. Cut from the same cloth.

Marlana's house looks just as dark and desolate as it did the first few times we came by. She's been teetering on the edge of giving up since Em offed her mother, and I can't feel sorry for her because I know Em did her a favor. She was on a similar path leading to self-destruction and now she has a chance to turn it all around.

"How did it go with Halbert Senior?" Emmett asks us.

"He has Alzheimer's," Travis huffs. "I couldn't stay there long because he thought I was his son."

"He sure remembers how much of a burden his son was with how many rapes he had to cover for him," I state as I park on the street outside of the house.

"Are you serious?" Emmett growls.

"Yeah, he's pretty useless to us." I shrug and shut off the Hummer.

"Let's get this over with." Travis nods toward Marlana's house.

"Rock, paper, scissors who goes to get her." Emmett's fist appears between me and Travis, just as his sister did in this very spot not too long ago. It makes me snicker as the memory only confirms their twintuition.

"We're all going in, bro." I chuckle as I swat his hand away.

"Ember would've played me." He sulks as he opens his door and hops out.

"And you would've lost... like last night," Travis retorts as we get out of the Hummer.

"True," Emmett mumbles as we walk up to the front porch.

Travis unlocks the door with a set of keys, the key chain hanging from the ring says Marlana. "How'd you get her keys?" I question as the door swings open.

"E had them," Travis explains, then heads inside with me and Emmett on his heels. It still reeks in here, and Emmett's gag has both Travis and I joining in.

"The bitch is rotting in here somewhere. Let's call it a day and get to New York," Emmett begs around his retching.

"Stop." I shove him, making him land against the wall, then laugh when he bounces back with a shudder. "She's probably in her bedroom."

"I could never get used to this smell. She's psychotic, not Ember," Emmett moans as he covers his nose and mouth with the sleeve of his sweater.

Sure enough, Marlana is in her bedroom, but her bags are packed and she's sitting at the end of her bed, dressed and waiting for us. "I want to get away from here," she rasps, her voice sounding as rough as she looks.

"Let's go." I pick up one of her bags and Emmett grabs the other.

"Emmett." Her voice cracks with defeat. "Will you sit with me and tell me about where I'm going?"

I expect him to have a comeback ready, something rude or funny, but surprisingly he doesn't. "Yeah, I can do that."

I look at him with a raised brow and he just shrugs his shoulders. As much as the Torres children like to act tough, they have marshmallow insides.

We're about a half hour out from the Rampage's warehouse, and I feel like if I hear Emmett snore one more time, I'll explode.

"Why do you think Moore hasn't questioned E yet?" Travis asks me quietly.

"He fears Ember," Marlana cuts in. I thought she was sleeping too as my eyes find hers in the rearview mirror. "I saw his face when I said it was her that killed my mother."

"So he should," I retort as my knuckles whiten around the steering wheel.

"There's something else." Her voice is small and unsure as she shifts in her seat nervously. "He wants Ember dead."

"How do you know that?" I question her as she turns her head to look out the window, her face filled with thought.

"Because he had the same look on his face as I once did. I wanted her dead too," she confesses, her tone filled with certainty.

"Wanted?" Travis reiterates as he turns in the seat to look at her. "What changed?"

"I don't know how I feel now." She slowly moves her head to look at him, her eyes filled with sadness. "But I can at least understand why she did what she did." I don't know what to say to that and I guess Travis doesn't either. The silence in the vehicle is deafening as he turns back in his seat. "She's in danger," Marlana warns, breaking the silence with her declaration. "Serious danger."

"I'll protect her," I vow, hoping she hears the threat in my voice.

"You're her greatest weakness," she counters and then rests her head back against the seat.

The compound looms in front of us as I nudge Travis awake beside me. He mumbles something incoherent before he finally rouses. "You didn't have to drive the whole way," he says with a yawn while stretching his arms over his head.

"I'm used to it." I shrug as I watch Marlana in the

rearview mirror.

Her eyes are wide as she takes in her surroundings. I know what the compound must appear like. It's vacant-looking, desolate, and holds an edge of danger. Perfect place to hide a body if you were a murderer, and I can bet her heart is beating out a wild staccato right now, wondering if these will be her last moments. I don't know what I ever saw in her before, but I can tell you what I see now; a girl so lost in a world where darkness reigned and the only way to survive was to become similar to the monsters that surrounded her. Deep inside though, she has something Em saw worth saving, and I trust what my girl sees.

"What is this place?" Mar's voice is soft, but tremors of panic coat each word.

"This is the primary base for The Rampage," Emmett answers as he stretches in the seat beside her. "I was born and raised here."

"That's so reassuring," Marlana answers sarcastically, the tone attempting to cover the fear she's feeling.

"Keep those comments to yourself, your head down, and change," I grind out as I exit the Hummer. Her eyes meet mine as she swallows down her retort, the fear once again prominent. If she doesn't humble herself now, she'll crumble here.

The parking lot is bare save for our vehicle, and I text Adri to ask how far out they are. The front garage-style door rolls up, revealing the intricate inside of what is seemingly an abandoned warehouse. Trent stands there with two guards and a smirk on his face.

"The family is here! I heard you've brought us a gift!" he calls out as we head toward him.

"If by gift you mean a large lump of coal in your stocking... then yes, we brought a gift." Emmett slaps Trent's shoulder as he passes him.

I turn when I notice Marlana hasn't gotten out of

the Hummer and cross my arms over my chest. Finally, her fading purple head appears as she gets out, the strands pulled into a high ponytail to no doubt hide the bald spot Ember gave her. She's dressed in baggy clothing to cover her frame and she looks around nervously. I grin as I revel in her fear.

"Where's your fiancée?" Trent asks as I lead Marlana inside and Travis takes up the back.

"On her way," I answer, giving him a one-armed hug.

He eyes Marlana and holds out his hand. "My name is Trent. I'm the head of security here."

"Marlana," she mutters as she takes his hand, her arm looking like a limp noodle.

"We have a room ready for you." He nods to one guard on his right. "Follow Dom and freshen up." She does as she's told, and we all stand there watching her leave.

"She's hot." Trent whistles and I roll my eyes.

"Trust me, brother. That is one pussy you want to steer clear of," I warn him with a shake of my head. With the blatant interest in his eyes, I can foresee some chaos erupting in the compound soon.

"Vin should know." Emmett smirks. "From experience." He wisely moves an arm's length away from me to avoid receiving a black eye.

"This is an ex?" Trent looks at me, surprised.

"Not an ex." I roll my eyes and then glare at Emmett while Travis covers his mouth with his hand, chuckling at his boyfriend's antics.

"And Ember is letting her live?" Trent looks astonished with his mouth hanging open and his eyes wide.

"Surprisingly." Emmett nods while I shrug.

"She has her reasons," Travis interjects, shutting

down any more speculation about Em's motives. He's always doing his part in protecting her.

"Let's get you all settled and then we can eat." Trent rolls down the door as my phone chimes.

Adri: We'll be there in about thirty minutes.

Me: Cool.

I make my way to mine and Ember's usual room as Emmett and Travis go to theirs. Then I take a shower, and when I get out, I find Em's bag on the floor beside mine, but she's not in the room. Throwing on some black track pants and a hoodie, I leave the room in search of my girl.

I have an idea where to find Emmett, and wherever he is, Em is always close by. I open the doors to the large dining hall and sure enough, I see Emmett shoveling food into his mouth as Travis sits across from him, shaking his head. Adri is leaning into Travis' side and sitting beside her is Marlana as she tentatively pushes food around on her plate.

Doing a quick scan around the room, I find Em and Carm standing off to the side in deep conversation. I head over to them and wrap my arms around Em's waist, needing to feel her after the long hours without her.

She instantly relaxes in my arms and sighs. "That's what I needed."

"So, this is her." Carm's gaze hasn't left Marlana. His interest is evident and just as dangerous as Trent's was when we first got here.

"Keep your dick out of her," Em growls, her body tensing with Carm's attraction.

His hands go up with a chuckle. "You got it, little sis."

"Seriously, Carm." Ember exhales as the fight leaves her tone, replaced with concern. "She's fucking damaged. Like from birth."

How he's looking at her tells me he has no intention of listening to his sister. Marlana is in his sights, and if I know anything about the Torres', it's that they always get what they want.

"Guess who's here." Carm finally breaks his stare from Marlana to look at us.

"No idea," I say as Em tips her head to the side in question.

"The Bishop."

Em straightens in my arms as she sucks in a surprised breath. "I remember our last fight like it was yesterday."

"I heard about that fight." Carm brushes his fingers through the hair on his chin.

"What fight?" I press as Em lays her head back on my shoulder.

"That fight will go down in the history of the Rampage." Carm whistles as he looks at his sister with pride. "The Bishop was our greatest fighter, undefeated, and his specialty was snapping necks. Then, a girl by the name of Blur called him out after one of his fights, demanding he fight her. It was a bloody one from what I hear, but our girl here reigned supreme that night and left The Bishop knocked out cold with her roundhouse kick." Her roundhouse kick is fucking impressive.

"It was the night Raph killed my mother." Her voice is small and my heart stops.

"Shit," Carm mutters, looking thoroughly chastised. "I forgot that it was the same night."

"It's fine." Em shakes her head and brushes it off. "What's he doing here?"

"He's looking for a fight." Carm grimaces. "With Blur. But I wasn't thinking when I brought this up. If you don't want to…"

"I can fight." She shrugs. I know her well, and so does Carm. He knew she wouldn't be able to turn this down, and I can bet he has a lot riding on this fight.

"He best not be planning on snapping any fucking necks," I snarl as my arms tighten around my girl. If she gets hurt, Carm will feel my wrath.

"Not if he wants to live." Carm snorts.

"I'm fucking tired," Em moans and turns her head into my chest. "Can we take a nap?"

"Let's go." I kiss her temple.

"I'll take care of our girl here." Carm points at Marlana and Em literally growls.

I can't see any of this ending well.

"Who is this Bishop asshole and why does he want to fight Ember so bad?" Adri asks as she shifts in her front row seat in front of the cage.

"Better yet, who is she coming out as tonight?" Emmett adds as his eyes shift toward the room Em is waiting in.

"Bishop was the guy she fought the night they killed her mother," I explain to Adri, then turn to Emmett. "I think she's Blur tonight."

The surrounding crowd is buzzing with excitement as they ride the high from the last fight that left the mat in the cage splattered with blood. Adri looks nervous as she clutches Travis' hand to my left and Emmett is sitting beside Marlana to my right. Usually, he's with Carm to walk Em to the cage, but tonight she requested just Carm so they could have a little chat. I'm not sure what they're talking about, but I can imagine it's to do with Marlana and Carm's obvious interest in her.

The lights dim and the crowd roars, making my heart slam up into my throat.

"Tonight, we are being graced by our favorite fighter!" the emcee yells into the mic. "Bodies" plays over the speakers and the noise becomes deafening. "Blur!"

I watch as Carm and Trent escort her down to the cage, her face a mask of indifference as the hoodie she wears rides low on her brow. I love her like this, tough and confident, so sure of what she's capable of.

Once she's in the cage, she whips off her hoodie, revealing her Nike sports bra and short shorts. Her hair is braided into two Dutch braids and her body looks toned and cut. She shakes out her limbs and smiles slightly when the crowd chants her name.

"It's a double feature tonight, folks," the emcee cuts through the music. "Some of you will recognize this next fighter, The Bishop!"

A hulk of a man struts down the center aisle and stops in front of the cage, then looks up at Em and fucking breaks out into the widest smile. Great, he's psychotic. My girl's psychotic-ass gives him one right back and motions him with her fingers to get in the cage.

"She looks like a psychopath," Marlana mutters as she shifts in her seat, her eyes never leaving Em.

"She is," Emmett answers, giving her the same smile his sister is currently wearing. "She fucking murdered your mother, remember?"

Sometimes the kid has no empathy, and I find it funny as hell.

"Fuck you!" Marlana snaps and crosses her arms

over her chest. She's always been the bully and never the bullied. It's about time she had a taste of her own medicine, even if it's at the expense of her dead mother.

The Bishop gets into the cage and holds his fist out to Em for a bump. She obliges, and then he walks to the other side of the cage and hops on his toes with excitement.

"This doesn't feel like a real fight," Adri mumbles as she looks around Emmett at me, her face pinched with confusion. "Why are they being nice to each other?"

"Because they have no hatred between them. Bishop hasn't done anything to Ember, it's just an old-fashioned fight," Emmett answers her as he wraps an arm around her shoulders.

The bell rings and The Bishop flies at Em. Her grin lights up her face as she watches him come at her. He grabs her by the midsection and throws her against the cage, making her bounce off the wire and hit the mat with a *thud*. I wince at the impact and curse her in my head. She better be playing him or have some sort of trick up her sleeve.

Before she can even get up, The Bishop grabs her leg and drags her back out to the center of the ring. Em flips onto her stomach, lifts herself up by her hands, and with the leg that's free, kicks out at his knee. He stumbles a bit, but his grip stays firm on her ankle.

He pulls her up and I watch as the love of my life dangles by one leg, her arms swinging wildly. Then the fucker throws her to the side, her small form slamming against the wire again. Her body hits the mat once more, hard, and we all wince at the impact.

My heart beats a quick rhythm as I fear my girl is losing.

Chapter Seventeen

Ember

I forgot how fast this man can be.

My back hits the mat for the second time as the air leaves my lungs in a *whoosh*. Fuck, how the fuck did I beat him the first time? Right. My life was a shithole back then and fighting was the only thing I enjoyed. I need to find her again, pull her out of me, and dance in the darkness for the next few minutes until I have him submitting or knocked the fuck out.

I also have a ton of shit on my mind. After my talk with Carm, I'm more unsettled than ever. I get back to my feet and watch as Bishop hops around the cage, cheering with the crowd. *Motherfucker.*

Shaking away all the other thoughts in my head, I focus on what's in front of me. He's a large man, bulked out, and tall as fuck. I've fought him once before and won, but the difference is The Bishop is a trained fighter and he finds the same enjoyment in watching people bleed as I do. Just because I won the first time, doesn't guarantee I will do it again.

Our eyes lock as he turns around to face me, and he raises his brow as if to ask, *What now?* Now, I fucking wipe the mat with his body. I let the uncertainty I've been feeling boil my blood, making it swirl deep inside me and course through my limbs. Finally, that familiar feeling bubbles up as I let the red take over my vision. From here on out, I can only hope I don't kill the bastard.

He sees it, the change in my demeanor, and corrects his stance to defensive. He remembers me and sees the anger vibrating from my very pores.

I stride forward, not in any rush to watch him bleed, and strike out my right fist. It hits the arm he blocks his face with, but he's not quick enough to block the kick I send to his solar plexus.

He staggers backward and again brings his fists up to cover his face. That's fine, because it's the thing I'm least interested in. I enjoy taking out the legs of my opponents when they're so tall. Their falls are always so satisfying.

I catch his attention by letting my fists fly out toward his face and he easily swats them away. Then I fall swiftly to my knees and punch his right kneecap twice before flipping backward and jumping to my feet. He lifts himself up from his knees and flashes me a grin before running at me, and I lift my hands up to protect my face. He punches me once, the blow landing on my forearm, and the pain reverberates up to my shoulder. I falter on my feet when his second punch finds purchase on my left cheek.

The force of the blow has me on my back again and blood flooding my mouth. I spit it out and watch as the red color soaks into the mat. I can't help the grin that takes over my face as I try to stand, but his foot comes out and connects with my stomach before I get the chance. Once again, I'm on my back and gasping for air.

I take in lungfuls as I feel the mat vibrate with the

force of his footsteps before I kip-up back to my feet and dodge his punch. My fist connects with his left ear, and then I'm behind him, my foot kicking out to meet his lower back.

He stumbles forward but remains on his feet as he swings around quickly, his elbow connecting with my left cheek again and I feel the skin split. I'm not sure what exactly triggers it, maybe the slow trickle of blood or the pain that's jarring through my head, but I roar as I jump and punch him once on the right cheek, followed by three more quick blows to the soft spot just under his ribs.

He stumbles again before falling to one knee as I rush forward, the blood dripping off my chin as I roundhouse kick him. My foot connects with his temple, and he falls face down on the mat.

I roll him over and he startles, his hands coming up to his face. Before I know it, I'm straddling his midsection and pummeling his face with my fists.

My name is being screamed, and it breaks through the red fog as I look up to see my family lined up against the cage, Travis' voice halting my actions.

"Ember! It's done!" he pleads for me to understand as his face fills with fear.

I look down at The Bishop to find his face a bloody, pulpy mess, but his chest moves. The fucker is still alive.

I get off him and shake his blood off my fists as the crowd roars and the emcee tries to scream something over the noise, but I don't care.

I want out of this cage and into Vin's arms.

"He wants to talk to you," Carm tells me when I finally leave my room, my ribs sore as fuck. He's standing against the wall, his face filled with tension and his arms crossed over his chest.

I tentatively touch my cut cheek and wince. Thankfully Vin was here to patch me up. "Why?" I ask Carm, raising my brow with skepticism.

"I'm not sure, but he says it's important. I'll have a guard inside with you." He pushes off the wall and drops his arms to pull his cell phone out of his pocket.

"That's unnecessary." I wave him off. He can be as overprotective as he wants with Emmett, but I'll always have my boundaries.

"Ember..." he begins his warning, but I'm ahead of him before he can finish, walking toward the room I know The Bishop is in.

"Em!" Vin calls out from our room's doorway. "I'll be right outside the door."

I wave my hand and turn the corner to where the room is. Without bothering to knock, I open it and enter the room. He's sitting on the bed, his face a mottled work of purple and blues.

"I remembered what the sight of blood did for you." His voice is deep as his swollen eyes meet mine. "Forgive me for hitting you, but I needed a fair fight." He holds up his hands in an act of truce and it takes me off guard.

"You wanted to talk?" I cross my arms over my chest and close the door, leaning back against the slab.

"Yeah." He gives me a smile that quickly turns into a grimace when the muscles in his smashed face move. "I heard what happened the first night we fought. I'm sorry."

I nod, but words escape me. Talking to him propels me back to that night and I feel all the overwhelming sadness and despair.

"I also know it was Raphael. When I was brought on here as a fighter, he was still in jail, and I had never met him.

I heard stories of his ruthless personality and disregard for life. I came here not to fight you, but I knew it was the only way to get you to listen to me. Don't trust the Torres, none of them." His warning has the hairs on the back of my neck standing on end as my stomach flips with apprehension. My back straightens as I narrow my eyes on him.

"I'm a Torres, Bishop." Then I tip my head to the side and look at him with confusion.

"My name is Johnny," he corrects, then groans as he grips his jaw. "I know what you are and it's not a Torres. You're not like them."

"Who?" I walk forward, his words intriguing me. "Who's them? I only know Emmett and Carm."

"I don't mean just the family. I mean this entire organization. Everything under this roof and beyond is Torres. I came here because I heard you were back, and I heard how you were connected to this place. I wanted to warn you." I can't say I understand what the fuck he's talking about, but a part of me has already come to this same conclusion. I already know who I can and can't trust. At least, I'm almost there.

"Thank you."

"Here." He holds out a card he already had waiting in his hand. "It's my number if you need me. I'm part of an extensive network of hired muscles. If you need an army, I can bring one."

"Why are you offering your help?" I question him, my eyes on the card he continues to hold out.

"Because I respect you, and sometimes we all need a little help." I already know I'll never ask him for it. I have Carm's men, and with my skills, I doubt I'll ever need more than that.

I stride forward and take the card. "While Raphael was in jail, did you spend much time here at the base?" I question him as he shrugs his shoulders.

"I was here for fights and sometimes called in for meetings. Why?"

I pull out my phone and find the picture of my grandparents. Then I hold it out to him and point to my grandfather. "Do you recognize him?"

He takes my phone from my hand and scrutinizes the photo. "No." I reach out to take the phone when he remarks, "But this woman is slightly familiar. There's something in her face that reminds me of someone, but I don't think it was here at the compound."

"She passed away a long time ago," I explain when he hands me back the phone.

"Maybe it's her face," he mumbles, his split lip beginning to bleed again with the motion. "Sometimes people just have familiar-looking faces. You kind of look like her."

"These are my grandparents," I tell him as I slip my phone into my hoodie pocket. "Anyway, thanks for this." I hold up the card and turn to leave as I put it in my pocket with my phone.

"Ember," he says as I reach for the knob. "Watch yourself."

I give a brusque nod and open the door. Both Vin and Carm turn and watch me closely as I step out and shut it behind me.

"Everything okay?" Carm is quick to ask, his face filled with concern.

"Yeah," I mutter as I mull over the entire interaction with The Bishop.

"What did he want?" Carm presses as his shoulders tense and his eyes narrow when I start to walk back toward my room.

"Just to apologize for what happened the last time

we fought." When the look of confusion comes over his face, my body stiffens with shock. There's no way he's forgotten a second time.

"What happened?" Carm has lost his fucking mind. There's no other explanation.

I suddenly stop mid-step before turning to look at him. "My mother was murdered by your father." My voice is low and deadly.

"Oh." He has enough sense to look chagrined. "Sorry, Ember, my head has been all over the place lately."

"Let's go to your office. I need to discuss a few things." I look at Vin, whose eyes are laser-pointed at Carm's head, and say, "Get everyone ready to leave."

Vin's eyes flick to me and he nods before heading off in the opposite direction. I lead the way to Carm's office with him following close behind me. The tension he's exuding is permeating the air around us and it's stifling. I know I snapped on him, but honestly, my mother's death will never be an easy subject for me to discuss.

Opening his office door, I step inside to find his desk a mess of papers and stacks of money. This must be my fight earnings. I take a seat at the desk as he sits on the opposite side.

"Ember—" he begins, but I cut him off.

"Carm, it's fine." I rub my temples. "What have you found out about the adoption agency?"

"There is no such agency now. They have completely disappeared, if they ever existed at all." He leans back in his chair and runs his fingers over his mouth.

"Okay... but what did you find out about them? They must have a paper trail of when they were open and running. Something." My hands clench into fists in my lap as I try my best not to lose my temper.

"There's no paper trail left behind. I tried looking through government files and found nothing legit with the name Love the Tots." He's looking me in the eyes, and I growl in frustration.

"You never answered me about the picture of my grandparents. Did you recognize them?" My words are clipped, but the exhaustion in his eyes has the anger subsiding.

"Sorry, Ember, I've been crazy busy." He scrubs a hand down his face. "I've never seen them in my life. They were never here."

"I see." I nod and feel a sudden onset of despair. Every lead I get pans out to nothing. Talia is slipping further and further away.

"Don't give up, we'll get something," he tries to reassure me, but it falls flat. My heart clenches when he stifles a yawn behind his hand as his eyes grow heavy, and I question again if I'm giving him too much.

"Yeah." I nod and shake out my hands, letting the frustration melt away. I love Carm, but it's clear I have to take the lead on a few more things. I stand from my chair and brush my hair back from my face. "Find something useful for Marlana, and I don't mean in your bed, buddy."

"You got it." He grins as he gets up from his chair to come around the desk to embrace me. "Are you sure this is the life you want, little sister?"

"It's the life I chose, Carm. I will see everything to the end," I vow as my arms slip around his waist. He feels safe, strong, and sturdy, but I can't help the nagging pit in my stomach.

"I don't doubt you." He kisses the top of my head. "Have a safe drive back." Then he hands me five of the ten stacks of bills on his desk.

"Thanks." I cradle them in my arms and wait for him to open the door.

"Nice stacks." Vin snickers when I get back to my room, our bags packed and ready to go.

"All in a day's work." I push them into my duffel bag.

"What did you learn from Carm?"

"I learned that we're on our own."

I'm stuck in a car with a singing Emmett and a giggling Adri. I should've somehow snuck into the Hummer with Vin and Travis.

"Ember," Emmett calls back to me.

"Eyes on the road, champ. You hurt Shelby and we're squaring up," I mutter as I press my forehead to the window and close my eyes, hoping for a little sleep before we get home.

"Can we go to the cemetery and see our grandparents' graves?" he skates over my comment like I didn't just threaten him.

I'm tired as hell, but I don't want to deny him. It's our family after all. "Yeah, but I'm dead on my feet. Can we make it a quick one today?" I open my eyes to find him watching me through the rearview mirror.

"As long as we can drop by the mausoleum so I can drop off flowers." He gives me puppy eyes and I feel myself caving.

I nod and rest my head back against the seat. A few hours later, we enter Whitsborough—the sign reading 'Love thy Neighbor'—and I snort at how serene it looks.

Soon enough, the cemetery pulls into view and Emmett stops at the front office. None of us know where exactly our grandparents are buried, and this cemetery is quite large. He comes out of the office and gets back in the car, his face filled with excitement.

"They bought a large plot on the outer edge, an older part of the cemetery rarely visited anymore. They said the ground is rougher back there," Emmett says as we drive past newer tombstones.

"Sounds like an adventure today," I mumble around a yawn.

"My grandparents are buried around there too," Adri adds. "We never visit them because it's not really taken care of back there." She's facing the window, her hand pressed to the glass.

"Hmm." Sleep is still saturating my senses as I look out my own window, my eyes growing heavy. I watch as the tombstones gradually grow darker and more obscured by weed growth as they get older. The trees are larger, casting more shadows than sunlight, and I exhale my breath when a haunted feeling comes over me. It's creepy back here. Blinking the last of my exhaustion away, I really begin to take in our surroundings.

Emmett stops Shelby and we all lean forward to look ahead. It's dense with foliage and the tombstones are half buried in the tall grass.

"This is kind of scary," Adri whispers, and Emmett nods his head.

"Oh, come on, pussies," I huff as I swallow down my own fear. "Let's get this over with."

I get out of the car and start walking along the overgrown cobblestone trail, swatting aside grass as I go while trying to read the names on the tombstones.

"Fuck," I gasp. "This one is 1920."

"Over here!" I hear Adri call out. She's about thirty yards to my right with Emmett not too far behind her. I trek it over to her and Emmett, trying not to trip on tree roots.

"Do you find it strange that our aunt and uncle didn't upkeep their graves?" Emmett asks me as he pulls away the grass and weeds.

"Kind of?" I shrug. "Or it's just in a weird spot."

It's just their names and the dates. Nothing about being loving parents or rest in peace. I can admit that's slightly strange, even the most disliked people get an R.I.P.

"Laurann J. Craven and Jack R. Craven," Emmett reads out loud as he shuffles from foot to foot. A twig snaps behind us and we turn to squint through the dense trees as my heart begins to race inside my chest.

"I'm done here," Adri says, throwing her hands up and walking back to the car.

"Me too." My shoulder bumps Emmett. "Kiss the stone or whatever and let's bounce."

Emmett rolls his eyes and crosses himself, then follows me back to the car. "A quick stop at the mausoleum and then we can head home," he states as he turns the car around.

"I don't want to go back to those graves." Adri rubs her arms. "It felt haunted."

"It's a cemetery, Adrianna," Emmett scoffs. "Of course it's haunted."

"I know what you mean." I reach forward and squeeze her shoulder. "I felt it too."

We pull up to our nice, manicured mausoleum with zero weeds and beautiful stone angels carved into its walls. A drastic difference from the graves we just left behind. Emmett leads us up the walkway and unlocks the door, holding it open. When I step inside, I exhale a sigh of relief. My mother is here along with my ma and dad. I can feel them here, more so than anywhere else.

"Ember," Emmett calls me. "Over here."

I turn to find him standing in front of Travis' birth mother's grave. I wanted Sonja in here too because she was just as much family as the rest.

"What is it?" I ask as I get closer. I swear to God, if something happened to her marker, I would sue the fuck out of this cemetery.

Emmett is pointing to the empty slot underneath Sonja's as I stand beside him. When I look closer, I see there's an inscription.

Thomas Williams - You were always family, no matter the blood. Rest in peace.

"Tommy?" My voice is hoarse as my hand reaches out to touch the brass plate. "But how?" I feel the tears gathering in my eyes.

"We found out he was cremated, and his foster home put him in a generic hole-in-the-wall at the cemetery in New York. I know who he was to you and thought he deserved better. We were granted permission to take his ashes, with some help from Carm, and placed him here."

Adri comes up beside me to wrap her arms around my waist, hugging me close. "He's family too," she whispers, and I lose it.

I haven't properly grieved Tommy. I have been pushing it down deep inside and telling myself one day I will acknowledge what happened and my part in it all. But now I'm forced to do it, and even though I'm happy he's here, I can't afford to lose myself in grief.

My hand shakes as I run my fingers across his name, and my mind spirals through all our memories. He was my first friend. He taught me how to ride a bike, took care of me at school, and we worked for a gang together.

He came to every one of my fights and made sure I always made it home safe. When we lived in the projects, he would stay with my mom when I had to work, just to make sure she was safe. Tommy was more than a friend. He was my brother too.

He's dead because of me.

My psychotic father thought he was a traitor because he wouldn't help them find me, because he warned me they were coming, and he tried his best to get to me first. His loyalty to me cost him his life, and I was unable to do anything to prevent it.

His face swims in my mind. His dark eyes, shaggy dark hair, and skin the color of honey. The pain is crippling, and I can't stop the sobs that break free from my chest.

I never got the chance to tell Tommy how much he meant to me and the impact he had on my life when I had no one else. He saved me from certain death inside my burning home and I watched helplessly as they killed him.

"Ember." Emmett's arms encircle me and Adri, crushing me to his chest. "He knew how much you loved him."

I continue to pour my feelings out into Emmett's shirt, my body shaking with the force of my sobs.

"Tommy was complicated with us, but he was always protecting you. Whenever Carm wanted a meeting with you, he would refuse and tell him he'd pass along any message. None of us could get close to you. That's why I never knew you existed. He loved you and he knew you loved him too." Emmett's words soothe the pain as Adri rubs my back, her sniffles filling the space between my sobs.

My phone begins to vibrate in my pocket at that moment, but I don't have the energy to pick it up. After the fight and now this, all I want to do is get home to Vin and snuggle into his warmth.

Soon after mine stops, Emmett's starts up. Since he still has me in his arms, Adri digs around in his pocket and pulls it out.

"Hey, Trav," she says in a low voice, her tone filled with sadness. "What?"

The sudden spike in her voice has me spinning. "What is it?"

"Where are you?" she barks into the phone and then puts it on speaker.

"Just past the Whitsborough sign. He just took him in. I'm going to head to the station."

"What the fuck is going on?" My voice rises as Adri looks at me with wide eyes.

"Moore just arrested Vin on suspicion of murder."

Chapter Eighteen

I don't remember leaving the cemetery or how the hell I got us to the station so fast, but I finally come to my senses when I pull up beside Travis and the Hummer.

"Where is he?" I jump out of Shelby and Travis grabs my arm.

"We have to be smart, E. I want to storm in there too, but we have a lot of blood on our hands. I called my father's old attorney. He's going to call the station and get back to us." His eyes are filled with fear and pleading. He's scared for his brother but he's also scared about losing me too.

"I'm going in there." They know better than to stop me because I will lay anyone flat who stands between me and my man.

I jog up the steps, taking two at a time as I begin to count backward from ten. It's been a while since I've had to use that technique to keep myself in check, but right now, knowing Moore has Vin behind bars, my rage is at a boiling point. One wrong move and everyone in this station will die until Vin is in front of me and safe.

Flinging the door open, I storm inside as the cop sitting at the front desk stands abruptly. "Young lady—"

"Where's my fiancé?" I cut him off as my chest heaves and my fists meet the front counter. I look around the room, finding only one cop while the rest of the station is silent.

"Who?" He looks confused.

"Fuck!" I turn on him. "Where is Moore?"

"C–Chief M–Moore?" he stutters a bit as his eyes skip from me to Travis.

"No, idiot, Demi Moore," I growl at him. "Obviously Chief Moore!" Someone grabs my arm, but I shrug out of it. I don't care if I'm acting irrationally. I want my soul back.

"Chief Moore is on vacation for the next week." The cop's face looks completely lost as his hand hovers over the gun strapped at his waist.

"That's impossible..." Emmett's voice drowns out as I let everything sink in.

"We need to leave. Now." Turning on my heel, I quickly head out of the station.

"Wait!" I hear Emmett calling behind me. "What's going on?"

I get back to Shelby and stand there quietly. I need to do this right. There can't be any mistakes. I turn and look at Travis. "You know what this is, right?" He nods solemnly. "Call the lawyer off, none of this can be done by the books."

"Guys?" Adri's shaking voice cuts through my thoughts as she hugs her arms around her waist, her eyes filling with tears. "What's happening?"

"Was Moore in uniform?" I ask Travis.

"No." He shakes his head as his hands grip the

strands of his hair in frustration. "Street clothes and an unmarked vehicle. I told Vin to stay in the car, but he just told me to call you."

"Moore has taken Vin." I pace as I piece everything together. "It's payback for fucking up his little side business of pervs here in Whitsborough."

"What will he do to him?" Adri asks as she steps into Travis' arms, her face settling against his chest. Seeing that only makes my heart hurt more. I want my fiancé.

"If it was me, I'd do nothing and use him as a bargaining chip for the bigger fish," I mutter, my feet still moving back and forth in a straight line.

"That would be you," Emmett says as he stands in front of me, forcing me to stop my pacing. "Sorry, Ember, but I'm not trading you for anyone."

"That would be my decision, Emmett." My hands slam to my hips as my eyes narrow on him, and his brows raise with surprise a second before they fall with anger.

"Like fuck it is!" he bellows, his hands clenching into fists at his sides. "I just found you, you're my family! You're my twin!"

"If everything goes right, nothing will happen to me, Emmett." I see the pain in his eyes, and I want to soothe him, but I know the words coming from my mouth will mean nothing if something has happened to Vin.

"Call Carm, please. I'm going to need his help and resources on this one," I plead with him, my hand pressing to his chest.

"What can we do?" Adri asks, motioning between Travis and herself.

"I need all of Moore's properties. Cottages, houses, and vehicles."

"We can do that." Travis nods as they break apart

and move toward Vin's Hummer. "Let's head home so we have the resources."

Making my way over to Shelby, I find Emmett talking frantically on his cell phone. Even though I know we need Carm's help, I'm also preparing myself to not get my hopes up.

I can only completely depend on myself.

"Carm is on his way. He's bringing backup as well," Emmett declares as he bursts into my office.

I have Google Maps open on my screen and my eyes are nearly crossed from surveying the land around Moore's cottage property. "Good."

"Do you think they're there?" Emmett asks as he stands behind me.

"I don't have the slightest idea. I think we will have to split up and hit up all three locations." Moore has his modest home here in Whitsborough, a cottage in the Kawarthas, and a vacant rental property in downtown Whitsborough.

"I think you and a few guys should check out this cottage, Travis and a few guys head over to his house, and Carm and I will check out the rental."

"So, you think he has him on the rental property?" Emmett asks.

"It's the most obvious choice, but I can only assume he would realize that. I would guess that anyway." I rub my temples to push back the migraine looming close by. I haven't slept, eating is out of the question, and my mind hasn't stopped the barrage of what-if situations.

"I texted Sharla from Vin's phone. I hate lying to her," Travis mumbles as he walks into the office.

"So do I, but I see no other alternative. If we tell her Vin is missing, we will have to tell her everything." I look up at Travis to find his eyes filled with pain. "She can't know everything."

"You're right, I know you are," he agrees as he releases a heavy breath. "Doesn't mean I like it."

"Besides, we'll have him back here in no time." Emmett grips Travis' shoulder and squeezes.

"Guys!" Adri calls out from the kitchen. "Come eat!"

"Oh, fuck." My voice drops low as I stare at them wide-eyed. "Did she cook?"

"I've barely spoken to her today," Travis confesses with a whisper. "I've been swamped."

"Me too." Emmett looks petrified as his hand slips into Travis'. I'd rather take on Moore and every other pedophile in Whitsborough at the same time than risk a dish of Adri's cooking.

"Fuck off!" she yells, her voice filled with exasperation. "I know you're scared I've cooked something. I ordered takeout!"

"Thank God for minor miracles," Emmett mutters as he releases Travis' hand to give himself the sign of the cross. Travis and I follow him out to the kitchen, our relief palpable between us. "I couldn't handle another disaster right now."

"You three are fucking assholes," Adri growls with her hands on her hips. "I knew you were worried about the food."

"Wouldn't you be if you were us?" I ask her, my brow quirking as a smirk plays along her mouth.

"Yes." She exhales with a roll of her eyes. "Totally. Come eat and let's hear the plan."

We eat the pizza as I lay out my carefully thought-out plan, all of them solemn as they listen intently. It's risky and I'm not sure if we will all make it out unscathed, but I don't have the time to make a completely foolproof plan. Vin is in the hands of my enemy, and I can only pray Moore understands his importance.

"Okay." Adri nods once I'm done and wipes her mouth with a napkin. "I will make sure Sharla and I are safe at the restaurant when this all goes down. I hate not being there with you guys. Promise me you will all be coming back." Her eyes swim with tears.

"I promise," Travis whispers and leans over to kiss her cheek.

"You're never getting rid of me." Emmett smirks and kisses her hand.

But her eyes haven't budged from mine. She's waiting on a promise I can't, in good conscience, make. So I dip my head and avert my gaze back to my plate.

I can only promise to make sure everyone else will come home.

VIN

"I love a good game of cat and mouse." Moore chuckles as his manic eyes find mine. "I bet you she's scouting all my properties. I mean, that's what I would do."

I keep my mouth shut and watch him pace in front of me with my one good eye. I knew exactly what was happening when Moore *arrested* me. He had reached his end and was feeling cornered, so his only option was to strike. He's been using my face as a punching bag since we got here, and I can fully see now that he's unhinged.

I think we finally pushed Moore over the edge and there's no coming back for him. I'm thankful Em wasn't in the Hummer with us because that's who he undoubtedly wanted.

"Your brother must've told her by now." He's repeated this line at least a dozen times since we've been here. "It's the only reason I left him alive."

"You left him alive because you knew she would kill you without thought if you didn't," I grind out, and his fist connects with my cheek.

"Shut the fuck up!" he screams, his voice pitched a little too high and his eyes bulging from his skull. "You really think I'm afraid of a child?"

The answer to that is yes, a loud, resounding yes. I don't say it though because I don't know how much more of a beating I can take without passing out.

He has my hands handcuffed behind me and I'm strapped to a chair. My face and upper body have been at the mercy of his fists, and each breath feels like someone is ripping my ribs out of my chest.

He storms out of the room and slams the large steel door behind him. I try to figure out where we are, but nothing looks familiar. I'm definitely in a basement because there are no windows, and the musky smell of moisture is thick in the air.

He'd pulled a bag over my head while we were going deeper into town, but I know we're still in Whitsborough. This place doesn't feel residential, more like a commercial or industrial building, but I still can't figure out where we could be.

All the buildings in Whitsborough are old and there's nothing remarkable about this space that makes it stand out. It's quiet, but every so often I hear multiple sets of footsteps above me.

He's not here alone, and that makes me more nervous for Em and my family. I worry they may walk into a trap, and knowing Em, she won't care about the destruction it leaves in her wake as long as I get out.

The sound of the door opening draws my attention, and I try to focus my one good eye on Moore as he reenters the room. "Looks like your girlfriend called in reinforcements." He shakes his head. "Is she planning a war?" She must've called in Carm, and I bet Moore placed an unmarked car to watch her house. I can only hope Em knows that and this is all part of her plan. "Nothing?" he sneers at me.

"How can I know what she's doing? I'm here, not there." I try to raise a brow, but the swelling makes it difficult.

"Who would come to her rescue? Maybe someone from New York? That's where she was found, right? Covered in blood with a loaded gun in her hand?" So he remembers what happened to Em. He was part of the investigation into her kidnapping and basically wrote it off as nothing more than a suspicious runaway. "Must be," he answers his own question. "She grew up there with a single mother and penniless. See? I did my homework too."

Not enough of it. At least, I don't think he did, unless he's hiding some of what he knows. He hasn't mentioned the Eastside Rampage or the fact that Em's father was the kingpin. He hasn't said anything about a brother in New York either.

"If she hasn't found you in a few days, let's send her a finger, shall we?" His face transforms into maniacal glee as he rubs his hands together.

I don't care how many pieces of me he sends, I just worry about Em leading with her anger and not with her head. My girl is a genius until her anger clouds every conscious thought.

"Not afraid? Maybe I'll do to you what she did to Halbert. I bet that's enough to put the fear of God into you." Is he trying to get off on my fear? Not going to fucking happen. I won't show him just how his words send my heart pounding into my rib cage or have sweat running down my spine.

"Boss." Someone knocks on the door. "We have movement."

Moore shoots me a look and winks. "Looks like something is happening... Finally."

I watch him exit and pray that Em is being safe.

Chapter Nineteen

Ember

"Emmett should head out now. How far is this cottage?" Carm asks as he paces the kitchen.

Carm came storming into my house about an hour ago with about fifteen of his men, their SUVs parked all over my driveway and a few on the street. He had gone into commander mode as he stationed the men outside, and now he's looking near frantic as he drags his hand through his hair and continues to pace. It's the most rattled I've seen him.

"Three hours and twenty-six minutes," I answer as my eyes follow his movements.

Not that I'm faring any better than he is. My nails are chewed and my nerves are frayed. Vin has been missing for half a day, and with each minute that passes, my fear only grows. Everything I'm doing suddenly comes into question and I begin to doubt it all. Why did I feel compelled to clear this town of its vermin and ignore the risk to my family? I haven't hidden the fact that the five of us are close, so close that we rarely find ourselves apart. Of course they would be used against me at some point. I just felt infallible for so long and I thought I would beat everyone else at their own game before they could even fuck with what's mine. I became too cocky and now Vin is paying for it.

"Travis, is your team ready to hit up Moore's residence?" Carm asks him as Travis nods from his place beside me at the table, his eyes flicking from Carm to me. He's worried, and I can't help but feel responsible. It's my fault his brother has been taken again.

I'm just glad Carm is here and taking the helm. I've come to the end of my patience reserve, and I can feel myself on the brink of an internal explosion.

"Little sis!" Carm raises his voice, pulling me out of my thoughts. I blink him back into focus as he studies me with sadness in his eyes. "Do you have a mailbox?"

"What?" I screw my face up as I look from him to Travis.

"Mailbox. Do you have one?" He stops in front of me with his hands on his hips, his eyes bloodshot and the bags beneath them bruised.

"It's at the end of the driveway," Travis answers for me as he reaches over to grab my hand.

"That's perfect." Carm nods. What the fuck does he need the mailbox for? Maybe some sort of surveillance? Right now, I can't focus on his plans, and honestly, I don't fucking care. I need to get to Vin.

I release Travis' hand and stand, my chewed nails once again ending up in my mouth. I can't just sit here and talk about mailboxes and plans. I want my man.

"Not much longer." Carm puts his hand on my shoulder as if sensing my volatile thoughts. "Everything will be okay, I promise." I believe him. He's my blood and has always came here when I needed him.

"It's been twelve hours," I whisper as fear clogs my lungs, preventing me from taking a full breath.

"Soon, I promise." He gathers me in for a hug.

Just as I'm wrapping my arms around his waist, I look over his shoulder to see Emmett leading a group of six men from the backyard toward the front door.

"Emmett!" I call out and break away from Carm's hold.

Emmett turns and gives me that lopsided grin identical to mine, and my heart crashes against my ribs. I rush to him and he sweeps me up in his arms. "It'll be okay, Ember, I promise." He's dressed in tactical gear, his knives encircling his waist and guns strapped to his chest.

"Please be safe." I pull away and hastily wipe the tears from my cheeks. "I love you."

"Don't say it like that." His face falls as he drags me back against his chest.

"Like what?"

Travis and Adri make their way to the foyer, both of their expressions reflecting fear. Travis is dressed similarly to Emmett, only missing the knives. The guns strapped to his waist will only be used as a last resort because he can't stand weapons.

"Like you won't see me again. Please, Ember, don't do anything that'll get you killed," Emmett pleads as his arms tighten around me. Words fail me, but even if I could speak, I don't think I could promise what he's asking. I would die for Vin, for any of them.

"Carm!" he calls out to our brother as Carm walks out of the kitchen. "I'm trusting you with her safety."

"I won't let you down, bro," Carm vows, the look in his eyes fierce as they move over me and Emmett.

"Ember, we all need you. I won't survive without

you. Do you understand?" Emmett's hands grasp my cheeks as he forces me to look at him, his words making my eyes cloud with tears as I nod.   He kisses the top of my head and squeezes me in another hug before he pulls away.

Turning and stalking over to Adri and Travis, he hugs and kisses them both as Adri softly cries and Travis clenches his jaw, his eyes filled with fear. Then he's out the door.

I lock eyes with Travis and he gives me a stern look. "I second what he said. I can't live this life without you, E."

Adri has tears coursing down her cheeks as she nods. "All for five and five for all."

"Travis," Carm interjects, his voice firm as men stand at the front door. "I have four men here who will go with you to Moore's residence. Are you ready?"

Again, my heart thumps, and I take a deep breath to dull the pain.

"Yes." Travis runs his hands down his chest as he exhales. "We'll drop Adri at the restaurant on the way."

Adri stands from the stairs and hurries over to me, her arms wrapping around my shoulders and her face burrowing into my neck. "I can't even put into words how much I love you and what you've done to change my life. You gave me a family and taught me what it means to love unconditionally." She sniffs, and I feel the wetness of her tears on my neck, threatening to crumple the wall I've so carefully built. "Don't take that away from me."

I hug her back and squeeze her tight. She's my sister, regardless of the blood running through our veins. "I love you too." My voice cracks with emotion.

She pulls back with a sob and hurries out the front door, her choked cries filling the silence that settles around us.

Travis stands in front of me next, his hands cupping

my face as he forces me to look into his eyes. "I knew from the very first day I saw you that you would come into my life like a tropical storm. Fast, tough, and destructive. I had a feeling you would swipe up all the small, broken pieces of my heart and form it back into something worthy of your love. Emberlise Craven, I have loved you from day one, and I will love you until this mended heart stops beating." His lips press against mine in a tender kiss. It's not romantic, it's filled with love and reverence.

He pulls away and rests his forehead against mine as tears finally escape my eyes. He thinks he's benefitted the most from our friendship, but he's played a large part in mending my soul. "I love you too, Travis. You will never know how much."

Then he releases me, and I watch his retreating back with my heart in my throat. Something keeps nagging at me, like we have this all wrong, and one of us—if not all—are walking into traps. I haven't heard from Moore. He hasn't called for a ransom or any demands, and I can't help but think this could be the last time I see my family.

"I see that look, sis," Carm says softly. "Nothing will happen to you while I'm with you."

"But what about them?" I turn on him, my voice breaking as my chin trembles.

"There's only one of me and I chose who it was I wanted to protect." His own eyes fill with tears and my heart pounds with his confession. He should've chosen Emmett, the younger brother he's always put before his own life.

"Why, Carm?" I demand as a sob escapes my chest. "Why did you choose me?"

"Because I have wronged you and I wanted to make it right." He's been harboring guilt for his part in my kidnapping all this time, and I wish I was clearer with my forgiveness of him.

"What happened to me in the beginning is all water

under the bridge now. You know you're my brother as much as Emmett, right? You have to know I love you just as much."

"Thank you." He nods, and I notice his eyes filling as well. "When this is all done and over with, you and I will have a talk. Go upstairs and change into the gear I've placed in your room. I will talk to my men and we'll hit up the rental as soon as dusk hits."

He strides outside as I head upstairs to my bedroom, my feet feeling heavy with every step. Once I enter the room and see the rumpled sheets, I fucking lose it. All I see in here is Vin. His scent is everywhere and his clothes are all over the place.

Sinking to my knees, I let the tidal wave of fear and despair pull me under. I've experienced this overwhelming sadness a few times before. My mother dying, Vin and Travis being taken by Carlos, and then Travis attempting to commit suicide. The only difference this time is this was all my doing.

Did I really need to purge this little decaying town? Did I need to put my family at risk to prove I was capable of such a colossal task? The answer is no, it will always be no, and if my actions put any of them in our mausoleum, I won't be too far behind.

I picture Tommy and his unwavering loyalty. I imagine him telling me to suck it up and take care of business as he usually would. My aunt and uncle are smiling at me and loving me despite my dangerous decisions. And finally, I see my mother. She's watching me with that small smile she always had when I made her proud. I realize then that she would be proud of me for what I came here to do and how I've avenged her.

None of them would want me to give up.

I have to believe that Moore wouldn't kill Vin, that he sees his importance and plans to use him to draw me in. That's what he wants anyway. He wants me.

"Ember!" Carm yells from downstairs. "Come down so we can go over this plan before we have to head out."

I once again bury my grief down deep under mountains of anger and get to my feet. My moment of weakness is done and now it's time to take out the rest of the trash.

"No one's here," I growl while I watch Carm's men surround the darkened house.

"Not necessarily. We have to think like him. Maybe he knows we've gathered forces and are scouting all residences. Maybe he's watching us now from a darkened room inside this place," Carm utters under his breath as we sit and wait in the SUV.

Travis called to say no one was at Moore's house, but they're going to stay there to see if he shows up. I haven't heard from Emmett, but he wouldn't be at the cottage yet anyway.

"I have a feeling, Carm." I shake my head and run my hand down my face. "Something is off. He's not in any of these places."

"Think, Ember. Where else could he go?" He lifts his phone and dials a number. "Enter the house and search it thoroughly," he barks at whoever is on the other end.

That's just it, I have been thinking. He's not at the police station because those cops looked more than surprised when we showed up demanding to see Moore. He's not in any residences with his name on the listing because that would be too easy.

Where the fuck are he and my fiancé? I run through all the places I can think of in Whitsborough.

"The place is empty, boss." I hear one of his men say

through the phone about ten minutes later.

"Of course it is." I nod and rub my temples. "Think, Ember."

"It has to be someplace secluded where no one would see him taking a hostage inside. Somewhere far enough away from others or somewhere soundproofed," Carm suggests.

"Fuck!" I yell into the car's interior, the sound of my rage echoing around us. I can't think of anywhere that would be like that.

My phone rings, and Adri's name flashes across the screen. My heart rate picks up as I brace myself to answer the phone. "Adri?"

"I know where he is," she whispers, her voice trembling.

"What?" I sit up straight as my mouth dries out and my heart pounds. "Adrianna Hinton, where the fuck are you?"

Carm looks at me and straightens in his seat as he starts the SUV, expecting us to need to leave in a hurry.

"I'm a few blocks from the restaurant. I dropped off a takeout order and I think I found Moore's vehicle." The wind blows against her phone, making her sound far away.

"Are you sure?" I press as I stare out the window toward Moore's property. "Why would he be parked out in the open like that?"

"He's not." She sounds slightly out of breath, like she's been running. "This is a side street. It's quiet here."

"Where is it?" I demand. When she tells me the street name, I realize exactly where they are. "Get back to the restaurant," I tell her and hang up before texting Travis and turning to Carm. "I know where they are."

VIN

My head snaps up when I hear a door opening. I'm groggy with exhaustion, my stomach is twisting in hunger, and my tongue is swollen and stuck to the roof of my mouth. Just the thought of water has my throat constricting.

"Your girl is as stupid as I thought." Moore chuckles as he leans against the doorframe, my vision swimming as I try to focus. "She even wasted precious resources by sending people to my cottage. It's three hours away." His laughter grows, the sound sending arcs of pain throughout my skull.

How long have we been here? There's no way to gauge time, and I've been floating in and out of consciousness for a while now.

"Looks like we might just have to cut a piece of you off and send it to her. Motivation to use that schoolgirl brain of hers." His smug tone stokes my anger and I gather what's left of my energy as I glare at him.

"Stop talking about it and just do it then." My hoarse voice cracks with thirst.

"Don't tell me what to do!" he yells as he strides forward and punches me in the stomach. "She has one hour, and then I'm starting with the fingers on your left hand."

The blow to my stomach triggers severe cramping as I gag. As long as Em is safe, nothing else matters, and I will take whatever Moore dishes out if it means Em won't have to.

Each breath is like a burning fire inside my chest, which means I must have a few broken ribs. The knife wound on my leg isn't feeling so good either. It's burning hot, and each time I flex the muscle, the pounding fire increases. Sweat gathers on my brows even though this room is chilly, and I can feel myself losing consciousness again. I try to stay alert by thinking of Em, my mom, and my family.

Em will find me, I'm sure of it, and she'll protect my mom because that's what she does. That girl was made for me, designed to smooth out all the broken parts inside of me, and created to teach me what the fuck this life is meant for. If I make it out of here, I plan on marrying her as soon as I can and putting a baby in her belly.

Life is short, and after everything, I can only assume ours will be shorter.

Chapter Twenty

"Are you sure this is the place?" Carm asks, his tone sounding unsure as we remain crouched behind a few bushes in front of the building.

"Yes." The town hall is completely still and dark, no noise and no movement, but I can feel Vin inside those walls. I texted Travis and told him to head over to the restaurant to be with Adri and Sharla, just in case they spotted Adri around Moore's vehicle.

"Emmett is turning around. We should wait until—"

"No," I cut Carm off. "No more waiting." Carm can stay outside and wait for Emmett for all I care. I will go in there alone to rescue my soul.

"This place looks empty," Carm protests, his eyes staying glued to the building in front of us. "There hasn't been any movement for over thirty minutes. Where would they be in there?"

"There's a basement," I explain to him. "It's where they had their very special perverted meetings before I started picking them off like flies."

"Is there another entrance?" He looks behind him, scanning the area for any movement. We left our SUV and the other filled with his men near Moore's car, waiting to see if he emerges.

"That, I don't know." I shake my head with frustration. "But I would assume yes."

"I would bet it's back around where that fucker parked his car." Carm snaps his fingers, and I look at him wide-eyed.

"Yeah, you're probably right."

We walk the two blocks back toward the quiet, residential street we came from. There are only a few houses here, but there is a large, densely wooded area behind them.

"Looks like we're hiking," Carm states as he motions for his men to get out of the vehicle.

"Wait, we could be in there all night searching for a fucking trapdoor." Irritation coats every word as I stare into the vast area of the forest. There's no way we could cover all this land between the eight of us in a decent amount of time.

"Or..." He raises a brow at me. "What if these inbred pieces of shit thought we would never discover them and made it really easy to find?"

"That's a big *if*, Carm." We don't have time to waste scouring a forest when Vin is trapped somewhere with a lunatic out for my blood.

"We can always go back and storm the front, but they're probably prepared for just that."

He's fucking right, and I can't put Vin's life in any more jeopardy than it's already in. I have to do this the smart way, so my anger needs to take the back burner. Once

I know my family and Vin are safe, then I'm giving it free rein.

We enter the forest with Carm's men in front and behind us. They fan out as I keep my eyes on the ground, looking for anything to lead us in the right direction.

A few minutes later, I hear a sharp whistle to my right and pivot. Carm's arm shoots up and the men that were behind us rush forward toward the sound.

"Ember," Carm whispers beside me. "I know you hate taking orders, but I need you to do me a favor. Once we're inside, I need you to listen to me. If I tell you to do something, please just do it."

I hate taking orders from someone else when this is supposed to be my mission, but I have no other choice in this. I need to trust my brother.

"Okay," I reluctantly agree.

"I promise we'll get to him."

"Okay," I repeat, because I believe him. I don't doubt Carm. He's saved us before and I know he'll do it again.

We follow the same direction as his men and a small building pops into view. It's made up entirely of cinder blocks and has a large steel door. Beside the door is a keypad and one small light to illuminate it.

"Beyond this point," Carm talks to his men. "Ember has the same rank as me. Whatever she asks, you will do. No hesitations. Understand?"

Most men nod and a few mutter their agreement. I turn and look at Carm because that couldn't have been easy for him, and I smile in appreciation.

"Open the door." He nods to one of his guys.

The guy pulls out a gun with a silencer and shoots at the keypad. I watch as the faceplate is completely blown off and sigh with relief when I hear the click of the door unlocking. Carm points to the two men, prompting them to enter the building before motioning for the rest of us to wait.

When the door opens, I see the faint yellow glow of a light and watch as the men disappear down a flight of stairs. So, this is an entrance to the basement of the town hall. We wait—not so patiently—for the men to come back.

Then I hear the faint whistle coming from inside and watch as more men enter the structure.

"Ready?" Carm asks me.

"Yeah."

Carm tries to hand me a gun, but I shake my head. I've never been too keen on them, and besides, my knife has always served me well. He rolls his eyes and motions with his head for me to go in first while he covers us from behind.

Inside is damp and the smell of musty mildew assaults my nose. The ceiling is dripping moisture and the lights swing precariously back and forth, creating shadows with their eerie, yellow glow.

"Watch your step," Carm murmurs behind me as I peer down into the cavernous space.

The concrete steps are green with mold and narrow, barely the width of my small feet. I try to hurry, feeling the anxious energy inside my chest the closer I get to Vin, but Carm has my hoodie gripped in his fist, refusing to watch me break my neck on the stairs.

I hear two pops farther ahead and jump down the three remaining stairs to hurry forward.

VIN

The door opens again, and Moore comes and removes the rope securing me to the chair. Then he waves to someone just outside the door, and I watch as two uniformed cops come in and lift me by each arm.

The fire that burns through my chest and my injured leg has me gasping in pain. They ignore my pained sounds though and continue to drag me out the door and then up a small flight of steps.

We're still in a basement, but the air is a little clearer, not so musty, and the room is large and open. It looks almost like a church with rows of pews and a large-looking altar at the front.

I'm dragged to the altar and thrown to the floor, the impact jarring my injuries as I grunt through the pain. I push myself up to my hands and knees as they place a chair in front of me.

"Tie him to the chair," Moore orders, and I wince as I'm roughly thrown into the chair. When I muster the strength to lift my head, I see more cops in the room. From a quick count, I can determine at least twenty men. That's almost the entire force here. "I want his hands free." Moore's voice breaks through my concentration. "I need those fingers spread out nicely."

My stomach rolls with the thought of losing a finger, and then the worry sets in for when Em receives it. We all might as well kiss the town of Whitsborough goodbye because she will raze it to the ground after this.

My hands tingle as the blood rushes through, my shoulders protesting when I try to bring my arms forward and they crack with stiffness. If I had more strength, I would fight them as they pull my arms forward and tape them to the chair. I'm weak from blood loss and lack of food, so I let my head fall to my chest as I accept what's about to happen.

Then, I pray for every soul in this room, because when she comes—and she will—they will all be decimated.

I feel my hand being stretched out and then hear Moore's chuckle. "Are you ready?" he asks, like the most cliché villain.

I chuckle right along with him and lift my head. "Are you?"

It's small, but I see a sliver of hesitation in his eyes, no doubt feeling the fear of what the repercussions of this particular act will be.

The sharp edge of his blade presses against my skin, then begins to cut through as I hiss through the agony. Just as the blade hits bone, I hear the doors crash open and gunshots ring around me.

That's the last thing I hear as the world goes dark.

265

C.A. RENE

Chapter Twenty-One

I'm running through a narrow concrete hallway when I hear gunshots going off just above us. "What the fuck is that?" I scream.

"I think my men found them," Carm replies, his voice low but his face filled with apprehension. I scramble up a small set of stairs and storm into the open door ahead of me where the gunshots are deafening. "Fuck!" Carm bellows from behind me just before his body slams into mine, forcing me to the ground.

He eases off of me and stands, shooting his gun into the ceiling. "Stop!" His voice rings out strongly.

The shots cease, and I lift my head from the concrete floor to find bodies lying across what looks like church pews, then breathe a sigh of relief when I see they are cops. Six of Carm's men took out a chunk of the Whitsborough police force, proving just how useless they were. More are standing in front of Moore, their guns trained on us, their eyes filled with fear.

I stand up and scan the room quickly until my eyes land on him. His chin is resting on his chest and he's tied to a fucking chair. His face is a mess of bruises and dried blood while his left hand looks like it's bleeding.

Behind him is Moore, holding a large hunting knife to Vin's throat—not unlike my own.

"My men will easily take out yours. You have fat lazy cops. I have military-trained men. Drop your knife and take your death like a man." Carm's voice is loud and clear.

"He's no man!" I call out as I stride forward.

"Ember!" Carm grinds through his teeth, but nothing will stop me from getting to my soul.

Vin's head slowly lifts, and he flashes me that crooked grin, his dimple still prominent amongst the blood. "Took you long enough. I was about to lose a finger because of your tardiness." His voice sounds like he's been screaming for hours on end.

I stop about halfway between him and Carm. He's only twenty feet in front of me, and I can't stop this anxious feeling of needing to have him safe in my arms.

"You know me, always needing to make an entrance." I smile back at him, knowing it looks forced and fake as fuck.

I take notice of a few things right away. Moore's men have their guns drawn, but none of their fingers are on the trigger. They have no idea exactly why they're here. Moore's hand is slightly shaking, his fear bleeding through even as he tries to hide it, and Carm's men are spread evenly around the room, being present in each corner.

I'm covered on all sides and that eases my anxiety some. One of Carm's guys shifts until he's a few feet from my front.

"I see you!" Moore yells out to him. "Stop moving!"

His eyes look manic and deranged. Probably a lot like my own. I watch as if in slow motion as Moore's fist swings out and slams into Vin's jaw. His head snaps to the side and blood runs down his chin, dripping onto the floor.

Don't ask me what came after, because all I could tell you is that my world became many shades of red as my pulse throbbed a rhythm of murder throughout my body and all the noise faded to a dull buzz.

VIN

Ember's body is stiff, and I can almost see the tension radiating off her in waves. I try to grin at her to calm her a bit, but she's not watching me. Her eyes are flitting around the room quickly, assessing and determining her next strike.

One of Carm's men is shifting slowly toward her, putting his back to her front, and I'm thankful someone is trying to protect her.

"I see you!" Moore's voice is like nails on a chalkboard. "Stop moving!"

My head is jarred once again by this motherfucker's fist, and I feel my mouth fill up with blood. I keep my head down and try to focus on not passing out, watching as the blood in my mouth slowly drips onto the wood flooring.

Before I can fully register it, I hear her moving. I force myself to look up and watch as she storms onto the platform I'm sitting on, and Moore's knife that was once at my throat hangs limply by his side as he watches her with wide eyes. One cop tries to run forward to cut her off, but Carm shoots him point-blank in the chest and he falls like a sack of potatoes.

Em barely pauses as she bends and picks up the fallen cop's gun, then hops over his body. In seconds, everything erupts into utter chaos. Carm begins to run and shots ring out in the place as I struggle against my bonds. I need to protect Em. I don't want her to get shot for me.

I feel the cool touch of the sharp blade against my throat again and Moore's heavy breathing on my neck. "If I'm going out, you're coming with me."

He digs the blade in deep, and the slow drip of my blood runs down my throat as Em screams. She lifts the gun and fires off a shot, and I feel its heat along my cheek before

Moore's blood sprays along the side of my face, warm and thick. My stomach rolls at the rusted stench as I breathe through my mouth.

Then her hands are on my face, cupping my cheeks, and scanning my injuries. Shots are still ringing out, men ducking behind pews as Carm runs up to us.

"Untie him and get him out of here," he barks to Ember as he shoots another cop.

I look around and am shocked to see more men coming from the same entrance Em came from. Someone called for backup and now we're severely outnumbered.

Em cuts away the rope and hoists me up out of the chair. I stumble but right myself across her shoulders.

"I'm not leaving you," she says to Carm as tears run down her cheeks.

"I will be right behind you." He nods, his throat working hard to swallow. A shot whizzes above our heads and his features harden. "Get the fuck out of here, Ember!"

"I love you," she tells him, a sob escaping her.

"Remember that." His eyes shine with compassion. "Remember I love you too."

Carm and I lock eyes, and what I see in their depths will forever cement my respect for the man. He gives me a brief dip of his chin and then pushes his sister toward a set of stairs that lead to another floor above us.

One of Carm's men grabs my other side and we flee as Em casts one final look back at her brother.

Chapter Twenty-Two

Ember

Carm's eyes meet mine as he gives me a sad smile. Then Vin's weight leans heavily against me as his head rolls from side to side, and I know I have to get him out of here now.

We hit the stairs when more gunfire erupts, and we rush up them to escape any notice.

The town hall is empty, and thankfully, with the help of another one of Carm's men, we drag Vin toward the front doors. When we step outside, my eyes are assaulted by the red and blue fluorescent lights of cop cars. A lot of them.

"Emberlise Craven," a voice sounds over a speaker system. "Hands up where we can see them."

"E!" I turn at the sound of Travis' voice and close my eyes in relief. Carm's man holds on to Vin as I slowly raise my hands in the air and step forward. "No!" Travis screams. "She didn't do anything. What are you doing?"

Two police officers rush forward, one yanking my hands behind my back while the other stands in front of me, reading me my rights. "Get Vin to the hospital!" I yell to Travis.

The rest of the police officers rush into the building as I send a silent prayer up for Carm. I hope he makes it out of there alive. I'm being dragged and pushed into a police car when I hear Travis behind me, causing a scene. He needs to snap out of it and get his brother to the fucking hospital.

Two police officers get in the car and look back at me. "What am I being arrested for?" I ask.

"The murder of Andrew Cox," one of them growls, and I exhale a huff.

"Whatever." My head tips back against the seat.

I'm too exhausted to think of a way to get out of this.

I've been denied bail and allowed no visitors as I await my trial. I've spoken to the family lawyer who is trying his best to get me out of this, but it's bad. They have video surveillance of me on the street where they found Andrew's body. It puts me there around the time of his murder. Then the police found Chief Moore with a gunshot wound to the neck and many eyewitness accounts from other police officers stating I did it, which I did.

I've been told only a handful of people survived in that basement, including Moore. My brother wasn't one of them. They found him with several gunshots to his chest, and I have yet another death to grieve later. He's been pushed down deep to settle in the same space with my mother, Tommy, and my adoptive parents.

"Ember, I need something here," my lawyer stresses as he sits across the table from me. "What were you doing on that street that day?"

"I was looking for Andrew. I was supposed to meet

up with him and he didn't show." I blow a piece of hair off my face, unable to use my hands as they're cuffed together and linked around my feet as well.

"But how did you know he was there?" he implores, his frustration hitting me square in the face.

"I didn't. It was a guess." I drop my chin to my chest. "My phone records will show that I received a text message from Andrew to meet up with him *after* his meeting with Moore. He didn't show. In another text message from Andrew, you will see he tells me where he's meeting Moore and that's where we found him." I look back up at him as he stares at me with thought. There are doubts swimming in his eyes, but he doesn't voice them, not here in the station where there are eyes and ears on us.

"Okay. I will petition the court for a warrant for the cell phone company, but that can take weeks. Ember, I'm afraid you'll be in here for a while." He gives me a sad look as he gathers up his stuff and slips them into his briefcase.

"I got nowhere else to be." I shrug, making the chains connecting my hands to my feet jingle.

That's a lie. I want to be home to make sure Vin is recovering. According to my lawyer, he spent one week in the hospital, just a few doors down from Moore, and was released to recover at home. I can only imagine the shitstorm Sharla has caused.

I'm escorted back to my jail cell and tossed—none too gently—back inside. They hate me here because I'm a cop killer. Little do they know I'm a pervert killer too, but that's neither here nor there.

I lie back on my cot and scratch another notch into the wall. Fifteen days. That's how long I've been in here. Fifteen days of food being thrown across my cell floor, male cops jeering through my bars as I piss, and random threats of violence throughout the day. I'm just biding my time and waiting for the perfect moment to strike. It may not be this week, month, or even year, but it will come, and I will bathe in their fucking blood while I dance naked around their bodies.

"We should come in there and show you exactly what happens to girls that misbehave," a cop calls out.

"Yeah, the operative word being *girls*," I sneer right back. "I know exactly how you and your chief liked to operate, but I think I'm a little too old for your tastes, right?"

I hear him grumbling as I chuckle inside my cell. Probably saying all the nasty things he'd like to do with my dead body. *Get in line, bitch.*

Chapter Twenty-Three

Ember

It's been twenty-one days since I've been arrested, and currently, I'm in a dark room only about ten square feet in size. I'm sporting a shiner and a busted lip from a guard whose elbow *slipped*. It's all good because my fist slipped afterward and I broke his nose. Hence, being thrown into the small windowless cell.

I've lost weight, mostly muscle mass, from not eating more than one meal a day. Having your food thrown on the floor will do that. I feel weak, and no matter how much I try to work out, I have no fucking energy.

I haven't spoken to anyone on the outside except for my lawyer, who brings me updates. According to him, my family has been working tirelessly to get me out, and he said he had to talk Emmett down a few times from trying to bust me out. Who the fuck does my twin think he is? Michael Scofield? He doesn't have the brain capacity to even attempt it. He'd end up bombing the place and hoping I'd make it through the explosion.

Just thinking about them has my chest squeezing. I miss them. Every time I think of their faces, I want to scream to release the building pressure inside my chest. It's not unlike how I felt while trapped at The Rampage's compound over a year ago. I push the thought away as I see Carm's face swim into my vision and the first time I found out he was my brother. There's no time to be depressed here. It's dangerous to lose my mind to it and leave myself vulnerable. I have to keep my guard up and prepare for anything to happen.

"Craven!" a pig calls out just before the door to the cell opens. I squint at the blinding light and wait for my eyes to adjust as I protect my face from any sort of attack. "Get up," the little piggy demands as he grabs my arm and pulls me to my feet.

"Am I going back to my regular cell now?" He doesn't answer me as I let him pull me down the corridor for a bit. Then I yank my arm out of his hold and glare up at him. "Keep your grubby hands off of me, pig," I spit out, and he shakes his head with exasperation. Or maybe it's from the stench of my body.

"Just follow me." I'm slightly shocked at the changed demeanor. Where are the threats of violence? Or better yet, the slipping of appendages?

I'm led into the intake room and I look around. A cop stands with the clothing I arrived in and a bag with my phone, shoes, and engagement ring. I'm relieved when I see that last item.

"What's going on?"

Of course they don't answer me as they throw me my belongings and tell me to hurry.

So I do because I am not looking a gift horse in the fucking mouth.

I knock on the door once I'm dressed, and a cop leads me to the front where I can see the outside world through the glass. I want to weep at the vision in front of me.

"Sign these," the woman behind the counter grunts as she slides papers toward me.

I read through them and my breath gets lodged in my throat. These are release papers and a few others that state the terms of my 'acquittal.' One being I am never to speak of what happened here.

"I would just sign it for now and we can look over everything later. I'm sure they were mindful to add all my *suggestions*," another woman says from behind me. "I think it would be prudent to get out of here quickly."

Quickly turning on the spot, I find a petite woman standing behind me with a large briefcase clutched in her hands. I don't recognize her, but that's because she's wearing a scarf over her hair and large sunglasses obscuring her face. She's not intimidating at all, but the air around her is charged with authority.

I do as she says and sign the papers. "I want copies," I tell the girl behind the counter and wait until she finishes photocopying them. Then I turn to the woman. "Are you working with my lawyer?"

"Something like that." She nods as she touches the glasses on her face.

I'm handed back copies of the forms, then I follow the woman outside. I can feel autumn in the air, and I know it'll soon be time for Vin to begin college.

"Who are you?" I ask as I turn around.

"I'm the one who sprung you out of here," she reveals with one hand on her hip while the other holds the briefcase. Something about her feels so familiar.

"Why?" I ask slowly as I draw in the fresh air. If I was alone right now, I'd roll in the grass and weep with my release.

"I have many reasons, but one stands out above the rest." She chuckles as her face transforms with mirth.

"I miss having you trying to chase me down. Life is utterly boring without it."

Her words hit me like a fucking freight train. "Jennifer Talia?"

"Ding, ding!" she singsongs, and I am left fucking speechless. "I think we need to have a lengthy conversation."

"Are you insane?" I ask her, shock lining my words as my hands curl into fists. "I should just fucking kill you."

"You could," she agrees, then takes a step back. "But then my men here would kill you and we'd never have the answers we both seek. Not everything is as it seems, Miss Craven. Or should I say, Torres?" My eyes scan the three men standing a few feet behind her and another leaning against a limo.

"It's Craven," I snarl as I step toward her.

"One is just as bad as the other if you ask me." She shrugs. She fucking shrugs like I'm not standing here imaging all the bloody, gruesome ways I want to kill her. "It's imperative we talk, Emberlise. It's been a long time coming."

"We do need to talk." I know exactly what I need to ask her. "I need some clarification on a few things."

"I know." She nods as she holds up her one free hand. "Can we call a truce? At least for today? And if you decide you still want to kill me, we'll continue as normal tomorrow."

"Fine," I grind out. I'm outnumbered, weak, and relishing my freedom. There's no way I want to be thrown back into a cell so soon.

"Excellent." She hands her briefcase to a man then claps her hands and points to another guy standing in front of a stretch limo. "He's been instructed to see you home safely. You now have more enemies than ever before, astonishing really."

"How do I know he won't kill me on your orders?" I stare down the goon who's now in charge of my safety, the situation feeling too precarious.

"You don't. You can walk home," she answers coolly. "But again, you have a lot of enemies, being a cop killer and all." She pointedly looks behind me, and when I follow her sight, I see a few cops watching from the window.

The fucking bitch has a point. I turn my back on her and approach the limo, to which the man hurriedly opens the door. *Trained dog.*

"I will come by and see you later!" she calls out. Of course she knows where I live.

I just flip her the bird over my head and fume as I hear her laugh. This world is a fucking mindfuck sometimes.

We pull into the driveway, and I know I'm about to be bombarded. Everyone's phones are probably pinging right now, alerting them to the fact that a limo is approaching.

Sure enough, as we stop beside the front door, my family is standing outside with varying degrees of annoyance on their faces. They don't know it's me yet because I wasn't able to call ahead to let them know I'm out. I take a minute and look each of them over. Adri looks like she hasn't slept in weeks. Her hair is greasy and her skin is an unnatural gray color. Travis has a fucking beard and his hair is shaggy and unkept... He also looks like he needs a bath. Emmett looks sickly and pale, the slouch of his shoulders relaying the stress he's under.

Then there's my Vin. He's standing with his arms crossed over his chest and his face stone-cold, not betraying any of his feelings, but I see it in his eyes. He's sad, and he looks like he's about ready to snap.

"This is the correct address, Miss Craven?" the driver

asks, breaking me out of my appraisal.

"Yeah." I open the door and stand, watching the expressions on each of their faces change from irritation to shock.

"Ember!" Adri is the first to react, and for once, I welcome that squeal.

She slams into me, throwing us back against the limo, her body shaking as she sobs into my neck.

"E?" Travis is standing behind her, watching us with wide, glistening eyes.

"Fuck, dude." I snort as I try to break the tension with some humor. "Did all grooming products get arrested with me?"

He ignores my jab and wraps his arms around the both of us. "Thank God," he murmurs.

"Guys." Emmett's quiet voice filled with sorrow interrupts our moment. "Can I please see my sister?"

Travis backs off and pulls Adri with him. Then Emmett is standing in front of me with tears streaming down his cheeks. The pain in his eyes could drown me in their depths, and my heart breaks as he steps forward, pressing his forehead to mine.

"I'm sorry," I croak, and my breath hitches with emotion. "I wanted him to come with us, but he wouldn't. He wouldn't move from that spot, Emmett."

"Shh," he says and shakes his head softly. "I don't blame you for that. He made the same decision I would've made too. I understand exactly why he did it."

"No." I sob and fist his shirt in both of my hands. "I am not worthy of anyone's life. Don't say that to me, Emmett." He pulls me forward into his arms and closes the limo door. Then he gives it two quick raps on the roof, telling the driver he can leave.

As much as I've missed Adri, Travis, and Emmett, there's one person I'm dying to touch and smell.

"Who owns the limo?" Emmett asks, but I don't answer as I pull away from him and look my soul in the eyes.

He hasn't budged, his arms still crossed and his face a mask over his emotions. He's been silently watching and waiting for me to come to him.

I slowly walk forward and stop in front of him. He still has a few healing marks on his face and a nice-looking scar on his neck from Moore's knife. Anger renewed pours through me as I look at them.

"There she is," he whispers as his finger comes out to stroke my cheek. "My rage-filled girl." His hand wraps around my throat as he drags me into his chest before he devours my mouth. His taste is a mix so tantalizing, nothing will ever compare. My hands immediately run up and under his shirt as his hand tightens, making me moan. "You need a shower. I smell jail on you," he says against my lips. "Then you're going to explain how you're home."

"Okay." I nod as he releases his hold on my throat. "I need some updates too. Like where the fuck Moore is now."

He nods in return and I feel myself slowly rejuvenating. I know they would've been keeping tabs on the man who tried to kill my fiancé and succeeded in the death of my brother.

The hunt is back on.

My fingers are like skinny prunes, but I can't make myself leave the warm stream of water. I've washed my hair three times and used an entire bottle of bodywash. I'm about to wash my hair again when the shower door opens and crashes against the wall.

Vin is standing there in all his naked glory, and my mouth waters as I run my eyes over all his defined ridges. "You're taking too long," he growls. I don't know if it's just me, but Vin seems a bit changed, harder and angrier.

"Sorry, it's all that jail smell." He ignores my jest and gets into the shower with me.

"I can't wait any longer, Em. It's been over a month since I've had you."

"I know," I whisper as I take in his body, the sight of him making my pussy clench in anticipation.

He wraps his hand into my hair and turns me to face the wall, my hands shooting out to brace myself before my face meets the tile. His hand runs down over my spine, then glides over my left ass cheek.

"I'm mad at you," he reveals, his voice filled with anger, but I can also hear how much he's hurting.

"I figured." I smirk as I try to diffuse the situation.

"You take too many chances with your life."

"Yeah," I agree with a shrug. If it means it saves theirs, then so be it. It's like he can read my unspoken response because his hand cracks down on my ass cheek. I gasp as the sharp pain spreads. "Vin." My voice holds a warning.

"You ran into the basement like this body is bulletproof."

Smack.

"You rushed Moore like there weren't twenty cops there waiting to get a good shot at you."

Smack. Smack.

"Then you got yourself arrested."

Smack.

"Hey!" I squirm as the stinging pain on my ass cheeks heightens. "That last one isn't my fault!"

"Pisses me off nonetheless," he snarls, and then he's pushing his cock inside me. Nothing about this is a sweet homecoming. He's pissed and he's making sure I feel it. I do, I fucking feel it.

I'm not prepared for him. Not only has it been awhile, but I'm also not lubed enough for his girth. Vin doesn't care though as he forces himself deeper, the pain only making me want more.

"This isn't for you," he snaps. *No shit.* "You don't deserve it." I try to breathe through the stinging, but it intensifies, and a whimper escapes. "Hurts?" He yanks my head back.

"Yes," I grind through my teeth, holding back the urge to struggle. He needs this, and I'd do anything for Vin. *Anything.*

"Good." That's the only warning I get before he releases my hair, grabs my hips, and slams himself home.

I scream as the pain becomes too much and tears run down my cheeks. He doesn't stop the onslaught, if anything, it spurs him on as his thrusts become harder.

Letting my head hang forward, I try not to tense through the pain. I know it'll only make it worse. I take no pleasure from this, and he knows it. This is the only way Vin could punish me and it's working. I've missed him so much. A part of me has been dead for nearly a month, and I envisioned this differently.

Vin is like a nuclear bomb. He holds all his emotions in, and in one critical moment, he explodes. He's exploding now, and I'm having to endure the damage. I will bear it though because I understand that my actions, my ideals, have brought him to this moment. It's my fault.

He finishes and withdraws from my body without

a sound. Nothing to enjoy, just a punishment I will never forget.

I stand up straight as my core aches, and I'm unable to press my thighs together because of the stabbing pain in my center. I rest my forehead against the tile and I'm shocked when tears fall from my eyes. I'm not crying from the physical pain. I'm crying from my broken heart, Vin's broken heart, and my family's broken heart. I feel the burden of all my choices and how it's affected each of their lives. Would they have been better off without me? Did my coming here set their lives down a path leading to death and despair?

Vin's hand lands on my lower back, and I tense as I wait for his wrath. "Em?" His voice sounds like the Vin I know, like home. "I'm not sorry for this." Right. I just nod, unable to answer him. "But this happened because of your total lack of regard for the thing I hold most precious." I turn to look at him and a sob catches in my throat. Vin is crying. His face is red from the effort of trying to hold it in and failing. "I can't live without you." His voice catches and he drops his chin to his chest. "I don't see a life without you. So I need you to see that. I need you to see we're one now. You die, I die."

I didn't see it that way. It was always their lives above my own, protecting them at all costs, and exchanging my life for theirs if ever need be. But when I turn the tables, putting myself in Vin's shoes, I can see how my disregard for my own life is a direct disregard for his as well.

"I'm sorry," I whisper. "I didn't see it before."

"I know, Em." He sniffs and I shakily reach my hand out to place it over his heart—over the infinity tattoo with our initials. His heart is pounding wildly, his breathing erratic, and his eyes shine with so much love and unshed tears. I have been wrong this entire time. Our lives are so intertwined that I don't know where I end and he begins.

"I love you, Vincent Greene."

"I've always been yours, Ember Craven soon-to-be Greene."

"I need an ice pack." I grab my sore vagina and step out of the shower.

Chapter Twenty-Four

I'm still not sure what came over me in the shower. I wanted to make love to her and show her how much she means to me, but then she acted so blasé about her life and it made me snap. After everything I'd been through, and then not having her here with me, I couldn't take that attitude.

I don't regret it and I would do it again if it meant we came to the same conclusion.

"She has bruises on her face and a busted lip," Emmett mutters as we sit in the family room and wait for her.

"I doubt she was treated well," I reply, my stomach souring at the thought. It makes me want to rage every time I see her face. "She was the one who shot Moore." His face reddens and he looks like his insides are boiling. Now we're on the same page.

I'm still trying to figure out how to tell her about the package we found in her mailbox from Carm. None of us has opened it, but Emmett has confirmed it's his writing. He must've put it there himself because the envelope has no stamps or mailing info, just Em's name. *Emberlise Torres.*

Carm's death has impacted us all, but Emmett is handling it badly. He was practically raised by the man, and for so long, Carm was his only family. It's also sad that the day his brother died, his only other sibling was locked away in a jail cell.

Emmett spoke about breaking her out every single day, and it took all three of us to talk him down... Every. Single. Day. He was a wreck and couldn't hide it. I was a wreck too, Travis and Adri as well, but we held it together. All of us felt like we were drowning under the stress of getting Ember out of jail, but we knew she would've wanted us to be strong like she would've been.

I don't know how she got out. We just finished speaking with her lawyer this morning, and he told us she'd be in there for the foreseeable future. He was still trying to pull phone records and video surveillance from the houses around Andrew's crime scene.

According to the judge, Em was a flight risk because of the amount of money she possesses. I know most of that was bullshit. The judge was looking to punish her too, but then she just shows up like nothing happened and everything is back to business. We lacked the evidence to get her bail decision overturned, and yet here she is, free and *acquitted.*

When Em went on her murder missions, I always took a backseat and let her do her thing. But for Moore? I want to be the one watching as he struggles for his last breath. Now I understand why anger possesses Em and she becomes the Black Slaughter. I feel it. It's almost debilitating, especially when it has no outlet.

I've been angry for most of my life, but that was based on resentment. Yes, it felt all-consuming at the time. I felt like I was a monster because I saw everything in a negative light. This is different. I'm filled with rage and I spend most of my days dreaming up different ways to dismember Moore.

"What's going to happen now?" Adri whispers as she wrings her hands in her lap. She's been a nervous wreck since Em was put away, and even though our girl is free, she looks petrified that she'll be taken from us again.

"Whatever Em wants to happen. With one exception," I answer her, holding up my finger.

"What's that?"

"I'm going to kill Moore."

"We all are," Travis growls, and my eyebrows shoot up in surprise.

"We are?"

"Yeah." His hands form fists as his cheeks redden with anger. "He fucked with our family and got one of us killed. We all plan his death and we pay him back with Greene revenge."

"I like that." I grin at him.

"Like what?" Em asks as she slowly walks into the room.

Still no regrets.

"They're talking about revenge." Emmett stands and pulls her in for another hug. Then he buries his head into her hair, and I know I'm witnessing the bond twins possess.

"My jam," Em purrs, and now I want to drill into her pussy again.

Her eyes meet mine, and I give her a grin. *I see you, baby girl. The way you're walking tells everyone I fucking own you.*

Travis pulls her over to him and she burrows into his chest. This is our family, nothing between us, no lines drawn. We love each other hard, and we'd kill to protect our sanctity.

Adri is next as she wraps her arms around Em's waist.

"I've been so lost without you. We've never been apart this long," Adri tells her, and Em wipes a tear from her eye.

"Never again," she vows. Finally, she turns and makes her way to me. I'm sitting on the single chair across from the couch, and she just curls herself up on my lap and sinks her face into my neck. "This is what home smells like," she murmurs against my skin.

"That's because it's where you belong." She kisses my cheek and adjusts herself in my lap as I wrap my arms around her waist, hauling her in closer. I'm betting my baby girl is sore.

"Where's Moore?" she asks, lifting her face from my neck to gaze around the room at each of us.

"How'd you get out?" I counter, making her turn her head to look at me.

"I promise, that story is going to take a lot of explaining. Let's hear about the Moore situation first." Her evasive attitude makes me grind my teeth together as my fingers dig into her waist, making her hiss and then swat my arm. I ease up, but only a little.

"We received some information yesterday," Travis starts, his eyes flashing with anger as his jaw tics. "Someone left an envelope on the doorstep. The video showed a man with a fedora on and a scarf wrapped around his face. Nothing stood out."

"This envelope contained actual court-ordered documents stating that Moore is in Witness Protection," Adri cuts in, making Em gasp with surprise.

"But not just that," I whisper into her ear as she squirms a little more in my lap. "Also, *where* he's being held in Witness Protection."

"I'd cream for that information, you know, if my pussy wasn't broken," she grumbles. I snort while everyone else looks different shades of amused. Except for Emmett, he looks slightly sick.

"Now your turn." I nudge her as her throat works on a swallow and she shifts once more in my lap.

EMBER

How do I tell them what happened and not start World War III? I don't know how to articulate my truce with Talia and somehow keep them calm at the same time. It's because of this woman that Adri was illegally adopted, Travis and Vin's father had dealings with her, and Emmett and I lost our aunt and uncle. I could say I agreed to just about anything to get out of there, but that's not completely true. I was intrigued and still am. I want to know what she knows, and I have so many questions regarding the dealings she's had with my family.

I take a deep breath, preparing myself to drop the bomb. "Talia."

"What?" Emmett leans forward, his eyes widening as his head tips to the side with confusion.

"Talia sprung me out of jail." *So far, so good.*

Vin is like a stone statue behind me, unmoving, Travis looks like he's trying to Google Translate whatever the fuck I just said, and Adri is as white as a ghost.

"Explain," Emmett says quietly, his calm voice a direct contrast to his stiffened body.

"I have nothing right now except I've been acquitted of murder in the first degree and she was there when I was released. I signed some papers, which I left in the fucking limo, so hopefully she brings those, and she told me she wants a truce for today to discuss things."

"Brings those?" Vin murmurs darkly.

Always so fucking observant. "Yeah." I nod, and a nervous flutter attacks my insides. "She's coming here to have a meeting."

"A meeting?" Emmett's eyebrows shoot up. "A

certified villain will be in this house?"

"One would argue I'm a certified villain too," I counter as his lips pull taut over his teeth. Not a good sign.

"You're having a parley," Travis interjects, his brows coming together as he works through what I've told them.

"Exactly!" I snap my fingers. "A parley!"

"A parley is done when opposing sides decide to come to an agreement." Vin is still speaking too calmly, his tone relaying danger. "Is that what this is?"

"It's a ceasefire to find out information." I hold my hands up.

"It's a good idea." Travis nods, which shocks the fuck out of me, but he's always been the most logical one. When everyone turns their eyes on him, I sigh in relief. "It is," he stresses as he leans forward on the couch to explain. "Think about it. This woman has had her hands in so many pots and she would know way more than us. She has years on us and she's always a few steps ahead. There's a reason for that. I want to know what she knows."

I've been nodding my head during his explanation, almost frantically so, and Vin slips his big hand through the strands of my hair to clench a fist near my scalp. I suck in a breath, rendered speechless at his new dominant behavior. I'm not sure I like it yet.

He pulls my head back until our eyes meet. "Stop nodding. You've already made a deal with the devil and we can't back down. It's done. When will this *parley* happen?"

I swallow the slightly fearful reaction I have to his stern words before making my voice strong and sure. "Today." I am Ember *fucking* Torres. No one—not even my soul—will intimidate me.

He releases my hair and nudges me from his lap. "I guess we should prepare, huh?"

I stand and watch as he speaks to Emmett. "Get shit together. It could be an ambush. This would be the perfect opportunity to take us all out in one shot. We need to arm ourselves." His narrowed eyes slide to me next. "Would have been better if we had a bit more time to call in some reinforcements, but it is what it is."

He turns and walks out of the family room, leaving me behind without so much as a backward glance. This is the most detached I've felt from Vin. He's not treating me differently, not really, *he's* just different, and I understand why. He was taken, beaten, starved, and held at knifepoint. That changes a person. I won't push him, and I can only hope he comes around. Even though it feels like my insides are being ripped apart.

"He's been through a lot," Travis echoes my thoughts.

"Yeah, I know."

"So have you. Don't think we've missed the bruising on your face." I don't answer, and instead, just shrug. "Find each other again," Travis suggests as he leaves the room next.

"Ember?" Adri speaks from behind me.

"Yeah." I turn and look at her.

"Carm left something for you." She bites her bottom lip as her eyes flick from me to Emmett.

"What do you mean?" The sound of my brother's name sends my heart into overdrive as my stomach flips with unease. I miss him, and if I dwell too long on it, I'll lose myself in the grief I'm straining to keep at bay. There's always someone to grieve.

"It's on the desk in your office."

"It's a large manila envelope," Emmett cuts in. "I would've opened it, but it didn't have my name on it."

I rush out of the room and right into my office, only

to find Vin sitting in the chair in the corner. "I thought they might tell you," he says as he scrubs his hand over his chin. "I won't be left in the dark any longer, Em. You open that with me here and then you're going to tell me exactly what you found in his office." I should feel some sort of anger toward his attitude, not this throbbing in my very broken vagina.

I don't answer him because I agree, he deserves to know everything. So I sit at the desk and stare at the envelope with *Emberlise Torres* written on the front. Flipping it over, I rip open the flap to slide the documents out. On top is a letter in Carm's writing, and the overwhelming rush of despair chokes me for a few seconds. I will never see him again. I won't be called *little sis* again. Taking a few deep breaths, I gather myself and read the letter.

Emberlise Torres,

Don't get mad, that's your name.

Reading that line takes me back to when he sent me my knife to Vin's cottage so long ago.

I want to start by apologizing to you. I'm sorry it took me so long to give you my complete loyalty, and you know why. You took that file from my office, and I know you've figured out what it all means.

With that being said, it's no excuse for what I've done, or better yet, what I haven't done to help you. Inside this envelope is everything I ever found on Jennifer Talia and kept to myself, including all business dealings through Love the Tots. I lied to you when I said I found nothing.

There were a lot of illegal dealings with them, but I can't see anything really wrong. They took children and infants from terrible homes and sold them to better homes.

Yes, they made a profit, but foster care is worse in a lot of cases.

If you're reading this, then I didn't make it out and I can only hope you did. If you did, don't blame yourself, because I did the right thing. I saved you.

Emmett needs you more than he's ever needed me. I can see your bond, and in a year, it's so much stronger than the one he had with me. I leave him in excellent hands, and I know you can take care of him. Let him take care of you too. He's more than capable, even though he can be an idiot.

You are the strongest person I have ever met. You see something impossible and work tirelessly to make it possible. You face down the most formidable opponents and laugh as you watch them fall. I have never been so proud of anyone in my entire life. I don't fear the Torres name ending with you having it.

You are not our father. You are nothing like him. He led with fear, but you lead with respect. I am trusting the Rampage to you, the Head corporation to you, and finally, the Torres empire to you. I trust you will do what's right. You always do.

I'm ending this in a confession, and since I am already dead, you can't kill me. Marlana and I slept together. I couldn't help how drawn we were to each other, and now that I'm dead, please continue to keep her safe. She can change. She can be good.

I love you, and please tell Emmett I love him too. He has always been a better person than me and his heart is ten times bigger than yours and mine.

Your big brother always,

Carmelo Torres

I wipe the tears from my cheeks and hand Vin the paper. He squeezes my hand before he takes it. As he's reading that, I sift through the papers on my desk. Some I already knew from the file I took, but others are a complete surprise.

I really need to know what the fuck Talia is up to.

All our phones ping with an alert and I know it's her coming up the drive. Call it intuition or some shit.

"Bitch is here," Emmett snarls as he opens the front door. I'm not going to ask him to be nice. She is a bitch, and to be honest, I may not be so welcoming either. After all the shit I read in that file, I want to throttle the little woman.

"She kind of reminds me of those old-school supervillains that were short and bossy, and the henchmen were always big and dumb," I state.

"I don't care." Emmett shrugs. "I'll still sink a knife in her eye." Sounds about right. He *is* wearing his belt of knives after all.

Standing out on the front step with him, we watch as three SUVs follow behind a limo—not unlike the one I rode in earlier. Four men get out and walk to the limo, opening the door for her fucking majesty.

"Is this real?" Vin says from behind me, his voice sounding amused.

"She is on enemy territory," I muse as the men make a show of standing around her. "I killed her son, remember?"

"Carm killed her son," Emmett corrects me, his eyes never wavering from the woman getting out of the limo.

"No, it all started with me," I argue with my stupid brother as Talia dusts off the front of her blouse.

"Shut up and get your heads straight," Vin snaps, sounding like the father me and Emmett never had. "We need to stay focused." There goes my broken vagina again. She's straight-up loving asshole Vin.

Talia steps away from the limo, spotting us on the porch, and raises her hand to wave at us like we're her fucking subjects.

"Bitch—" Emmett growls and takes a step toward her.

I reach out just in time to grab his shirt and drag him back. "Keep a calm head, *little brother*," I grind out, the sentiment sounding close to what Carm would say.

"Trust me, Emmett," Vin cuts in as he watches Talia walk toward us, an eerie smile on her face. "I will hold her down for you if shit gets out of hand."

"That sounds close to non-consent and gross," I mutter. "She's a little past her prime."

"Fuck off." Vin snorts, the sound making me whip my head around in time to catch his grin. The sight steals my breath as my throbbing pussy clenches.

"Hello," Talia breathes out as she faces us in her scarf and sunglasses. "This is a pleasant house. Debra and Scott had excellent taste."

"Don't fucking say their names," I growl and step forward with every intention of ripping her tongue out of her mouth and slapping her in the face with it.

"Yes!" Emmett says excitedly, his hand reaching for a knife. "Can I get stabby?"

Talia's men crowd around her, each of them with their hands on their guns as Vin warns, "Guys."

"Let's talk and clear some things up, shall we?" Talia asks with her head cocked to the side. I get the distinct impression that this bitch isn't all there.

We all collectively move aside for her to step into the house first, followed by three of her four armed guards. "Follow me." I guide them to the kitchen as Vin and Emmett take up the rear. "Want something to drink?"

"Yes, please." She sits at the table while her men line up against the kitchen wall, their hands crossed in front of them and their expressions blank. *Stupid henchmen.* "Anything sealed, that is." I snort and pull out a bottle of water, hoping the bitch drowns in a mouthful.

Adri and Travis come into the kitchen, and Adri warily watches Talia while Travis doesn't keep the disdain off his face. "Talia." He says her name like it's a mouthful of poison, spitting out each syllable. "You've been a thorn in our sides."

"Call me Jenna." She glosses over his statement as Emmett and I take a seat across from her. Travis sits beside Talia and Adri beside him as Vin takes the head of the table.

"Jenna... Talia?" Emmett looks around the table at each of us. "Is this a bad *Austin Powers* movie?" Adri was taking a drink while Emmett was talking and now said mouthful is sprayed all over my face.

"Funny." Talia chuckles as she opens her bottle of water to take a sip. "Very much like her."

"Like whom?" I ask as I wipe the water off my face.

"Your mother of course." The room becomes still with silence and the tension weighs us down like a humid summer day.

"I'm going to need an explanation." My mouth feels dry as my tongue works slowly to speak.

"That's why I'm here." She gives me a smile as she exhales, sounding slightly exasperated. "But let's start with the information you possess regarding your brother, Carmelo Torres."

"No." Emmett seethes as he rises a little from his

chair. "We call the shots, and you're never to speak his name."

"Hold on, I know where she's going with this." I pull him back down into his chair, keeping my hand on his arm. "This is important." Emmett looks at me with shock as I grab his hand. "I didn't purposely keep any information from you guys. I did it because I couldn't validate any of it. Carm had a file in his office that contained a letter from Talia and a DNA test."

"DNA test?" Emmett's brows crease in confusion as his eyes well up with the mention of our brother.

"Yes. One that states a certain Jennifer Talia to be his biological mother." Adri gasps as Travis' mouth falls open with shock.

"That's impossible." Emmett shakes his head as a tear escapes his eye and he angrily brushes it away.

"You're correct," Talia confirms as she sips her water. "Ember, dear, those documents were forged, as you well know."

"Yes," I agree as I continue to stare at Emmett, his heartbreak making my grief want to rear its head. "Carm left me an envelope containing proof that Talia is not his mother, and he had only just found out the truth last month." My voice breaks as I swallow down the pain.

"Why did you lie to him?" Emmett's chair screeches as he pushes it back, his eyes on Talia as he prepares to stand.

"I didn't." Talia shrugs as I grip Emmett's hand tighter, our eyes meeting as I plead with mine for him to stay. "But I have an idea who did." Emmett reluctantly sits back down and motions for her to continue. "I'll start at the beginning."

Chapter Twenty-Five

There's just something so oddly familiar about this little lady and the feeling is creeping me out. I can't put my finger on it, but every time she cocks her head or shrugs, it throws me off.

She seems slightly unhinged—not that it's something I'm unaccustomed to—but not in a maniacal way, more subtle and… contained, maybe?

"I'll start at the beginning," she begins and waves her hand about her head. With that movement, I'm knocked into a state of shock. I know why this woman is so familiar and I open my mouth to say it, but she beats me to the punch. "My name is Laurann Jennifer Craven."

No one speaks.

No one moves.

I can hear the creaks of the house, the wind hitting the windowpanes, and the accelerated breathing of my family.

"Well, I've captured the house, boys," she says to her men with a giggle that matches Ember's to a T, right along with that wave. "I am Ember and Emmett's maternal grandmother."

Em's mouth is opening and shutting like a fucking fish and Emmett looks like he's about to pass out.

She finally removes her sunglasses, and I can see it in the shape of her face, so much like Ember and Emmett's, but it's her eyes that finally sell me. They are Debra's eyes, a dark, chocolate brown.

Em sees it and covers her mouth as she looks over at me. Her face pales as her body begins to tremble, her eyes bulging from her head. I stand and immediately make my way over to her. She needs me, and I will always be there when she feels weak. Family makes Em weak in the best possible way. It gives balance to all her fierce strength.

I gather her up in my arms and sit in her chair before placing her on my lap.

"Yes, you're Sharla's boy." Jenna nods as she smiles. "Rebecca would be proud to know her daughter ended up with you."

"You don't look like your wedding photo." Emmett is the first to speak, his voice hoarse.

"No, I wouldn't. I've had work done to look unrecognizable." She lifts the scarf off her head and points to a scar running from her ear to her collarbone. "I've had many enemies in Whitsborough because I killed my husband. After he tried to kill me of course."

"I'm so lost." Em shakes her head as she rests it against my shoulder.

"Bear with me," Jenna says as she smoothes down her mahogany hair. "I've never told this story before." She takes another sip of her water and looks at Emmett. "I'm sorry you never knew your mother. You are so very much like my oldest daughter. It makes my heart ache with how much I miss her. Rebecca was eight years old when I noticed how closely Jack would watch her. At first, I chalked it up to her enigmatic personality and how much she loved life. Debra was different. She was an old soul in a young girl's body. She was practical while Rebecca was innocent."

Em whimpers a little, too quiet for anyone but me to hear, and I kiss her forehead, hoping to ease some of the pain. She's been acting strong, thinking I didn't notice how grief has been leaving her shoulders hunched and her eyes hollow.

"Rebecca would trust just about anyone," Jenna continues, a nostalgic look on her face. "I had to keep a close watch on her with gardeners and pool boys because she could've been swayed to do just about anything. Sometimes Debra acted like the older sister despite being three years younger. They worshiped their father, not seeing the monster that lurked just beneath the surface, and I felt trapped, unable to stand up to him. Jack liked to have his way, and if anyone stood up to him—especially a woman— he had no problem knocking them back into place, whether it was with the use of his fists or his harsh, degrading words. Over time, I learned I had to remain silent or die trying to change him. So I waited until I could strike. That moment came when I found out Jack was having an affair... with Constance Germaine."

She's looking right at me as I stare back at her, willing her to tell me she's joking.

"It's true." She nods sadly. "I'm sure they planned her husband's death together as well. I can't prove that though, it's just a theory." Her words are like knives as they stab through my chest, hitting my heart in fatal strikes.

"My mother told me about my grandfather's death and how they came to work here for you." There's no way my nana would ever want to kill her husband, Jenna is confused or she's fucking lying, trying to paint a believable picture. Then she looks at me with sadness, her eyes glossing over as she presses a hand to her heart, and something inside me tells me she's being honest.

"Sharla." She smiles wistfully. "Just as much a daughter to me as my very own. She was as sharp as a whistle and just as rambunctious as Rebecca. She had so much attitude and would put anyone in their place. I loved her."

"Yep." Em snickers, breaking the heavy feeling inside my chest and bringing a smile to my face. "That's her."

I snort and kiss the side of Em's head. It looks like she's slowly coming out of her shock. Travis and Adri are so engrossed in the story that they haven't moved an inch since Jenna started, but Emmett still looks skeptical.

"Constance and Jack were in love and that's why I had my suspicions about what happened to her husband. Well, as much in love as Jack could be, which isn't much I'm afraid. He also liked to use her as a punching bag, but the woman continued to love him. Gradually, I backed off and tried to become a part of the shadows in the house while they played the married couple. They hid it well in front of our children. Constance never allowed Sharla up to the main house, and Jack remained hidden most of the time unless it was to groom our oldest daughter. I foolishly thought the man would let me go because he had a new love interest, and I broached him with the idea."

"Your mother never mentioned anything about this?" Emmett asks me as Jenna takes a drink of her water. I shake my head as Emmett slowly turns back to his grandmother, waiting for the rest of her story.

"I wanted to leave, but I wanted to take my girls with me. By this time, Rebecca was starting high school and slowly withdrawing from her father as she became a young woman. This angered him more and more each day. He berated her constantly, calling her a whore and chasing down any young man that dared to step on our land. Sometimes even brandishing a shotgun."

"We heard about that," Travis adds, his head shaking

with disbelief. "Everyone talks about how crazy he was."

"He was certifiable," Jenna agrees with a scoff. "He wouldn't hear of my leaving, and he especially wouldn't let me take Rebecca, although I could take Debra. I became enraged, and he cut my throat with his hunting knife, miraculously missing my artery." She fingers the scar as her hand trembles. "I would've bled out on that floor if Constance hadn't found me and stitched me up. That's when I knew I would never be free of him as long as he was alive. So that's when I started my plans to kill Jack Craven. It took a few years to plan and I watched my girls grow, and in Rebecca's case, fall in love. Raphael wasn't who I would have chosen for her, but he was a lesser evil than her father, or so I thought. I will always bear the guilt of my part in their meeting."

"How so?" Emmett asks as he leans on the table.

"I knew about the business relationship between both of your grandfathers. Antonio Torres was going to help my husband fake his and Rebecca's death so they could have a life away from me together. I couldn't let that happen, and when I gained the courage to call the man, I found out his son, Raphael, had taken over. In a sense, I was sheltered in my life here in Whitsborough. I didn't have any dealings with Jack's business associates and I was never accustomed to backhand dealings. So at the time, I didn't know that Raphael had killed his father and brothers just to take over the Rampage."

"The night he told me that, along with confessing to my mother's murder, altered me forever," Ember confesses as Jenna's eyes soften on her.

"I know, dear," Jenna sympathizes. "He told me he preferred to be called Ray and promised he would help me kill my husband. He agreed to come to Whitsborough and help with the planning, even orchestrating it. He came and he met Rebecca. I can only imagine he fell in love with her as so many others had. Suddenly, our terms had changed. He would help me kill my husband only if Rebecca could go back with him to New York. I made him agree to eventually take me in as well."

"What?" Ember straightens in my lap as her hands hit the table. Jenna holds up her hand and shakes her head.

"He was my only option to get out of here, and Rebecca's too. I needed her away from her leering father. What would you have done if it was your child?" Jenna's voice rises as Ember falls back against my chest and nods her head. "Rebecca ran away as soon as her father found out about her rape—which nearly killed me—and accused her of being the town whore. Robert Greene had just started his reign of terror in Whitsborough, and my daughter had been one of his first victims. I only found out about him years later and I was happy to hear he killed himself."

"I killed him actually," Em says proudly, and Jenna smiles.

"I know."

EMBER

The more I look at her, the more I see Aunt Debby. Her eyes are the same and the way her mouth curves into a grin is identical. It makes my chest constrict with how much I miss my aunt and uncle, and mother too, but I'm waiting for her to explain her part in their deaths. How could she kill her own daughter?

"It wasn't too long after that I was ready to put our plan into motion, and Raphael sent me the men to help. By this time, Jack and I had found out Rebecca was pregnant, and he disowned her for good. I had to play along with the farce because I was planning on faking my death with my husband and I needed Rebecca to believe it." Jenna's eyes cloud over with sadness as she exhales, her chest expanding on her next deep breath.

"She was his prisoner," I snap as the memories of what Raph told me so long ago come flooding back.

"I didn't know she was being held against her will. That I traded her away from one monster only to deliver her into the arms of another. It's my biggest regret." Her head falls as her chin hits her chest, shame rolling off her.

"Shouldn't your biggest regret be killing your daughter, Debra, and her husband? They were my parents, loved me unconditionally, and gave me a home," I tell her as the pounding inside my chest intensifies.

"Killed my daughter? Once you become a mother, you'll see how impossible that is, no matter the consequences." She drinks some water and continues, "Let me finish and then you can decide whether you want me to leave, and we'll continue our game of who can catch whom, or we join forces and seek revenge."

I wave her on and cuddle back against Vin's chest.

"Jack, Constance, and I had lunch every Friday at the country club. It was something we did to keep up appearances. I was to look like the doting wife, and Constance was our hired companion. It was disgusting and I hated every second of it, but that was the way of life in Whitsborough. I tried to warn her, and I even told her to stay home, but she thought I was just trying to move in on my own husband. Jack had her so brainwashed that she actually thought he loved her. Even after everything he'd done."

"What did he do to her?" Vin asks, his voice sounding deadly low and filled with creeping anger.

"I'll get to that. Trust me, son. Everything is so tangled together, and this is the first time I am unraveling it for anybody." She looks at me and smiles, so much like Aunt Debby. "I am doing this for you because I don't want to see anything happen to you. I made some big promises."

I don't have the slightest idea what she's talking about, but all I know is I want to hear more about my family.

I nod to her and she carries on, "Raphael sent Trent to me—who at the time was a fresh addition to the Rampage at sixteen—and a few other men."

"Wait," Emmett interrupts. "You know Trent?"

"Yes. Trent and his family mean a lot to me. I survived because of him." She looks at Emmett and smiles. "I helped his family get out of the cartel and gave them jobs to help me hunt down the head of the cartel."

"Trent is a double agent?" He slaps his hands on the table, the betrayal clear on his face. "Is he the one who gave Wade's guy the knife that stabbed Ember?" I'll give him this, he connected things a lot faster than I did and now my mind is reeling with all the things Trent could have done to protect Talia and betray us.

"He loves you very much," she assures Emmett and then looks at me. "He wasn't the one who put the knife in that cage. If I can continue, we will get through everything."

"Let's hear the rest," I say to Emmett, eager to hear more about our family.

He nods, still looking skeptical and I don't blame him. All of this can be intricately woven lies and we're actually sitting at the table with our greatest enemy.

"Thank you," she murmurs as she shifts in her seat. "That day will always be a hard one for me. Like I said at that time, I wasn't a murderer. Honestly, I'm still not." Her voice shakes a bit. She's either being genuine right now or my acting skills come straight from her. "We got in our Rolls Royce because your grandfather loved to flash our wealth, and drove the ten minutes to the country club. About five minutes in, we were sideswiped by a large industrial van, causing us to roll a few times into the ditch. Your grandfather wasn't much for seat belts—deeming himself above death— but Constance and I were, thankfully. I couldn't tell you if he survived the initial crash, but if he did, he wouldn't have survived much longer. He was pretty beaten up. Constance was alive and screaming for Jack as I remember undoing her seat belt and begging her to get out of the vehicle with me. She refused."

Vin's arms tighten around me as he sucks in a deep breath, his chest moving against my cheek. It can't be easy hearing this about his grandmother.

"I tried forcing her, but Constance was much larger than me. We ended up struggling, me trying to get her out and she just hating me. I knew we didn't have much time, that the second phase of my plan was coming and there could be no stalling. I tried to drag her, but she kept trying to get to the front seat to Jack. Us lowly women were to always ride in the back, never up front with him." She wipes at the tears escaping her eyes, her long, red nails flicking the offending moisture to the side.

"What a sick bastard," Vin snarls as I rub my hand along his arm.

"Finally, I got ahold of her dress and yanked her back. She fell into the backseat with my effort and her body hit the side door. There was a piece of protruding metal and it sunk easily into the back of her neck. She died instantly." A sob erupts from her throat as she covers her mouth with her hand, more tears skating over her cheeks.

"So she didn't die in the accident as my mother was told," Vin mutters, his heart beating quickly against my ear.

"What you won't read in those reports given to you by McKay is that they covered the entire thing up. They didn't think it necessary to tell the town every detail because it was gruesome. They also covered up this next part." She lifts her bottle, but it's empty, so Adri gets up to get her another. "Thank you." She smiles at her like a sweet old woman and drinks some. "Trent dragged me out of that car, even though the deal was for me to get out or I would die as well. I was just so overcome with grief at what I'd done."

"Why would you be so overcome with grief?" Vin questions her. "Didn't you hate her?"

"God, no!" She shakes her head vehemently. "I'm not telling this well. Constance was my only friend in Whitsborough. Yes, she hated our situation, but she knew I didn't love my husband. She also knew he would never leave me and marry her. That's just how it was. For him to marry me, I had to suppress my heritage and was accepted only because I was white-passing enough."

"White passing enough?" Travis echoes.

"Yes, I am actually a Spaniard. My maiden name is Talia, and my family sent me here to Whitsborough to marry into a rich, aristocratic family. Jack's family knew he was a deviant, just as the whole town knew, and they wouldn't find him a wife anywhere close by, but they also wanted that wife to come with wealth and good breeding."

"You were a mail-order bride," Adri says, and I snort.

"Essentially," Talia answers and fires me a look to

behave. I squirm in Vin's lap because that look is so much like the one my mother would use on me. "I was heartbroken as I watched Trent and his men douse the car in gasoline and set it aflame, but I couldn't give up, I had to continue."

"There were three bodies in that car," I interject as I sit straighter in Vin's lap. "And your dental records matched one of the bodies."

"Right!" She snaps her fingers and opens her mouth wide. She's missing four molars in the back of her mouth. "These are all crowns. I had my teeth removed in a painful procedure a month before the accident. I paid the dentist a hefty sum to give me the teeth, and over the span of a month, I had crowns installed. The third body? I didn't know who the woman was because Trent had brought the cadaver himself with my loose teeth in her mouth. Sounds strange, right? That the police found a skull with only a few teeth? They glossed right over it. Whitsborough police were so amateur and just downright lazy."

"Still are," I agree as my teeth gnash together with what I've recently endured.

"Then I left for New York that same day with Trent and a new name. I dropped the Laurann and Craven, then assumed my very popular maiden name."

"Our mother was still alive then," I say to her. "Did you go to her?"

"I did." She nods, and I watch as this formidable enemy I've been chasing for a year tears up in front of me. "I essentially traded one daughter for another. Rebecca needed me more than Debra, and I needed Debra to believe I was actually dead. She inherited the family fortune and married Scott. So believe me, being out of her life was for the best."

"I doubt Aunt Debby felt the same," I retort as I envision my aunt as a younger woman, scared and alone. Sure, she had Uncle Scott and Sharla, but that's nothing compared to having a mother.

"Maybe." She shrugs, her face looking forlorn. "Rebecca was pregnant when I got to New York, huge with you twins growing in her belly. I found out that same day that she was just as much a prisoner with Raphael as she was with her father, and it broke my heart. So I had yet another nearly impossible task in front of me. I now had to escape that place with Rebecca and two newborn babies."

"It's true then, our father was never really in love with our mother," Emmett cuts in quietly.

"Oh, no. Quite the opposite. I believe he loved her, but he was also deranged, and his love equated to obsession. Rebecca had just found out that Raphael was not monogamous and he never would be. He had a six-year-old son already from a teenage pregnancy. The mother was nowhere to be found, and according to Trent, they disposed of her. I'm guessing she was murdered. We also found out just what the Rampage did for a living. They recruited prostitutes, organized illegal fighting rings,"—for this, she looks directly at me—"and pushed drugs all over New York. Raphael was essentially setting up his own cartel, and he was looking to expand with a new organization called The Heads."

My heart gallops inside my chest at the mention of the Head Organization. I'm one of them.

"I know you are one of them," she says, as if reading my very thoughts. "I heard you stopped the prostitution, child sex trafficking, and drug distribution in Toronto. I was so proud of you for that but also worried. With doing that, a lot of attention was focused on you and this little town in Canada."

"I'm used to it now." I lift my chin as she gives me a sad smile.

"I know you are. Your mother and I found out a lot about Raphael's dealings because he would come talk to her, believing she couldn't leave, and I began dating someone who was very close to Raphael's finances and money laundering. His name was Emmanuel Vergara, and he was kind but also corrupt. He had strong ties to government officials and politicians sat in his pocket. Your mother and I listened quietly to both men, gathering all the intel we would need. I obviously couldn't be involved with the takedown because my new persona could so easily be blown apart. Your mother was tough though, and I smuggled her a burner phone I found in Emmanuel's office. She found an agent in the FBI who worked with her for months building a case."

"Which would ultimately end in her death," I mumble under my breath as Vin kisses my head, letting me know he heard me. "Why didn't she tell me about you at all?"

"Because I eventually became the enemy." Her mouth turns down as she takes a deep breath and toys with her fingernails. "It'll become clear in a bit. The day she gave birth to you two was an emotional one. She was instantly in love and so was I. There you two were, completely identical but with such contrasting personalities. Ember, you were intense from day one. You were quiet and observant, watching every single thing. Emmett, you were loud and demanding, wanting everyone's attention."

"Nothing's changed there." Travis snickers as Emmett shoots him a glare.

"Wait," Emmett cuts in, his eyes moving from Travis to Jenna. "You can settle something once and for all. Who was born first?" I gasp as my eyes widen on Emmett, his face slowly turning to look at me as his mouth curves upward. "This is it, little sister." He smirks deviously.

"Ember was born first, you were eleven minutes later." Jenna startles as I let out a loud whoop, and Emmett falls back into his seat with a long groan.

"*Little brother*," I taunt him as Jenna purses her lips to keep from grinning.

"Some things will never change, because like now, you were both a handful back then, and Rebecca was often so exhausted that the conversations with the agent fell to me. Your mother didn't want him knowing about the babies, and I agreed with her. Trusting people around us had become hard. She'd given birth in that compound with doctors employed by the Rampage. They weren't poor doctors, the opposite really. They did a great job and your mother recovered quickly, but she still wasn't allowed to leave the compound and doctors would come to her and you two regularly for check-ups. Finally, with stolen documents and our testimonials, the FBI moved in on your father and he was arrested. They turned the Rampage upside down, and I had to get you babies and your mother out of there, but that wasn't proving easy. Calen had taken over in his place and the man despised anyone who was weak, especially women."

"Tell me something I don't know," Emmett mutters, and I watch with shock as Talia reaches for his hand and Emmett doesn't pull away.

"I am sorry we left you with that man. I will always blame myself for that." She pulls her hand back and looks at me. "The night we were supposed to leave the compound, Rebecca only had Ember with her. Ember was fussy whenever she was with anyone but her mother, and Emmett really couldn't care less who he was with as long as they fed him. Raphael hired a nanny, and the woman was kind. Her name was—"

"Cassidy or Mama Cass as I knew her," Emmett interjects, getting a faraway look in his eyes.

"Yes, Cassidy was a great nanny, and she would take Emmett during the nights to help Rebecca sleep, but Ember wouldn't leave her mother. It was the same on this particular night, and there was no better time to leave. Rebecca was insistent we both go to get Emmett, but I knew that would alert the guards all over the place. So I promised her I would get Emmett, and she was to leave the way we planned. She did as I asked and trusted me to get you, Emmett," she confesses while looking at him sadly. "I failed, obviously. Emmanuel was looking for me that night because a few of the documents the FBI showed Raphael could only have come from me."

My heart grows heavy inside my chest as I stare at my twin's profile, wishing it all could've ended differently and we escaped together that night.

"He found me, captured me, and let Calen torture me for information for three months. When I wouldn't break, Emmanuel deemed me worthy to be by his side. They finally released me from my cell, and when I went looking for you, you were long gone. Emmanuel assured me you were with the nanny, but I could never see you. I tried for months to find out where you could be, and I tried to get in contact with Rebecca, but failed at both. Thankfully, I left some money for Rebecca before I came to New York, but it wasn't nearly enough. I knew I had to find her and help her, especially with a newborn." She takes a sip of her water and brushes her hair back from her face as she shakily releases a breath. "Every time I asked Emmanuel where you were, he would just say the same things, that you were fine and doing well. We eventually left the compound, and I moved into Emmanuel's estate. I found out he had a wife, a son, and another baby on the way. You could imagine my surprise since he and I were together in the carnal sense."

"Ew." Emmett shudders.

"Oh, knock it off." She waves Emmett off. "You're over here with a boyfriend *and* a girlfriend. You're getting it a lot more than I am."

"Ew!" he reiterates, and Travis chuckles.

I just want to hear the rest of this story so I can decide if it's okay to relax or plan how to take this woman down.

Chapter Twenty-Six

She has the same sarcastic, dry humor as her grandchildren. I keep seeing all the similarities and the look in her eyes each time she stares at one of them. It really tells me everything I need to know. We fucked up. We've been chasing down the wrong enemy for nearly two years, and the thought of all that wasted time is exhausting.

"Vincent looks like maybe he needs a break," Jenna suggests with a small smile.

"I feel exhausted, but it's not because of your story." I shake my head. "I believe you are who you say you are, but I can't seem to figure out why we played this game for years. Why didn't you reveal yourself to us before now?"

Her eyes widen as a smile ghosts her mouth. "Thank you. I didn't come forward because of Carmelo and the confusion surrounding us."

Em is staring up at me, and I finally lower my gaze to hers. "Seriously?"

"Yes," I answer honestly before kissing her nose. "But I need more explanations for the tragedies that happened and were blamed on you," I say to Jenna.

"I promise we're close." She nervously grabs a piece of her hair, her fingers raking through the strands.

"Please continue," Travis presses, knowing we need answers quickly.

"Emmanuel set me up in his house and I played mistress for a few months. It was weird and uncomfortable, but I was protected. He gave me updates on you, Emmett, and also on my daughter and Ember. Everything seemed to be fine, and I was patiently waiting for my time to get away. I was still a prisoner in every sense. His son was four years old when I arrived, and I took an immediate liking to him. His mother was pregnant with their second child, and from what I could gather, suffered from depression. She didn't want to spend too much time with him, and I took on that maternal role. Carlos was a handful, but he was extremely intelligent."

"Hold on," Em interrupts her. "Carlos wasn't your biological son? I have a file that states otherwise, right down to the scars on your belly from a cesarean section."

I watch as Jenna stands up and lifts her shirt. There are a few scars running vertically over her torso, but none that match a cesarean procedure.

"Again, you received a forged document. That file originally belonged to Emmanuel's wife." Her tone sounds a little exasperated as she shifts once again in her seat.

"Who would forge these documents?" I press her, needing more than a brush-off for answers.

"I'm getting there. Sorry if it's slow. I want to make sure you have all the facts." She pats down her hair. "I guess I can skip a few years at this point. Emmanuel's wife gave birth to her second son, Anthony, and when he was three years old, she killed herself. Do I know for sure she actually killed herself and wasn't killed? No, but I was in love with Emmanuel by then and believed everything he told me, even about my family being completely fine. He told me he was sending anonymous envelopes of cash to Rebecca and that Emmett was receiving the best education and care. I knew in the back of my mind that Rebecca wouldn't rest until she found Emmett, but I also let myself believe that if he was well cared for, then surely raising one child was enough for her to handle. I know I was wrong, but it helped me sleep at night."

"As a mother, you should've known that Rebecca was most likely tortured every day she was away from her son," I snap, anger lacing my words.

"Yes, deep down I knew she would never give up. I want to say I agonized about it, that I wanted Rebecca to claim her son back, but I'd be lying. The years of torture and captivity had hardened me. I no longer cared about familial ties, and I grew to just look out for myself."

"I understand that," Em concedes, even though she's been through so much and still holds her family in high regard. "But I can't help the resentment I feel for the life Mom and I lived because of it. Or Emmett for that matter. His life was even worse."

"I had no idea, and you're right, I should've cared," she admits with a nod of her head. "After Emmanuel's wife died, he wanted to be married, but I convinced him they would notice our connection, and I couldn't further my career to benefit us both. It was his idea for me to join Congress. I leaped up in ranks and held a lot of power. I amassed money and slowly hired people to work for me. I wanted information on those who made my life hell. I planted spies everywhere. Here in Whitsborough and also New York. I had people infiltrate the Rampage and kept older affiliates under my thumb, like Trent and a few others. I moved out of Emmanuel's home and took his sons with me. There wasn't much he could do because I became too powerful, even for him. I let his sons believe their father and I were married but separated. Anthony has always been close to me, but Carlos was tougher to convince. He grew apart from me and his father. He began running in the wrong crowds and doing things I couldn't control without attracting the media's eye and disparaging my reputation." She exhales a sigh of regret, her eyes sad as she falls bad into her memories.

"He was an asshole," Em states as I fight to keep the grin off my face.

"I know you searched him out, Ember, and it surprised me to learn you let him live. Surprised and relieved. I will always believe Carlos had the potential to be great, but his resentment for his father and me caused him to do things he thought would hurt us. I became cocky in my new persona and thought my cover was infallible, but I was wrong. Someone figured out who I was and my connection to Whitsborough. Someone who knew what I did here and wanted revenge, but they didn't just want revenge on me, they wanted it on the girl who was causing ripples all the way from Canada to New York. This girl they figured out to be my granddaughter. They got to Carlos and convinced him I was corrupt, I killed his real mother, and eventually I would kill him too. They asked him to grab Vincent and try to get information out of him about how much Ember Craven knew."

"Who's 'they'?" Ember asks, now leaning forward with interest.

"At the time, I had my suspicions, but I wasn't sure. I only just recently found out with the help of your brother, Carmelo. I promise I'm getting to that, but first, I want to explain all the events that had you convinced it was me. The retaliation for Carlos' death, the guard who was murdered and had the message carved into him was not by my hand. They set it up to look like me to get you off their case. You were closing in on them and they needed you to change your trajectory." Jenna is taking her time getting to the point and I can sense Em becoming impatient.

"And?" she pushes, her eyes riveted on her grandmother.

"Your aunt and uncle—my sweet daughter, Debra—being murdered was not by me. It was also this person. Again, you were getting too close to the secrets here in Whitsborough and they set the whole thing up. I mourned my daughter and tried my best not to blame you." She looks at Em, her sad eyes filling with tears. "I knew what you were doing was for the greater good, and anything that extreme will always have collateral damage. They sucked your brother, Carm, into believing I was his mother for the longest time to cause a rift between you two and foster the intent of distrust. You were becoming impenetrable, and it was nearly impossible to stop you. When you three went to Spain, following my coattails, Carm had done everything to keep you one step behind me. Don't hate him for that. He truly believed I was his mother."

"Did you ever speak to Carm face-to-face?" Emmett asks her.

"Yes," she admits, her mouth pressing into a thin line. "For the first time last month, just before he came here to help you, Ember. I told him everything I could without telling him everything. Mostly, I told him about what I finally discovered, and he was suddenly in a rush to get here."

"He wrote me a letter, apologizing for everything he did wrong. There were a few pages he left me I didn't understand, but now I do. You moved a few kids around with your Love the Tots agency and he highlighted a note that said you took a child from Whitsborough. Who?" Em's voice becomes laced with irritation as the answers she seeks are close, yet still out of reach.

"Almost there. First, let's talk about your fight with Wade. Did you believe he planted that knife?" Jenna directs her question to Em with a tip of her head.

"I had my doubts that Wade did it." She rubs her forehead. "But I couldn't see any other way."

"Without implicating someone close," Jenna finishes the thought.

"Right," Em mutters, her back stiffening as Emmett looks between them, his face contorting with confusion.

"Carm gave the man the knife," Jenna reveals, and we all tense with shock. All of us but Em.

"I thought he did." Her shoulders slump. "I was hoping I was wrong."

"What?" Emmett turns on Em, his voice filled with outrage.

"When I questioned Wade and even when I fought him in the cage, he was genuine about not planting the knife. I continued to fight him because he wasn't a good person," Em replies, her voice soft to ease the pain of her words.

"Ember," Emmett croaks, his face filling with agony. "He was our brother."

"I know, Emmett, and I still love him regardless. If it wasn't for him, Vin and I could've died." Her hands press to her chest as her voice breaks with emotion. "I will forever be grateful for him and what he did to protect us."

"He admitted to me in a tearful confession about planting the knife. He was going to confess to you what he did, but then the town hall debacle happened. He did it because I gave him an order, or so he was made to believe. This person threatened to kill Emmett if he didn't. He said he knew you would still come out the victor," Jenna says while smiling at Em.

"Think that covers everything." Em slaps her hands to the table, finally meeting the end of her patience. "I'm ready to learn who my opponent is."

"Opponents," Jenna corrects.

EMBER

"Opponents," Talia corrects me, her eyes boring into me with intensity.

"Spit it out," I growl at her as my hands curl into fists on top of the table. As much as I've been thankful to hear her side of the story, I'm tired of waiting around for the answers.

"It all started with Constance and Jack," she starts as Emmett falls back into his chair with a groan.

"Another story?" Emmett huffs, and I feel his fucking pain.

"A short, interconnecting one." She gives us both an apologetic smile before continuing. "Something happened between Constance and Jack that, if it had become known, would ruin us all. They fell pregnant."

"My nana had another baby?" Vin asks, his voice filled with skepticism. "But my mother would've known."

"It was soon after your grandfather was killed, and they did well with hiding it from everyone. When the child was born, he was five years younger than your mother," Talia explains to Vin as I stare at her in shock.

"Obviously he's dead, right? Or else I would know my uncle," Vin argues as his body stiffens behind me. It's a huge revelation, and the hardest one to believe yet.

"You know him very well, Vincent." Talia's eyes widen as she continues to answer him. "The child was born, and we, of course, could not keep the child around. We couldn't pass him off as Constance's because her husband was dead, and looking at the child, you couldn't mistake his uncanny likeness to Jack. They gave him up to an orphanage, and he spent many years in group homes and foster homes until finally, a nice family adopted him when he was twelve. You see, Mary-Beth and Gregory Moore couldn't have children,

"

so they turned to adoption."

My heart fucking stops before it ricochets off my ribs. "Chief Moore?"

"Yes, William Moore, named after Constance's deceased husband. Strange but true." Talia grimaces as my lungs cease to draw in air. Vin is a statue behind me, and when I turn to look at him, his face is pale with disbelief.

"I thought his name was Bill?" Emmett asks, but I'm too fucking disturbed to make fun of him right now.

"Bill is short for William," Adri tells him as she pats his hand.

The room is just buzzing around us. We're all so quiet, I can hear the hum of the fridge and the whirl of the ceiling fan above our heads. Still, Vin hasn't moved a muscle.

"He's my uncle," he finally breaks the silence.

"Yes," Talia answers him. "But no one else knows that in this town. Only us in this room and himself. He became chief and got his hands on his closed adoption papers. He's known this whole time who you were," she reveals to me and then turns to Vin, "and how he's related to you."

"He's our uncle too," I mutter to Emmett as his face turns a weird shade of green.

"You and Vin?" He's trying to find a connection in his head, which looks like a bad case of constipation by looking at him.

"No." I shake my head. "We're not related."

"You said *opponents*," Travis reminds her, bringing us back around to our original purpose.

"I did." Talia faces me once more. "This may be a hard pill to swallow."

"None of it has been easy. I can handle it," I assure her as I rub a hand along Vin's arm, soothing his tumultuous mood.

"I recently found more on William and knew I needed you out of prison and safely at home. So I found surveillance that was deleted by William in his computer's trash bin at work. It showed him shooting Andrew point-blank, and then he deleted another video of a house that gave a perfect view of Andrew Cox's brain-splattered head resting against the glass before you even got to his car. I've kept the shooting one to myself but used the latter to have you acquitted. I'll give it to you if you want his justice served in a courtroom, but I think I know you well enough that you would want to serve your own particular brand of justice, am I right?"

"Yes," I answer empathically, my teeth clenched.

"William's life hasn't been a walk in the park. His foster parents died when he was seventeen in a tragic robbery gone wrong, and that's what encouraged William to join the force. The actual story is he killed them to inherit their riches. He was soon to be a father, and the mother was a pitiful woman. A prostitute by the name of Tonya." Once again, the room around me ceases to exist as shock rips through me.

"Marlana's mother?" I glance up at Vin. "Did you know Marlana had a brother?"

Before he can answer, Talia cuts in, "No one knew. His good friend, Robert, put him in touch with me, and I took the child once he was born, placing him in foster care. A good group home in New York City. They were a little crowded, but I didn't have a family who wanted a baby boy at the time. He continued to flourish in the home and stayed there even when he was past the legal age to leave. He helped with his foster siblings and took to one in particular. A troubled boy who reminded him of himself. His name was Jason." My mouth dries out as my brain tries to catch up on the information overload.

"Jason?" My mind is running at high speed as it tries

to connect every fucking dot.

"Thomas Williams. I gave him that last name so his father would forever know who he actually belonged to." She brushes her hand over her hair as she gives me a pointed look.

"Tommy?" His name is heavy on my tongue, and the grief I've been tamping down threatens to surge.

"Yes." Talia looks at me sadly. "It's actually amazing you guys found each other."

"He's not my opponent," I retort with a sarcastic scoff, thinking I've caught her in a lie. "Tommy is dead and buried in my mausoleum."

"Is he?" she asks as her head tips to the side.

"I saw Carm shoot a bullet into his skull. I saw the blood on the mat," I snap, hating reliving my memories.

"Yes, all that happened. Carmelo grazed his skull right here." She points to her right temple and drags her finger to the back of her head. "Carm thought he was dead and asked one of his men to drop his body off at the foster home to be found. The man he asked was actually one of *my* men and he called me immediately because he knew who Tommy was in relation to me. He told me that Tommy was actually still alive and would recover from the wound, although it looked bad. I asked him to bring me the boy, then I called the foster home to tell them I found Tommy a job overseas. I housed him and called doctors in to assess him and make sure he was healing fine."

"I don't believe it." I stand up from Vin's lap, anger making my limbs vibrate. "Tommy would've come to me. We have been best friends since we were children. He wouldn't stay away from me." Rage begins to boil inside of me as the vibrations intensify. Grandmother or not, I will fucking kill her and her men if she continues to push this narrative.

"He would if he knew his family story, he would if he knew you were trying to kill his father, and he would if he knew that your family wanted him dead," Talia counters, her brows lifting.

"I have his ashes in my crypt!" I yell, unable to keep the emotions at bay. "The foster home is the one who told us where he was buried!"

"That woman works for me." She winces as she wraps her hand around her throat. "I asked her to tell everyone that he was dead, to give him a fresh shot at a new life overseas. I provided a fake funeral for his foster home siblings and even buried ashes."

"Whose fucking ashes are in my crypt?!" I scream, and Vin clasps my hand, trying desperately to ground me.

"Anthony's dog died of cancer that year and we had him cremated." She looks remorseful but also not at the same time.

"That's fucking messed up," I breathe out as the rage begins to slip away and hurt seeps through me. I drop Vin's hand to pace the kitchen. "So where is he then?"

"Trent has him held at the Rampage compound. Ember, he's not the same man he was before. He knows who his father is, he knows where his family is from, and he knows you want his father dead. If I let him go, I can assure you, he will find his father and they will both try to kill you." Talia really believes what she's saying, but I know Tommy.

My mind is shifting between believing her and wanting to knock her out. Actually, I just want to knock her out. People I trusted kept so many things from me, and now my fists want so badly to sink into flesh and watch it bleed.

"I can't believe that Tommy would want to harm me. He tried to save me from my father, he put my life before his! He told me to kill him to save my own life, that's not someone that would kill me," I argue as my hands fly over my head and my feet continue to walk a line back and forth.

"Em," Vin interjects. "Maybe the injury to the head changed him somehow. We can't be sure of anything."

"I agree, E," Travis cuts in. "I'm not risking your life like that. Head injuries are very unpredictable."

"He saved me from a burning building. My number was up that night, and if not for him, I wouldn't be here. I wouldn't know you! Any of you!" I look at each of them, willing them to understand. "He tried to get to me when he found out my psycho father was coming. They captured him, tortured him, and then killed him because of it. He accepted it, knowing he was protecting me."

"I'm with Ember." Adri stands up, her chin lifting with her admission. "Us girls have an intuition that boys don't. If he's pissed, then only she can fix it. He's her family. She needs to go to him."

"I love you." My vision is suddenly clouded by tears at her decision to stand with me.

"I love you." Her response is immediate. "I'm staying here to help Sharla with the restaurant. One of you needs to stay to monitor Moore." She looks at the boys. "And then the rest of you get to New York and find out what you can about Tommy. He's family, and he deserves to be with us."

I rush over and wrap my arms around her. Adri sees what I do in the name of our family and trusts me wholeheartedly.

"Just please be careful," she whispers in my ear.

"I will," I promise her as I squeeze her a little tighter.

"I'll stay here with my men and keep a close watch on William and make sure your family is safe. I can assume you received the intel I sent for where William is being kept under a protective order?" Talia interjects.

"Yes, I received it." It's hard to trust someone you've hated for so long, but she's proving to be on our side.

"I'll stay too." Travis stands, and I am instantly relieved. I wanted him to, but I didn't want to have to ask. He's someone I can trust to look after everyone and make the most logical decisions in my absence.

"Thank you." I nod to him.

"Looks like we're taking a road trip, bro," Emmett declares as he slaps Vin's shoulder.

Vin looks at me and raises a brow. I know he's wondering if I believe all of this, and now, with Trent firmly under Talia's thumb, we have no idea what we could be walking into at the compound.

"I know you doubt me, and it's the smart thing to do. I can only tell you I am being genuine. If I wanted you dead at any point in the last few years, I could have done it easily." Jenna's words ring true, but I still can't completely get rid of my doubts. Like she said, I have to see it for myself.

The thought of Tommy being alive leaves me excited and scared at the same time. If he is alive, I can understand why he'd hate me. Because of me, his life was completely uprooted.

"I need to get there quickly." I stride out of the kitchen and pass by Talia, looking her in the eyes as I threaten, "If at any point I learn this is all a grand lie, I will completely enjoy gutting you open and playing with your intestines... while you're still alive."

"I wouldn't expect anything less," she answers with a grim look.

One of her men growls at my words, and I turn on him. "I'll tie you down to watch. Remember whose house you're in."

Emmett snickers as he lifts his arms. "Why don't I show you three out?" Then he looks at Talia with a smirk. "If you need anything while we are gone, you can call Travis and Adri. Okay, Grandma?"

I smirk when she visibly shudders. "We'll have to work on a better title," she grumbles as she follows Emmett to the front door.

"Bye, Grandma!" He waves exaggeratedly as he watches her leave.

"If all of this is true, how much do you think she'll regret having us as grandkids?" I ask him with a chuckle.

"We should take bets on when she'll stage her own death again just to get away from us." He snorts.

"With you constantly hounding her… Two weeks," I mutter.

"With you coming home every other day coated in someone's blood… One week," he retorts.

"With how annoying you both are… this is the last you will see of her," Vin interjects, making us both laugh.

"Do you really believe her?" His green eyes meet mine as he shrugs.

"For some reason, I do." He smiles. "I see a lot of Debra in her."

"Yeah, me too," I agree.

"Let's get ready and on the road. We have a long drive ahead of us," Emmett suggests as he starts up the stairs.

"It's going to be weird going to the compound without seeing Carm." My words slip from my mouth as my chest burns.

"I know." Vin wraps his arm around my shoulders and kisses my forehead.

"Trent says he's waiting for us." Emmett holds up his phone. "Looks like Talia called him beforehand."

"I figured she would," I reply with a shrug.

I'm eager to get there, nervous to discover everything, and scared to face the first person I ever trusted. When my family only consisted of my mother, Tommy was the first to break my walls, and I trusted him with everything. Even my life.

The same can be said for him. He grew up without a proper family, and when he and I met, his walls crumpled for me too. I was his little sister in every sense of the word, and my mother accepted him as her own. Now that I think back on it, she was probably trying to fill the space Emmett's disappearance left behind.

"Tell us about him," Emmett says when he notices I'm deep in thought. "I can tell you're worried. Talk it out."

"Tommy's group home was three houses down from my apartment complex when I was six. It was a shady part of the projects, but we all looked out for one another. Just because we were poor didn't mean we were criminals. Some families worked around the clock to provide a roof over their heads. I know our mother did." I rub my hands together as I exhale, my eyes growing misty as I swallow the lump in my throat. I still have so much grieving to do.

"Being poor isn't the problem with the criminal system." Vin reaches over and grabs my hand.

"One day, I was left at my school's afternoon program. It was for parents who worked late and didn't have a sitter. We were at the local park and a bunch of rough-looking older kids showed up. We overheard them talking and found out they were from the group home. Anyway, I ended up falling from the top of the climbing bars and I really hurt my arm—thankfully it wasn't broken, because Mom wouldn't have been able to afford the bills—and the boy who helped me was Tommy. He didn't even think, he ran over to me and checked it out right away, bending it to make sure it wasn't broken."

Emmett chuckles from the backseat as Vin squeezes my fingers. "You've always spoken so highly of him. I can see why."

"The next day, he was back at the park again, but

this time without his tough-looking friends. He sat on a bench and watched all of us as we played. Afterward, he came to ask me about my arm. It went on like this for a week straight, and I could feel myself slowly warming up to him. Yes, he was a few years older, but I quickly saw that he was kind, and it just grew from there."

"Let's say everything that woman told us is true," Emmett says. "How do you want to handle this with Tommy?"

"The way we always handled disagreements... With a fight."

Chapter Twenty-Seven

Vin

The compound is quiet and looks like it's in mourning. Even the weather is gray and gloomy, a reflection of my trepidation about Tommy being back from the dead situation.

"Trent's on his way up," Emmett informs us as he opens the Hummer door.

We exit the vehicle and I keep a close eye on Em. She bottles everything up inside until it explodes, and I would say she's due for an eruption soon. If this Tommy truly is alive and well, I can see it being the one thing that sets her off or breaks her.

The garage-style door opens and we see a smirking Trent. Now that I know who he really works for, I can't help but feel like I never actually knew him to begin with.

"Boss!" he calls out to Em. "I guess I have someone here to see you."

Em strides forward, her steps sure and filled with a

purpose. When she stands in front of Trent, I almost choke as I watch her fist smash into his nose.

"Fuck!" Emmett yells and rushes forward.

I take my time, knowing my girl can take care of herself.

"What was that for?" Trent asks as he tips his head back to staunch the flow of blood.

"Did I break it?" she asks nonchalantly.

"You know you did!" His voice sounds nasally because of the broken bone.

"Good. I've been wanting to do that from the first day I met you, and now I recently learned you're a double agent. Tell me,"—she places her hands on her hips—"did Carm know?"

"No, he didn't." He rips his shirt off and holds it against his nose. "I would never two-time him. He was my brother!"

"Oh, yeah?" She gets closer to his face, and I watch him flinch with satisfaction. "What if she asked you to kill him?"

"She isn't like that!" he protests.

"*She isn't like that*," Em mocks him, and I snort. "I'll ask you again, and if you give me a shitty answer, I will take your balls and your life in that ring... in that order."

"If she asked me to kill Carm, there would have had to have been a damn good reason. Like maybe he was going against his brother and sister, her grandchildren. Then, and only then, would I consider it. I will say it again. He was my brother." Despite the water collecting in his eyes, I can see the sincerity there.

"Did he tell you about believing Talia was his mother?" She's firing on all pistons right now, and I'm so fucking hard while watching her.

"Yes," Trent admits, his forehead wrinkling.

"Why wouldn't you tell him she wasn't? He was your brother, no?"

"Bro," he wheezes while looking at Emmett, "tell her we were brothers."

Pure fury crosses Em's features as Emmett shuffles nervously. Then she steps between Trent and Emmett to peer up into Trent's face. "Was I talking to him?" she growls, and my dick throbs. "Don't take my threats idly. I'm waiting for any excuse to watch you bleed to death."

"I'm sorry," he mutters, shifting his gaze from Emmett to Em. "If I told him she wasn't his mother, he would've asked for proof. Guess where that would've had to come from? Her. You know how she found out about the whole fucked-up situation? Me," he sneers as he drops the shirt from his bloody face.

I want to fucking laugh so hard right now. Trent is trying to act tough, and regardless of what he's saying makes sense, he's purposely taunting my killer girlfriend. She bares her teeth before her knee slams into his balls... Hard. Emmett and I blanch at the impact. Trent crumples to the ground as his breath comes out in a rush, his skin growing pale. Then he begins to retch as he holds his balls in his hands and rolls onto his side.

"We're not done. Especially considering the fact we haven't even gotten to Tommy yet." She walks farther inside, and Emmett hurries over to Trent.

"Bro." He tries to help him up. "Why did you hide so much shit though?"

I don't think he's expecting an answer since Trent is currently upchucking his dinner. I shake my head and hurry past them to catch up with Em as she gets into the elevator. "I bet they have him in some cell somewhere, chained like a monster. I will kill people if he's been mistreated, literally paint this motherfucking compound red." Her body is taut and her fists clenched as she heaves out a breath.

"Maybe you should've asked Trent that before immobilizing him," I suggest with a chuckle.

"You're probably right." She nods as we step out of the elevator and head to our usual room. "Fuck, I'm just so angry with all the fucking secrets."

"Yeah, I don't know how many more surprises I can take."

"This whole Talia being my grandma is the fucking cherry on the cake," she mutters as she throws open the door.

I haven't even processed how my mother is going to feel about all this. Jenna Craven killed my grandmother unintentionally, but still. Then I have to somehow tell her that Moore is her half brother and he has a son who was Em's best friend in New York, and then he was killed by Em's unknown older brother who is also dead now, but the best friend is actually still alive. Feel my pain?

"Do you think we should go find them and check on Trent's balls?" I ask her with a grin on my face.

"I need to know where Tommy is, so yeah." She inhales a deep breath as a rare expression comes over her face. Hesitation.

I toss our bag on the bed and lead her toward the cafeteria. I've learned throughout my years at this place that everyone chills in there. I hold the doors open for her, and we both step inside. There's a buzz of chatter as I walk over to check out the food lineup.

"Vin?" I hear behind me. I turn and find the very faded, purple hair on Marlana's head, her bald spot covered by a beanie.

Em stands beside me and looks at Marlana from head to toe. "Heard you banged my dead brother. Did he pay you for your time?"

Marlana's face turns a dark crimson. "I cared about him," she whispers.

"Well, he's dead now," Em growls, and I'm stunned by how callous she's being. "I have no one to watch you, so I might as well kill you too."

"Stop threatening her."

EMBER

He's standing right behind her and his features are exactly as I remember them, save for the scar on his right temple. He looks angry, nothing like my happy childhood friend I once knew.

"Surprised to see me?" His voice sounds too calm compared to his turbulent features. "I get it. You left me for dead."

"Hold on," Vin cuts in. "You're Tommy?"

"At least you had the decency to tell people about me. Did you tell them how I saved your life?" He's filled out a bit in the years I thought he was dead, his body thicker.

My ability to speak has been wiped clear from my brain and I can't stop my eyes from roaming all over his face. His olive skin is paler than usual, his black hair still a mess of waves on his head, and his equally black eyes are sunken. I can't believe he's actually alive and standing here in front of me.

"She did," Vin continues to fill my silence. "Your death devastated her."

"But I wasn't dead!" he yells, and the room falls silent.

"Tom." Marlana grabs his arm, and my sight locks on to the motion like a missile.

"Tom?" I finally say and look back up at his face. "Do you know the shit this girl has done?"

"Yeah, she told me some. She also told me how you killed her mother and then fucked him over her dead body." He glares at Vin before bringing his eyes back to me, their depths filled with rage. "I also know the fucking killing spree you've been on since your psychotic father got ahold of you."

"It's true." I won't ever lie to him. "You were gone when I came back."

"And that was it? You just believed people you barely knew when they told you I was dead?" He takes a step closer to me.

"Watch it," Vin growls and holds his arm out.

"I saw you get shot in the head, *Tom*. It's what triggered something in me and I killed my father."

"I would've never left you bleeding on the ground." His face is pure fury like I've never seen it before.

"There's only one way to handle this," I tell him and watch as a sadistic smile crawls across his lips.

"Is this a good idea?" Vin asks for the twentieth time as I pace the room's length.

"It's our way." I shrug.

"You're seriously going into the ring with this guy?" Emmett huffs as he watches me.

"It's our way," I repeat. *I just hope he doesn't kill me.*

"It *was* your way," Vin corrects.

"I have to do it, and you're not to open the cage door unless I say so," I warn them both.

"I can't agree with that." Vin shakes his head.

I don't argue because I'm hoping it doesn't get that far. Have Tommy and I fought before? Hell, yeah. We were childhood friends. My first real shiner was from him when we had to duke it out over the last slice of pizza.

I'm not stupid. I can see the hatred and resentment he has bottled up inside, but this is our way. We'll fight it out, and after, it'll be squashed. I just hope the same rules still apply.

"Let's go." I open the door.

"What about your music?" Emmett asks, and I roll my eyes.

"It's just us, jackass."

Tommy is already in the cage, his taped hands by his sides as he leans against the wire. When he sees me, his hands slowly curl into fists. Okay, that's a bad sign. It's never been this contentious when we've decided to fight it out, and it sends my heart pounding throughout my chest.

"I can't promise I won't kill the fucker properly this time," Vin snarls, his face filled with menace.

"Don't, Vin." I turn and look into his green eyes. "This is the only way to fix it. It might get messy, but I can handle it. Trust me." He rolls his eyes but finally gives me a nod.

I get into the cage and stand still, watching Tommy for any reaction.

"No 'Bodies hitting the floor'?" he taunts me.

"Is that the type of fight you want?" I ask him quietly. "A fight where one of us doesn't leave this cage on their feet?"

"I want to give you the same courtesy you gave me." He nods.

"I wouldn't kill you." I shake my head. "You know damn well Carm shooting you was out of my control."

"I've always put my life on the line to save yours, Blur." His use of my nickname clogs my throat and breathing becomes difficult.

Then, like a tornado of limbs and fists, he's in my face. I have just enough time to dodge him, but it's difficult because anger has him punching hard and in quick succession.

After a few minutes of his punching and my dodging, I realize two things. One: I am tiring him out and his hits are becoming slower. And two: His anger is only getting worse with each dodge. If this is going to work, I realize I need to take a few blows.

"Haven't really been on your game for the last few years, huh?" I taunt him. "Looks like you're about ready to pass out."

"Recovering from a head wound would do that!" he bellows and comes at me again.

This time, I let him, and when his fist connects with my jaw, I'm jarred with the force of the impact. *Yeah, he's fucking pissed.* I stumble back and move my jaw back and forth, checking to see how bad the damage is. It'll be bruised, but that'll be the least of my worries when I leave this cage.

"That's it?" I chuckle. "Those arms need some extra gym time." His dark eyes flash with a dangerous glint as he bares his teeth and spit flies from his mouth. I've seen this look before, but it was never directed at me, and to be completely honest, it's a little startling. "Do it." I nod at him encouragingly as my hands remain at my sides. "Do what you need to."

He doesn't hesitate as his taped knuckles slam into my cheek. Even expecting the impact, I'm still thrown to the mat with his force. My vision blurs, but I still get back up to my feet. This isn't over yet.

"Hit me back!" he roars, and his fist sinks into my stomach, effectively stealing my breath. As I try to suck in air, I fall to my knees.

"I'm not angry with you," I speak slowly, still trying to catch my breath.

He hits me again in the same spot on my cheek and my body meets the mat once more. My vision fades to black, but I take a few deep breaths to stave off unconsciousness. My mouth is filled with blood and I spit it out, bright red against white. Then I get back up to my knees and wobble slightly as my world tips on its axis.

"Hit her one more time, motherfucker, and I will kill you!" Vin screams from outside the cage.

I hold my hand up toward my soul, asking him to stop, because this isn't his fight. This has nothing to do with him. He wants me to care more about my life because he and I are forever tied as one, but I know Tommy doesn't want me dead, just hurting.

Call me masochistic.

My head is pounding with the blood swelling under my skin. I never let myself get hit this often, so I don't ever feel this way during a fight. "I got this," I say loud enough for Vin to hear.

"Do you?" Tommy chuckles, and the sound coats my blood in ice water.

I raise my face so we can look at each other, eye to eye. "Yeah." I nod slowly. "You don't want to hurt me."

"Think again," he snaps as his fist flies out again.

This time when he connects with my head, he hits my left temple, and blackness erupts behind my eyelids before I even hit the mat.

Chapter Twenty-Eight

Ember

"It's just what we do." I hear Tommy's voice as I'm coming to.

I can feel myself lying on a bed as someone presses a cold cloth against my face. At least he sounds remorseful and less angry, closer to the Tommy I know and love.

"What happened to you isn't on her." Emmett's angry voice filters through. "If anything, she should be pissed at you for being such a good soldier to our father."

"She was a good soldier to your father too, remember? She has been a Rampage fighter since she was thirteen years old." Their arguing is giving me a worse headache, and I groan as I open my eyes. "Blur?" Tommy exhales with relief.

"Are we good now, asshole?" I ask him and savor the sound of his chuckle. I thought I would never hear that again.

"Sorry, but I'm not sorry." He laughs, and again it's like music to my fucking ears.

"You never are. Did you make me ugly?" I reach up and hiss when my fingers touch my tender cheek.

"Impossible," he says as he brushes the hair off my forehead.

"If you want to keep that hand intact, I suggest you remove it from her face," Vin growls, his voice promising violence.

"This one is serious," Tommy muses, trying to hold in his laughter. "You went and found your exact double in a dude."

"I know." My eyes flick to Vin's as warmth gathers inside me. Tommy is back. I look up at Vin as he presses the cool cloth against my cheek. "Thank you."

"Is there a sign-up sheet somewhere? I think it's my turn to get you in that cage." He looks serious, but I can hear the humor in his voice.

"Don't threaten me with a good time, Greene." I chuckle, but the movement causes my vision to swirl.

"It's time to talk, Ember," Tommy tells me, and I nod slowly.

"Where have you been this entire time?" I ask him. "Were you here?"

"No." He lifts the hair off his head and I see the long, jagged scar running along the side of his scalp. "This was a long recovery. I had short-term memory loss and my speech was affected. Jenna had me placed in a facility that specializes in head wounds and serious brain trauma. It still took a year to recover."

"Why didn't you try to contact me?"

"Because my memories of that night were baffling. I couldn't place timelines, and yours was the only face I could remember. For a while, I believed you were the one holding that gun. After a few months, my memories cleared up, but not enough. I remembered you didn't shoot me, but you were the reason I got shot. I was angry." He shrugs. "Still am."

"And your memories now?"

"Like Swiss fucking cheese, but that final hit in the cage, watching you being knocked out and falling to the mat, unsettled a lot of things in my brain." He smiles and his eyes look clearer. "It's not the first time I've knocked you out and for a lot less too."

"Like for the last slice of pizza?" I snort.

"Or because you took a dangerous job."

"Or when I stole your skateboard." I waggle my eyebrows, the motion sending pain skating along my scalp as I take a deep breath.

"Yeah! Then sold it to some kid!" he exclaims, the sound making me wince as my head pounds.

"Because he needed it more than you!" I argue, the pressure mounting behind my eyes.

"Guys," Vin interrupts, giving me a reprieve. "As sweet as this is, we have pressing matters to get to."

"Right." I nod, then clench my teeth against the throbbing. "So I'm guessing you know who your birth father is?" I ask Tommy.

"Yeah, looks like we both come from the same town."

"My blood and Vin's blood flows in your veins," I explain to him quietly as I relax back into the pillows, and then relay the story of his heritage as best I can.

"So we're all cousins," Tommy says when I'm finished, and Emmett bursts out laughing.

"No," I refute vehemently. "You and Vin are cousins, and then you, Emmett, and I are separate cousins. Don't lose that in one of your Swiss cheese holes."

Tommy throws himself back in his chair and lets out his genuine belly laugh, the sound making me tear up. Emmett and even Vin laugh along. It's almost too good to be true.

Finally, when the laughing stops, Tommy's face turns somber. "My bio dad is a fucking corrupt cop who likes to help distribute child porn and kill people in his spare time. Now it all makes sense." He shakes his head.

"What makes sense?" I raise my brow.

"Why I was taken away from him."

"There's more." I cringe. "Tell me you haven't fucked Marlana."

"God, no." He shakes his head. "She's a great friend, but not even close to my type." I deflate with relief and both Emmett and Vin laugh. Tommy looks from them to me and his eyebrows smash together in confusion. "What am I missing?"

"You share the same mother." I bite my lip and count to five before saying, "The one I killed and fucked Vin over her dead body."

"Marlana told me. She also said her mother was a bad person."

"She said that?" Vin asks, clearly as surprised as me.

"Yeah, something about raping a kid and helping a rapist? Fuck, it's sad that these people are my parents."

"I will kill your father too," I mumble.

"What the fuck are you? The Terminator?"

"*I'll be back*?" I say in the worst Arnold Schwarzenegger impression.

"You've become harder, if that's even possible, and you've jumped from beatdowns to full-out murder. But something in here,"—he points to his head—"is telling me

I can trust you completely. If you think you should kill him instead of a courtroom handing him a sentence, then I'm with you."

"Really?"

"Yeah." He smiles at each of us. "We're family, right?"

Chapter Twenty-Nine

"Wow." Tommy whistles when I press my thumb to the scanner by the front door. "I knew you were rich, but this is rich-rich."

"I thought the same thing when I first moved here." I chuckle and lead him inside.

"Am I staying in the garage?" Marlana's snarky voice hits the back of my head and I roll my eyes.

"Don't fucking tempt me, bitch. I hate that you're here, but there's literally no one left to watch you," I warn her, snapping my head around to glare at her as she takes a step back on the driveway.

"Looks like you're having my old room." Emmett swoops in before my hands wrap around her thin neck. "It's across from mine, Adri's, and Travis' room. So enjoy that." The thought of Marlana having to endure one of their sex-filled nights has the anger washing away as I grin.

"I still can't believe I'm about to meet my first

throuple," Tommy says, and I snort at him.

We head inside the house as Emmett leads Marlana up the stairs and Vin travels slowly behind them. He was quiet for most of the drive back, his face looking a little troubled sometimes. We're nearing the end of our mission, and I pray he can hold on just a little longer. I couldn't do this without him.

I lead Tommy over to my aunt and uncle's old room, and even though I said I never wanted anyone to use it again, the thought of him being in here settles something inside my soul, like it was meant to be this way.

"Wow, ground floor suite." He whistles again as he nods his head and looks around, so similar to my reaction that very first day Aunt Debby showed me around.

"This was my Aunt Debra and Uncle Scott's room." I open the door and step inside. "They died last year. Actually, your father killed them."

"Shit," he groans and looks around again, then his eyes flick to mine, guilt shining bright in their depths. "Are you sure you want me in here?"

"Yes, I'm sure."

"I can see why you would want him dead, among other reasons." He drops his bag to the floor and moves to sit on the bed, giving it a little bounce. "This is fancy."

"Yeah." I point to his private bathroom. "Get cleaned up because Miss Jenna Talia will be here shortly."

"Jenna... Talia. Wow." His eyes widen. "I've never said her name like that before. Is it some kind of joke?"

"I fucking wish." I leave the room and call back, "I could deal with more jokes in my life." Then I head upstairs, hearing Emmett and Marlana bickering down the hall. I ignore it and head to my room instead. Vin is sitting on the bed, staring down at his hands and shaking his head. "What's up?" I ask him.

"I need this to be it."

"What are you talking about?" I kneel in front of him.

"Like the final fucking showdown, Em." He looks at my face and cringes. Yes, it's a mess of bruises from my very best friend. "I don't want my whole life—our whole lives—to be like this."

"I can't guarantee there will be no other battle to fight. I won't ever lie to you like that. But I will say this: I promise you, Vin, that after this, my sole focus will be on you and our family. I want nothing more."

He sinks to the floor in front of me and gathers me into his arms. "My soul is tired. It just wants to grow old with you."

I kiss him softly before pressing my forehead to his. "Let's go wait for Talia, Travis, and Adri to get here. Then the only planning after this is for our wedding."

"Really?" His green eyes brighten.

"I promise."

"I'm glad to see the two of you worked things out." Jenna looks from me to Tommy, a small smile playing along her mouth.

"Will there be any more supposed-to-be dead people popping up?" I ask her as I eat my chocolate muffin.

Adri chuckles. "Or like, people who-are-alive-but-should-be-dead disappearing soon?" She looks straight at Marlana.

"Anal Ram is here to stay, for now." I wink at Adri.

"You people really were meant to be together," Jenna muses as she shakes her head.

"You can't fake this chemistry." Emmett flutters his eyelashes.

"Anyway." She waves off our antics. "We're set, right? My men will take out the guards around the house. That means you have ten minutes—fifteen, tops—to be in and out. Is it doable?"

"Yes." I nod and look at Vin.

"Yeah," he agrees. Tonight, it's going to be Vin and me infiltrating Moore's little hideaway. After a lot of complaining from the others, we explained Vin should be the one to take him out. Tommy doesn't care either way, and Travis wants to make sure everyone is safe at home. "You sure you don't want to meet your father before he meets his maker?" Vin asks Tommy.

"I'm sure I'd rather forget I even came from him. We should never acknowledge someone so evil ever again. I was much better off as an orphan." Tommy's eyes flash with disgust as his jaw pulses with anger.

"We could talk about evil fathers for days, right, Trav?" Vin turns to Travis.

"Yeah." Travis nods solemnly. The sins of his father will always bear weight on his shoulders, and he'll gladly carry it if it means it breaks the cycle.

He's been lukewarm toward Tommy, but only because he fucked up my face. Adri is just grumpy about having Anal Ram in the house, and we're all eager to see this final chapter close.

"Oh!" I snap my fingers and point at Jenna. "Since getting me out of jail was such a breeze, I need you to get Rodney Jones out. Watkins was a racist piece of shit and locked up a first offender as if he were a lost cause."

"I wouldn't say it was a breeze, but I will see if we can get him some community service and set him on the straight and narrow with proper opportunities." Jenna pulls out her phone and begins to tap her fingers on the screen. "Rodney

Jones of Toronto. Got it," she murmurs.

"That would be nice," Travis adds.

"I think we're ready." I nod to Jenna as her eyes lift from the screen of her phone. "Question, what *do* we call you? Nana? Grandmother? Granny?"

"Oh dear." She rolls her eyes, and it's like Aunt Debby is back and listening to one of my rants.

"Grandmammy!" Emmett yells, and we all burst out laughing.

"Jenna is fine." She waves us off, but she's smiling.

"Jenna Talia, it is." Emmett rubs his hands together.

"You may want to bring back the Laurann," I suggest to her. "You've given him unlimited ammo."

"I guess I have some making up to do." She shakes her head. "I'll let him keep it."

Vin and I leave them at the kitchen table to bicker and talk. Tommy needs to become one of us and there's no one better to help with that than Emmett. He'll bring Travis on board and the rest will be easy sailing.

"Are you doing your makeup?" Vin questions as we step into our bedroom.

"You bet your sweet ass," I reply and head into my bathroom. "This may be the last time."

I'm applying the white to my face when I realize I'm ready to hang this shit up. I want to finally experience this world around me without it being tinted by the color of evil and watch as life blossoms in crystal clear purity. Do I deserve it? I don't know, some days I think yes, but then there are those dark, dreary days when all I see are the souls of my victims as they wander around me.

I've walked a highway of pain in my few short years on this Earth, and I can only hope my bloody tasks shine with good intentions. I hope once this highway ends, I can begin my travels on the road to redemption. I don't care how rough the terrain or how narrow the path is, as long as I can see my ending being worth the journey.

I need my pain to be worth the journey.

VIN

I can already see the men dropping like flies around the house. "Are you ready?" I ask Em and grin when she snorts.

"Baby, this is my nine-to-five." She giggles and gets out of the Mercedes.

I follow her lead and keep an eye on her back as we run up the path to the front door. We were assured it was just Moore inside, and the tremors of anticipation flows through me. I can understand how Em finds this so addictive.

She throws open the door and it bounces off the wall behind it. "Oops." She snickers.

The place is dark and there's a muffled noise coming from upstairs, like a TV playing on low. "You think he's sleeping?" I whisper, and she shrugs as she makes her way up the stairs. "Take it easy. He could have a gun," I chastise and grab the back of her hoodie. She slows down and lets me take the lead. Besides, Em has had her fun with blood and torture. It's my turn.

We reach the room with the TV on, finding the door ajar. I peer in and see a sleeping Moore lying on the small twin bed, a gun resting on the pillow beside his head. I point it out to Em as she creeps into the room while I head to the foot of the bed and wait until I'm sure she has the weapon safely in her hands.

"Wake the fuck up," I growl into the room before ripping the blanket off his body.

He sits up and automatically reaches for his gun, but Em knocks it into the side of his head and cocks it. "Looking for something?" she taunts, her voice sounding sinister.

"How'd you find me?" He sounds disoriented as he grabs his head, but not too surprised to find us here.

"Looks like you made too many enemies," I inform him as he blinks me into view, his eyes hardening. "The enemy of our enemy forced us to pair up to take you down."

"Ahh... Talia." He actually grins. "I didn't see this one coming. When they told me they released Emberlise Craven, I wondered how."

"Get up," I order as Em bites her lip. Is she fucking serious right now? How can I concentrate when I know how wet her panties are?

Moore does as we demand and stands from the bed, his eyes flicking to Em. "Are you here because of what happened to your idiot brother?" He has the nerve to chuckle, and it makes me wonder why he's being so complacent.

"I'm not liking your tone, Chief Moore. Especially knowing all about your lineage. We have a lot in common." His body stiffens at Em's words. "Oh? You couldn't see that coming as well? You're my uncle."

"Mine as well." I let my full-tooth grin free.

"Twelve minutes," Em murmurs, and I know it's time to start.

I take the gun from her hand and point it at the center of his forehead. Then I watch from the corner of my eye as Em withdraws her brass knuckles from her hoodie pocket. I will never forget the first day I saw those in the Precious Blood parking lot.

She slips them on before rearing her arm back and slamming it forward into his right cheek. His head snaps to the left in a spray of blood and teeth, and I chuckle as I hear some hit the floor with a *clink*.

"You bitch!" he roars and spits blood onto my girl's hoodie. "I was the one that popped your brother's chest full of bullets. I made him look like a bowl of fucking Froot Loops."

"That's good." She nods, her voice calm and void of

emotion. "Now we have an excuse to make this as bloody as possible."

I pull the clip out and toss the empty gun on the bed. "No more time to waste."

Grabbing him by his hair on top of his head, I haul him toward me and headbutt him. His nose practically explodes on his face, spraying more blood everywhere. Em leans against the wall, watching us as she bites her lip.

Moore falls back onto the bed with a groan. "Hey, William," I taunt him with his first name. "Your son consented to us coming in here tonight, knowing we were going to kill you."

"I don't have a son," he croaks as he tries to sit up. "I was nothing but a donor."

"He'll be happy to hear that," Em says as she picks at her nails. "He feels the same way." I grab the front of his shirt and haul him back up to his feet, his head lolling from side to side. "Eight minutes," Em says as she peers at the watch Jenna gave her around her wrist.

"Looks like I'll have to *cut* this short." I hold my hand out to Em and she places her large knife into it.

"There's more of us. When one of us dies, another takes our place."

"And we'll always be there to cut you all down," I grind out as I stab the knife into the soft flesh of his belly.

He makes a choking noise, his mouth hanging open and his eyes widening as I slash the knife horizontally along his abdomen. The warm blood runs out and over my hand, feeling like a lover's kiss.

"Checkmate," Em whispers.

Pulling the knife out, I stand back to watch as he falls to his knees, his hands trying to hold in his own entrails. I hold my hand up and stare at the amount of blood that runs down to my forearm.

Em strides forward, kicks Moore's body to the side, and grabs my face with both hands. "Five minutes. Let's make it worth it."

Then she's on her knees, in Moore's blood and intestines, as she opens the fly on my jeans. I run my fingers down her cheek, smearing her makeup, and decide the bloodred color looks good on her face. She pulls me out of my boxers and has me in her mouth quickly, and I groan at the feel of her mouth around my cock before grabbing her hair into my fists.

She said to make it worth it.

I slam my hips forward, hitting the back of her throat, and grin when she gags around me. Her throat constricts and her eyes water as her tears run through the blood and makeup on her face, making me want to paint this picture.

"Let me down that pretty throat, baby," I beg her just before I slam back in and moan as my balls slap her chin. The sounds of her gags and chokes are like music, along with Moore's dying gurgles.

My thrusts become harder and faster, my balls tightening with the all-consuming feeling of my impending release. My orgasms with Em are better than I've ever experienced with anyone else.

Sirens sound in the distance as I tighten my fists in her hair, and I thrust one last time before coming down her throat. My girl sucks it greedily along with my soul and swallows it whole. It's always belonged to her anyway.

Epilogue

ADRIANNA

"Mommy!" Sonja screams from across the yard. "Ivy is being mean!"

"Sonja," I reprimand her. "You know what I'll say to that."

"She'd say toughen up," her twin, Samuel, taunts her. He's five going on thirty.

Yeah. I ended up with twins and they remind me every day of the original set. Their eyes even shine the exact same shade of blue. Only Samuel looks more like Ember while Sonja is like Emmett.

"Ivy's an asshole," Ember states from beside me as she rubs her very pregnant belly.

"She's like you." I chuckle as I sip my glass of wine.

"I want to guzzle an entire bottle of that shit," she moans as she watches me drink with longing.

"Soon," I promise her and smooth down her hair. "You look ready to pop. Maybe after this one, you can tell Vin to get himself snipped."

"Three is good." She nods.

"Three is perfect," I reiterate.

"When will your parents get here?"

"Next week," I groan and tip my head back. "The thought of having them stay with us for a month is exhausting."

"It's amazing how good they are with the kids though." Ember laughs at the irony of my parents. "Nothing like how they were with you."

"And the fact that they accepted I have two husbands? It's freaking astonishing." I drain the rest of my wine and set the glass back on the table.

Six years ago, I married Travis in a courtroom, officially becoming a Greene, and then two weeks later, we had a garden wedding for the three of us here at Ember and Vin's house. It was perfect. Vin was Travis and Emmett's best man, and shockingly, Marlana was my maid of honor. She's changed a lot and the two of us grew closer over the years. She's matured into a caring woman who has discovered the importance of family. Ember even got herself ordained and officiated the ceremony herself. It was amazing.

We built our house on Travis' family's land. It took some convincing, but he finally relented and we all pitched in on the design. He was so worried about the land being evil and penetrating our new home, but that couldn't be any further from the truth. Our home is bursting at the seams with love that we can hardly contain it.

My life is nothing like I ever imagined it would turn out. I went to community college here in Whitsborough to stay close to my family and to help Sharla with the restaurant. I took Early Childhood Education classes and graduated early to attend teachers' college.

Now, I am the current principal of Precious Blood Academy. Watching the teenagers there with all their angst and anger brings me back to my adolescence every day.

Life is what you make it, and I believe us resilient Greenes made it the absolute best we could've.

EMMETT

"You should've seen this bust!" I exclaim to Vin as we stand at the barbeque. "It was the biggest in Whitsborough history."

"Bro." Vin chuckles. "That can't be that much compared to what they get out in Toronto."

"Mountains of white shit, trust me." I nod and take a sip of my beer.

I watch as the twins run through Ember and Vin's lawn like two forces, their laughter echoing back at us. Those two came from my sac, there's no fucking denying it. Ivy stands and watches them while deep in thought, likely planning their demise. So much like my sister, it's uncanny.

I wasn't sure what I wanted to do with my life, but I knew I wanted to do my part in keeping Whitsborough clean and safe for our family. So I went into the police academy and started out in parking patrol until I crept up. Now, I'm better known as Police Chief Torres. Plus, those handcuffs were a blessing.

"Is this going to be your last kid?" I ask Vin as my sister waddles inside the house to answer the ringing phone.

"Not if I can help it." He grins at me. "If I keep her pregnant, it keeps her from running off doing dangerous things."

"That's true. Until she blows up from a life of normal activities. It may be your murder scene I stumble upon next."

"You're probably right," he admits and continues to grin. "But we always did like a little blood play."

"Gross." I gag and choke on my beer.

"Uncle Tommy! Aunt Mar!" Sammy comes running over. "Look, Daddy! Look who came."

I turn to find a smiling Tommy with Marlana. They always remained close and even married into the same family. Marlana married Charles—our high school friend—and Tommy married Charles' older sister, Amy. Speaking of, I watch as they come outside behind them.

"What's up?" Vin calls out. "Grab some beers and whine to me about that football game last night."

"Fuck you." Tommy grins and comes over to us. "Bro, Ember is a fucking whale this time around. How many little Cravens are in there?"

"That's an evil thing to wish such an atrocity on people." I point at him.

His head tips back as he laughs. "True," he agrees as he watches Sammy and Sonja tackle Marlana.

"Heard about the bust, bro," Charles interjects as he sits down in the chair beside me. "Fucking sweet."

"Yeah, man. Biggest in Whitsborough history. Bet you can't top that." I wink and take a swig of my beer.

"I'm the fucking Fire Chief. I couldn't top that, idiot," he states as he chuckles and shakes his head.

"That's right, loser," I say. "How're the kids?"

"Carmelo is sulking because we dropped them off with my parents." Charles rolls his eyes. "Sabrina is good. We just learned she's gifted."

Carmelo Jr. Yep, that's right, Marlana ended up being pregnant with Carm's baby and there was no need for a DNA test. The kid came out looking exactly like him. When she came back here to Whitsborough, she saw Charles and they reconnected. They also have a daughter as well.

Thankfully, after Carm passed, no one else was buried in our mausoleum. We kept our promises to each other and lived our lives, not just for ourselves but for the whole family.

Tommy's plaque is still in there though, because we're all a little morbid like that.

TRAVIS

"Father, I didn't mean to wet my pants." Gabriel looks at me with his large, chocolate-brown eyes. "I just didn't have time to come inside."

"You have to make the time," I chastise him as I towel him down from the bath. "This is your last change of clothes."

"Okay." He nods solemnly as I dress him.

He's so much like Adri, it makes my chest hurt with how much I love him. Our twins are five and Gabe will be three in a month. Our kids are my absolute pride and joy. There's nothing I wouldn't do for them.

I won't lie, when I found out Adri was pregnant the first time, I panicked. My childhood consisted of physical and emotional abuse, and I thought, how could I do any better?

E could see the battle I was having within, even when no one else could, not even my husband or wife. We've just always been like that, connected on a level we could never explain. She took me aside and told me she had an idea. She wanted to build a center for children who had experienced trauma and she asked me to run it. It was exactly what I needed, to help children like I was never helped and to see how far I truly came.

After our first year of being open, I wrote a memoir. It has every detail of what happened to me and I've never felt freer. I can finally let go of all the hatred buried inside me and have forgiven everyone for their grievances against me.

My father's company is still in my name, but I don't have much to do with it. The board makes the decisions and I sign checks, then funnel all the money I make into our shelter.

"Come on, Father!" Gabe yells from the hallway. "Sammy and Sonny are going to have all the fun without me!"

"Alright, alright." I laugh as I scoop him up and bring him back outside.

"Everything okay?" Adri asks as I watch her little mini-me scoot across the lawn toward his family.

"Perfectly okay," I whisper and grab her chin. Then I pull her in and kiss her softly, her breath hitching as she presses in closer.

"Hey, you two!" our husband calls out. "Let me know when I can be tagged in." Adri snorts into my face as I flip him off over my head.

"Maybe we'll get another set of twins!" Vin calls out.

I turn to look at him over my shoulder and grin. "Maybe you're having the next set for us!" I chuckle as I watch his face blanch.

"Ember is carrying bigger this time," Adri muses.

"Nah, the doctor is sure there's only one in there, but it's fun to scare him anyway."

My life was never a walk in the park, more like a stroll through Hell, and I couldn't see an end to the inferno's heat. Then Emberlise Craven waltzed into my life, doused the flame, and laughed like Hell was her own personal playground.

I am a prime example of damaged goods. I could've let it kill me, and I almost did, but she showed me how to grab those demons by the horns and make them my bitches.

VIN

"Ivy gets this look that makes me want to apologize in case she stabs me," Emmett admits as he watches my daughter scowl at his children.

"She's her mother's daughter through and through," I say with pride in my voice.

A few weeks after we killed Moore, Em found out she was pregnant. I was over the moon and forced her to marry me the next month. I decided as much as I loved acting, it just wasn't feasible while I had a wife and a baby on the way. So I did the next best thing. I took up Scott's classic car acquisition business and grew it even bigger. Now it's run on a global scale and I have multiple HQs around the world.

I'd like to think I've made him proud.

"Daddy?" I hear a little voice behind me.

"Hey, Saxon, what's up?" I look at my young son.

His tear-filled green eyes stare up at me as he pouts in that adorable way only a four-year-old can. "Ivy says I'm adopted." My daughter will be the reason I'm prematurely gray.

"Sweetheart, you tell Ivy she's actually Uncle Emmett's child and we took her to be nice."

"Okay!" he squeals and runs to find his troublemaking sister.

"What the fuck?" Emmett looks at me in shock. "First off, fuck you. Second, that could seriously scar her."

"Nah, man. Like I said, that girl is her mother through and through. She'll wake me up tomorrow morning with a punch in the face as retaliation."

"What a peach," he murmurs with adoration in his

eyes. "Oh! Grandma is bringing potato salad and her special fruit punch. You know what that means."

The guys all groan as I laugh. Jenna has a fruit punch she brings to every cookout and the thing must have a gallon of alcohol in it. We can all safely say we've knocked up our wives after a night of drinking that shit.

I don't have to worry. I can fuck the shit out of my wife tonight. Not that I wouldn't if she weren't pregnant.

"Do you know what you're having this time?" Charles asks, and I shake my head.

"Nope. Same as the others. We like surprises."

"That's what Amy and I did too." Tommy nods. "Cameron was an 'it' until the day he was born."

Watching everyone laugh and be a family unit has me thinking about the road that got us here. Nothing about it was easy, but fuck, if I had to do it again, I wouldn't change a single thing. I got my happily ever after with my soul's mate and a family anyone would be envious of.

Can I say I am one-hundred-percent content? That my heart doesn't quicken when I look back over the things we did to cleanse our town? The answer is no. My dark undercurrents will always be there, and I have a wife who has hers to match.

Like a pair of murderous vampires who lust for the sight of blood.

C.A. RENE

EMBER

This kid weighs like a hundred pounds, so waddling to a ringing phone is torture. Also, the pressure on my vagina tells me it's coming soon.

"Hello," I growl into the phone, a little breathless and a lot pissed off.

"Crazy girl," Trent says with a chuckle.

"Fuck, I almost gave birth rushing to this phone."

"Good," he says. "We need to get back to training you. You're the size of a van."

"I'm hanging up on you now, you cunt."

"No, wait." He's laughing harder, and the sound my clenched teeth make has me worrying I cracked one. "The Head meeting, you wanted a rundown."

"Right," I grind out, and he has the audacity to chuckle again. "Just because I'm pregnant doesn't mean I forgot how to break a nose, asshole." He falls silent, then clears his throat. Yeah, I figured that would shut him up.

"Everything is operating as you had hoped. The Heads have a final tally in and we're looking at five child rapists, three corrupt foster homes, and thirteen rescued sex slaves. That's just last month. You were right. This underground system really is working."

"Can you say that again?"

"What?" he asks, sounding slightly confused.

"The part where you said I was right. I want to record it and get myself off to it later." He barks out a laugh, and I smile right along with him.

"Hi, sweetheart!" Jenna's voice calls out as she comes through to the kitchen.

"Hey." I smile as she comes over and kisses my cheek.

"Are you taunting Trent?"

"No way." I shake my head and she chuckles softly.

"Tell her how you threatened to break my nose again!" he shouts through the phone's speaker.

"No!" I whisper harshly. "She won't let me have any of her cobbler."

"Hurry and push that kid out. I have jobs lining up and everyone is asking for the Black Slaughter."

"Fucking right, they are. Why have shit when you can have the best?" I singsong.

"How's Emmett and the throuple?"

"Emmett is his annoying self, and now that someone gave him the chief's badge, it's only gotten worse," I huff.

"You have to admit though, you never saw this coming for him."

"I knew he would be great at something, but being a cop was the furthest from my mind," I admit.

"Emberlise!" Jenna calls out—only Emmett can call her grandma. "Help me get this punch in the bowl."

"Oh, fuck, Trent, I gotta go. Grandma here has the baby-making punch ready, and I need to bet on who's getting knocked up next."

"Alright." He laughs. "I'll be up there in a few weeks, hopefully around the time my new niece or nephew is born."

"Okay, brother. See you then."

I hang up the phone and turn to Jenna. "Thank you for bringing the fuck juice. Let's watch these heathens lose their minds." I rub my hands together.

She's having trouble holding her smile in as she

reprimands, "Ember, watch that mouth. You have a child inside you."

"What?" I grasp my belly in mock-surprise. "I thought this fucker was a beach ball."

"You're impossible," she huffs, but I hear her chuckle as I go to her and pour the punch into a large bowl. Yep, this shit is strong. I can smell the rum three feet away. "I'll carry it out," she offers while looking at my stomach. "With that beach ball, surely you can't see your own feet."

"Fucking rude," I mutter before following her outside.

I find Vin, Emmett, Adri, and Travis by the barbeque and head over there.

"Grandma!" Emmett stands and yells for Jenna. "You brought my favorite punch."

"Yes, my boy," she coos, and I mock-gag. She'll always be making up for the guilt she feels in her part of losing him as an infant.

"I have my cooking class tomorrow evening," Adri tells Emmett. "Don't have a hangover and not be able to try my food."

"Yes, honey." He looks at me, his eyes wide with fear.

Yeah, Adri can take a million classes, but her cooking never gets better. At least she's persistent. I'll give her that.

"Rodney is going to be late," Vin says as he flips a burger. "He found a classic Impala we've been searching for."

Oh yeah, we also got Rodney out of jail, and when people wouldn't hire him because he had a criminal record, we gave him a job with Vin.

"That's cool." I shrug, not knowing what the fuck an Impala is.

I look out and watch as our children all run and scream, mostly from Ivy being a little sadistic. It makes me feel justified in everything I did to get to this point. I did it for everyone here right now and some who aren't.

Through the eyes of my family, I finally found my redemption.

"Guys!" I spread my arms out toward our children. "Check out the Whitsborough Progenies."

For all book updates and social platforms, check out my website

C.A. Rene lives in Toronto, Canada with her family, where most of the year varies from chilly to frigid. Most days you'll find her wrapped in her many blankets in bed while reading or writing her next dark, twisted story.
Her stories boast of inclusivity and refusal to be conformed in any small box. Writing across genres is a hobby and drinking wine is a must... Or coffee ... with a splash of Baileys.

ALSO BY C.A. RENE

<u>The Whitsborough Chronicles</u>

Through the Pain

Into Darkness

Finding the Light

To Redemption

<u>The Whitsborough Progenies</u>

Ivy's Venom

Carmelo's Malice

Saxon's Distortion

Gabriel's Deception

<u>Desecrated Duet</u>

Desecrated Flesh

Desecrated Essence

<u>The Reaped Series</u>

The Reaper Incarnate

Hunting the Reaper

Claiming the Reaper

<u>Hail Mary Duet</u>

Blue 42

Red Zone

<u>Fusion Core</u>

Tension

Release

<u>Steel Dragons MC</u>

Dragon Slayer

Dragon Strife

Dragon Scorch

<u>Hell's March MC Duet</u>

Hell's Viper

TBA

<u>Second Chance Standalones</u>

Fighting the Tide

* 9 7 8 1 9 9 0 6 7 5 9 0 4 *